Joel Cook, Philadelphia Public Ledger

An Eastern Tour at Home

Joel Cook, Philadelphia Public Ledger

An Eastern Tour at Home

ISBN/EAN: 9783337191177

Printed in Europe, USA, Canada, Australia, Japan

Cover: Foto ©Andreas Hilbeck / pixelio.de

More available books at **www.hansebooks.com**

AT HOME.

BY

JOEL COOK,

<small>Author of "A Holiday Tour in Europe," "England Picturesque and Descriptive," etc., etc.</small>

REPRINTED FROM THE PHILADELPHIA PUBLIC LEDGER.

————•————

PHILADELPHIA:

DAVID McKAY, PUBLISHER,

23 SOUTH NINTH STREET.

1889.

INTRODUCTORY.

It is the belief of the writer of the prefatory note to this book that neither the book itself nor its author needs to be introduced, for its contents already enjoy high favor with a large portion of the reading public by reason of the original serial publication of the articles in the *Public Ledger*, and the author is widely known through his other contributions to this class of descriptive literature. Still, as the Publisher prefers an introduction, the undersigned performs the ceremony of presentation with real satisfaction.

While the volume is entitled AN EASTERN TOUR, it is not to be understood that it means a tour in "Oriental" countries. On the contrary, it is limited to that near-by region embraced in the Eastern States of our own country between Pennsylvania and Maine, including portions of the States of New Jersey, New York, Rhode Island, Connecticut, Massachusetts, and New Hampshire as well—a region much more important in all ways to every-day Americans than any Oriental country can be, and in many respects quite as interesting.

Mr. Cook has certainly made his narrative extremely interesting, so much so as to cause a demand that his serial articles should be reproduced in collected form in a book. He has the faculty of seeing in familiar scenes and places notable features and aspects usually overlooked by other writers, and of giving to his narrative and descriptions the sparkle of sprightliness, freshness, and life, in company with marked graphic power. These characteristics give such a charm to his descriptive writings that many people are at a loss to couple them with his matter-of-fact and prosaic vocation of Financial Editor of the *Public Ledger.*

But the volume has merit of far more importance than commonly comes with a tourist's narrative. The book, besides the general interest always aroused by vividly-described travel, is valuable because of the interwoven facts, data, history, tradition, poetry, and anecdote that exhibit the very life, great activities, and wealth of resource of the country traversed by the author.

W. V. McKEAN,

Editor-in-Chief.

PUBLIC LEDGER OFFICE, }
    October 1, 1889. }

CONTENTS.

AN EASTERN TOUR.

I.

THE BOUND BROOK ROUTE.

DURING several years past the Philadelphia and Reading Railroad has had in successful operation its new line between Ninth and Green streets, Philadelphia, and New York, popularly known as the "Bound Brook Route." It passes out through the northern suburbs, and, skirting Germantown, crosses the lowlands beyond Wayne Junction, bisecting diagonally Mr. Clayton French's magnificent avenue of overarching trees leading up to his residence, and then goes on to the picturesque scenery of the North Pennsylvania road. Its rails are laid in a lovely section, the train now darting into rock-cuttings and over purling brooks and beside pretty sheets of water, and then out upon the open, rolling ground dotted with beautiful villas, gliding by charming little stations and across field and meadow, moving swiftly and smoothly as the car-windows display in dissolving views the gorgeously variegated panorama of Philadelphia's fascinating scenic environment upon a balmy summer morning. Past Ashbourne and Ogontz and Chelten Hills, with a brief halt at Jenkintown, the train leaves the North Penn road and rushes across country, seeking the Delaware River above Trenton. There are broad farms and many villas, sloping lawns and bits of woodland on the hillsides, the delicious green of grass and foliage varied by brown fields and waving grain.

7

Many cattle graze and the farmers are out at work. The villages are all growing settlements, their new cottages placed on pleasant sites. Somerton is passed and the Neshaminy crossed, its little waterfall just above the railway-bridge being the momentary centre of an attractive landscape, the narrow lake above having on either hand a sloping grove where picnic-parties gather under the shade of the trees. Langhorne is darted by, its newest cottages having huge overhanging red roofs, and the village getting ready to become a town of pretension and summer fashion. Beyond, the surface flattens as the Delaware is approached, but it is good land and superbly cultivated, the level fields appearing, were it not for the trees and patches of woodland, much like a far Western prairie. Soon the river is reached at Yardley, the railway crossing upon a long trestle and bridge. Here, as the Delaware flows in almost straight course through the flat valley, is displayed a quiet rural view of forest, meadow, and stream. Each bank has a canal or two, and long stretches of river are visible far up and down. A short distance above is another bridge, while below a narrow island is set in the scene, with the Trenton steeples and pottery-smokes making a distant background.

CROSSING NEW JERSEY.

The train runs into New Jersey, and, moving over the dark-red soils beyond the river, the low, outcropping spurs of the Highlands come gradually into sight to the northward. Then higher hills are seen, at first dimly blue in the long view over the intervening surface, but, approached nearer, rising more boldly as the route skirts the level land stretching to their bases. Forests cover their sides, and occasionally they go far away from us. Little houses may be seen among the trees, and some peep out on their summits. Thus moving, we cross the Lehigh Valley Railroad, which comes out from among these hills, and the Raritan

River that drains them, and soon stop at the little winding Bound Brook that feeds the latter. This stream has named the village which has grown up at the junction of the Reading and Jersey Central roads, and the place nestles under the shadow of a great ridge, with the Raritan washing its southern edge. The Lehigh Valley Railroad, coming over from Easton on its way to Amboy, now keeps us company for a brief space as the train starts up again on the Jersey Central tracks and moves through the valley south of the long, high, forest-clad ridge bounding its northern verge as far as eye can see. This railway traverses a section that seems almost like one continuous town, it is so thickly settled, and heavy traffic moves upon the line in coal and other freight. Past Dunellen and a dozen other settlements, and still skirting the base of the dark-green ridge, we rush through Plainfield and many villages beyond. The route has turned eastward, and at length gradually leaves the hills behind as distance fades them into hazy blue. The Lehigh Valley line also goes off on the right hand toward Amboy. We pass many suburban settlements peopled by the overflow from New York, and, having moved far away from the hills and out on the flat land, the train enters the city of Elizabeth, its broad and shady streets being laid upon the dark-red, level soils that border the little Elizabeth River. In the heart of the town we diagonally cross the tracks of the Pennsylvania Railroad, also bound to New York.

Elizabeth rapidly dissolves into Elizabethport as we run along the meadows and to the northward see Newark spread broadly across the view. As the terminals on the kills and the sounds are approached, the railway-tracks multiply, and the long lines of coal-cars show the trade that is conducted. We glide past the extensive works of the Singer Sewing Machine Company. Over the broad expanse of Newark Bay the train trundles upon a long trestle bridge, with the boats of the fishermen and oyster-dredgers dotted upon the smooth waters, and the hills of Staten Island off to the eastward. Beyond the bay is the town of Bergen Point, and the railway is then laid near the bank of the Kill von Kull, with the attractive sloping shores of Staten Island on the opposite side. We have thus come upon Paulus Hook, the tongue of land, with its rocky backbone of Bergen Hill, which is thrust out between Newark Bay and the Hudson River. Our railway avoids the hill by going around its lower end, while the others have to pierce it by tunnels or cuttings. Swiftly gliding through the villages amid a maze of tracks, with coal and oil freight-cars by hundreds stored everywhere, suddenly in front of Bayonne is got the first glimpse of New York harbor. The great Liberty statue on Bedloe's Island, with uplifted torch, is in full view, while behind the Gallic goddess rises the Brooklyn bridge, throwing its distant span across the East River, some eight miles away. Brooklyn is beyond, its hills stretching across to the Narrows seen over the water, with ships in the offing and many craft sailing about under the stiff breeze. This splendid view develops as we move along the edge of the harbor and approach Communipaw, the lower end of Jersey City. Here is Port Liberty, the Reading coal-shipping port, with the Liberty statue out in front as a guardian. The passenger terminals are upon a peninsula just at the mouth of the Hudson, pushed out between the harbor and the capacious basin of the Morris Canal, which is led over here from Newark. In a moment we glide into the magnificent new station of the Jersey Central and Reading lines, the finest in Jersey City, and the railway journey is ended. It is a broad and capacious structure, just completed, built of ornamental brick, with an impressive front elevation and surmounted by a clock-face of large dimensions, making the most attractive building seen on the Hudson River front of Jersey City. There are ample train-sheds and ferry-slips, and a regiment of troops could manœuvre in the capacious head-house of this great station.

THE HUDSON RIVER.

We go out upon the ferry-boat for the transfer across to
New York. Before us flows Hendrick Hudson's famous
"River of the Mountains" that has made the metropolis.
Across its broad bosom are the docks, sheds, and shipping
of the great city, with the buildings rising behind them
that are the stranger's first view of New York. Directly
opposite is Castle Garden, the low, circular building originally a fort and afterward a place of amusement, but now
the dépôt where the immigrants land on their arrival in the
New World. Alongside is the attractive foliage of the
Battery Park, and just below the little round yellow Castle William, on Governor's Island, which, with the Battery
Castle (then called Clinton), was the original defender of
the town. The great Produce Exchange tower and the tall
Washington Building, one on either side of the Park, stand
up as sentinels at the lower end of Broadway, while behind
them stretch far to the northward the many huge buildings
and steeples marking the line of that famous street, prominent among them being the graceful spire of Trinity Church.
As the ferry-boat carefully threads its way among the vessels by the aid of much screeching of the steam-whistle,
and moves out into mid-stream, turning northward, it
brings into full view both sides of the great river. On
the left hand, the Jersey City front for miles is occupied
by railway terminals, making successions of docks, ferry-
houses, and grain-elevators. Here come in all the lines
from the West excepting the New York Central, and from
these dépôts and wharves their rails extend to the most remote parts of the continent. Yet Jersey City is entirely a
growth of the present century, at the beginning of which it
had a population of only thirteen persons, living in a single
house. Its great expansion has come from the overflow of
New York during the development of the railway system
in the past thirty years. While spreading upon much sur-

face, yet it has little attraction beyond its enormous railway terminals and the factories that are adjacent. Jersey City is adjoined to the northward by Hoboken, where, in strange contrast with the commercial aspect of everything around, the river front rises in a bluff shore crowned by a grove of trees and running up into a low mound, whereon is the "Stevens Castle." This was the home of Edwin A. Stevens, one of the pioneer railway princes of New Jersey, and a projector of the famous "Camden and Amboy Railroad," which was formerly the pride and the despot of that State. He endowed the Stevens Institute of Technology at Hoboken, and spent his declining years in building, at great expense, a noted warship for New York harbor defence—the Stevens battery—which he bequeathed to the State of New Jersey, and that thrifty commonwealth shortly after sold to the highest bidder, to be broken up for old iron.

Beyond is Weehawken, where Aaron Burr killed Alexander Hamilton in the duel of 1804 that caused such a commotion—then a pleasant rural retreat, but now also absorbed by railway terminals. Behind Jersey City rises the long ridge of Bergen Hill, whose outcroppings above Weehawken come forward to the Hudson River bank in the grand escarpment of the Palisades, stretching to the northward. These remarkable columnar formations, extending for twenty miles along the western shore of the river, are of trap rock, and in part appear to be built up of basalt, not unlike the vast amphitheatres adjacent to the Giant's Causeway in the north of Ireland. Occasionally patches of trees grow on their sides and tops, while the broken rocks and rubbish that have fallen down make a sloping surface from about halfway up their height to the edge of the water. In some places these strange rocks rise five hundred feet. Thus, stretching from Communipaw to the end of the flat land where it is encroached upon by the Palisades, are the wide-spreading lines of Jersey terminals, while over on the New York side the long covered piers are thrust out, with great steamboats, car-floats, lighters, and huge ocean-steamers in their intervening docks. As we take in this unrivalled exhibition of the vast paraphernalia of commerce, the boat gradually turns into the ferry-slip, and, after sundry bumps and gyrations, is made fast, and we are landed in New York.

II.

THE METROPOLIS.

WE have come to the American metropolis, which the geography says is upon the island of Manhattan. Why the city is called New York we know, but why should the island have been named Manhattan? There is a vague legend that the first European who looked upon this magnificent harbor was the Florentine Verrazani, who came as early as 1524. The redoubtable Hendrick Hudson, however, is universally recognized as the authentic discoverer. Searching along the American coast for the "North-west Passage" to the Indies, he steered his fifty-ton ship into the bay in 1609, and when he saw the great river was sure he had found the long-sought route. So he landed on the island with his crew and sundry kegs of seductive "schnapps;" soon made good friends with the Indians; and Ticknor in his guide-book tells us that "from the scene of wassail and merriment which followed the meeting of the sailors and the natives, the Indians named the island Manhattan, 'the place where they all got drunk.'" Thus at its birth did the infant settlement acquire a reputation which many visitors say exists with undiminished lustre in its maturer years. Hudson being a Dutchman, the settlement was called "New Amsterdam," and the land across the East River "Nassau," the earliest name of Long

Island. But five years were occupied in firmly fixing the
colony on Manhattan, which, when fairly started in 1614,
was a small palisade fort with four little houses.   Here
originated the Dutch aristocracy of the " Knickerbockers,"
who impressed their peculiarities upon the early metropolis, but whose descendants are giving place to a newer
aristocracy of wealth and an army of immigrants from all
races.   The colony was of slow growth, and land-values on
the island had not advanced much when old Peter Minuit
bought it in 1626. He was the Dutch governor, and, again
making judicious use of " schnapps," bought the whole of
Manhattan from the Indians for goods worth about twenty-
four dollars.   That sum doesn't go very far on any part of
the island in these days.   There were a thousand people
here in 1644, and to mark the northern boundary of the
settlement a fence was built along what is now the line of
Wall Street.   An Indian scare ten years later caused this
fence to be replaced by a wall of cedar palisades, and this
ultimately developed into the city wall.   Thus enclosed,
New Amsterdam became a walled city, around which His
Honor the mayor was required to walk every morning at
sunrise, unlock all the gates, and give the key to the commander of the fort.   When the duke of York's expedition
came over in 1664 and overturned the government of old
Peter Stuyvesant, surnamed " the Headstrong," and knocked
out his " Knickerbockers," at the same time changing the
name of the city, it had three hundred and eighty-four
houses, while in 1700 the population had increased to
about six thousand.

TRINITY CHURCH.

The ferry-boat, landing at Liberty Street, has set its
freight of passengers and vehicles ashore.   Emerging from
the ferry-house to the street, it seems as if Bedlam were
broken loose, such is the horde of shouting and scuffling
hackmen trying to capture the people and their baggage;

and as they noisily contend it requires only slight imagination to convince one that their prevalent brogue indicates an arrival at "New Ireland" as well as at New York. Swooping down on their prey, those not trying to get possession seem anxious to drive their hacks over you. West Street, stretching along the Hudson River bank and having a street-railway, fronts the ferry. It is muddy, and almost impassable from the jam of vehicles of all kinds trying to move in various directions, while a few sparsely-distributed policemen endeavor to maintain a semblance of order. An effort is required to break through this struggling blockade, but the plunge is made amidst a conglomeration of wagons, people, cars, horses, policemen, and mud; the gauntlet is run, and we are soon on the way through Liberty Street to Broadway. This wonderful highway, the artery of the metropolis, is quickly reached, and, turning southward, a few steps take us to the "Westminster Abbey" of New York—Trinity Church. This famous edifice stands on Broadway at the head of Wall Street, and its chimes morning and evening summon the restless brokers to attend divine services, yet few pay heed. It is a wealthy parish and maintains a magnificent choir. The old graveyard stretches along Broadway, and in Church Street, behind it, the elevated-railway trains rush by every few minutes. It is part of the valuable domain of Old Trinity that the "heirs of Anneke Jans" have for many years been trying to get away from her possession. Anneke Jans Bogardus was an interesting Dutch lady who died in Albany in 1663, after having survived two husbands. Her first husband owned the whole of the Hudson River front of New York from Chambers to Canal Street, with a wide strip running out to Broadway. Her heirs sold this to the British colonial government, and it was known as the "King's Farm," being afterward given as an endowment to Trinity Church. It is now worth millions, and the anxiety to get possession of it has given "the heirs of Anneke Jans" a world-wide reputation.

It was in 1696 that the first Trinity Church was built, being afterward burnt, while a second church was built and taken down, to be replaced over fifty years ago by the present fine brownstone edifice, whose magnificent spire rises two hundred and eighty-four feet. Its chancel contains the splendid Astor reredos of marble, glass, and precious stones, the memorial of the late William B. Astor. From the steeple there is a superb view over lower New York and the harbor. The Battery Park, with its dense foliage, is half a mile away, and beyond are countless vessels on the water. In the foreground is Governor's Island with its forts, and on the other side of the channel is the Liberty statue, while seen far off over the harbor are the blue hills of Staten Island and the water-route through the Narrows to the sea. The roar of Broadway, with its endless moving traffic, comes up to the ear, and, turning northward, the great street can be traced far away, with its rows of stately buildings hemming in the bustling throng. Descending to the churchyard, it still remains a mass of worn and battered gravestones, resting quietly in the busiest part of New York. This tree-embowered spot has been a burial-place for nearly two hundred years, and near its northern side is the "Martyrs' Monument," erected over the bones of the patriots who died in the prison-ships moored on the Brooklyn shore during the Revolution. It is darkly hinted, however, that it was not so much the reverent memory of these martyrs that prompted the erection of the monument as the desire of the vestry to stop the proposed opening of a street through the yard. It is also noted that while these patriots were in prison dying, among their relentless foes was Dr. Inglis, the rector of Trinity. When Washington came into New York in 1776, he desired to worship there, and sent an officer to Dr. Inglis on Sunday morning to request that he omit reading the prayers for the king and royal family. The doctor refused, and afterward said: "It is in your power to shut up the churches, but you cannot make

the clergy depart from their duty." The oldest grave in
the yard dates from 1681, and among the most noted is
Charlotte Temple's, under a flat stone having a cavity out
of which the inscription-plate has been twice stolen. Her
romantic career and miserable end, resulting in a duel, have
been made the basis of a novel. William Bradford's grave
is here—one of Penn's companions in founding Philadelphia, but he removed to New York, and for fifty years was
the official printer. A brownstone mausoleum covers the
remains of Captain James Lawrence of the frigate Chesa-
peake, killed in action in 1813, when his ship was captured
by the British frigate Shannon, his dying words being,
"Don't give up the ship." Here are buried Alexander
Hamilton and Robert Fulton, with other famous men, and
almost the latest grave is that of General Philip Kearney,
killed during the Civil War.

THE NEW YORK FINANCIAL CENTRE.

Opposite Trinity Church is Wall Street, leading, with
winding course and varying width, down to the East
River, following the line of the ancient palisade wall,
which it has replaced. Here are the bankers and brokers. Its chief point of concentrated attraction and the
financial centre of the United States is one block down
from Broadway, where Broad Street enters from the south
and the narrower Nassau Street goes out to the north.
Here stands, at the corner of Wall and Broad Streets, the
white marble Drexel building, while on the opposite corner
of Wall and Nassau Streets is the United States Treasury,
with the Assay Office alongside. The three leading bank-
ing-houses of the country are at this street intersection—
Drexel, Morgan & Co. at one corner, and, diagonally across,
Kidder, Peabody & Co. and Brown Bros. & Co. Mr. J.
Pierpont Morgan in the intervals of his financial diplo-
macy can look out of his office-window at the Stock
Exchange on the other side of Broad Street, which is the

2

theatre of vast transactions, and at times of enormous activity, while adjoining his office is the towering Mills building, the home of many bankers and brokers, extending down to the next corner, Exchange Place. These structures at Broad and Wall Streets are the most valuable real estate in the world. The Treasury and Assay Office contain in their vaults most of the gold and silver owned by the United States, and at the latter the kegs of gold are made up that go to Europe. It holds millions in gold bars, whose duty it is to make annual excursions in fast steamers across the ocean and back again to adjust our foreign exchange balances. The Treasury is a white marble building, fronted by an imposing colonnade and a broad flight of steps, and here is a statue of Washington on the spot where he was inaugurated the first President of the United States in 1789, the location then being occupied by the old Federal Hall, where the first Congress met. Standing by the statue and looking down Broad Street, one can see the great square tower of the Produce Exchange, at the foot of Broadway. Upon these Treasury steps are convened public meetings when grave subjects stir the financial centre or the politicians desire to invoke Wall Street aid in important elections. Proceeding farther along Wall Street, the next corner is William Street, and here is the Custom-house, with its long granite colonnade, where the Government collects the larger part of its revenues from imports. Here are controlled an army of placemen who make a powerful "political machine," and more than one President, who has been harassed by the intrigues for its spoils, has described this Custom-house as giving him more anxiety than all the rest of the country besides. A short walk down William Street, past the Custom-house and across Exchange Place, brings one to a low, broad granite building of two stories, with heavy-columned portico, having over the centre doorway the inscription, "Chartered 1822." This is the "Farmers' Loan and Trust Company," with a million dollars' capital and an enormous surplus. Some farmers may have started it, but they don't have much to do with it now. It is a financial institution of wide renown, whose shares of twenty-five dollars' par value each command five hundred and fifty dollars, and it makes 40 per cent. annual dividends. This prodigious success as a money-maker is the outcome of its fidelity in executing trusts, good faith being a factor in New York.

THE BATTERY.

Turning westward through Exchange Place, and passing the offices of more bankers and brokers, we are soon at Broadway again, and see the palatial brick and brown-stone building of the new Consolidated Stock Exchange, the rival of the older institution on Broad Street. Below this Broadway soon comes to the Bowling Green, a triangular space of about a half acre having a small oval park in the centre. This green ends the street, which divides into two smaller ones, Whitehall on the one side and State Street on the other. In the early days this place was the court end of the town, surrounded by the homes of the proudest Knickerbockers. Here in the Revolution lived Cornwallis, Howe, and Clinton. Benedict Arnold occupied No. 5 Broadway, and Washington's headquarters was in No. 1, then Captain Kennedy's house. The site of these on the west side of Bowling Green is now occupied by Cyrus W. Field's great Washington Building, an immense structure filled with offices, which rises nearly three hundred feet to the top of its tower. To the eastward is the broad stretch of the Produce Exchange, with its huge square tower, part of the ground it stands upon having been the site of the house where Robert Fulton lived and died. Talleyrand once lived on Bowling Green, and the leaden statue of King George III., which was there at the opening of the Revolution, was melted down to make bullets for the Continental soldiers, so that it was facetiously said at the time that "King George's troops will probably

have his melted Majesty fired at them." The space south
of the green was the site of the old Dutch fort guarding
" New Amsterdam " which afterward became Fort George.
Six fine residences were built here, which are now the favorite locality of the offices of the great steamship lines. Beyond, the island ends in the Battery Park, over which the
elevated railways come from both sides of the city, joining
at the point of the island in one terminal station at the
South Ferry. This park superseded the forts after the war
of 1812, and in the earlier years of this century the fashionable people took their airing here. But they long ago left
it, as the residential section moved far up town. It is a
pleasant place and well kept, and into the spacious rotunda
of its old Castle Clinton are brought the immigrants—
sometimes thirty thousand in a single week—and its occupants overflow the entire neighborhood. It is wonderful to
see the place filled with men, women, and children of all
races, who bring their old-country clothes and languages
with them, and reproduce the ancient Babel of tongues as
they ask information, change their money, and buy railway-
tickets for the Far West. At Whitehall slip, the point of
the island, is the Government barge-office. This pretty
foliage-covered park at the Battery is an attractive spot,
and a fitting terminus for the famous island of Manhattan.

III.

A SURVEY OF MANHATTAN ISLAND.

THE long and narrow island of Manhattan, upon which
New York is built, stretches about thirteen miles, while it
is not much over two miles broad in the widest part, and
sometimes narrows to a few hundred yards, particularly in

the northern portion. The corporate limits of the city are extended also over the mainland to the north and east of this northern portion, so that while the island area is about twenty-two square miles, the city covers altogether forty-one square miles, its boundary going about four miles eastward from the Hudson to a picturesque little stream known as Bronx River, which separates New York from Westchester county. The Harlem River and the winding narrow strait of the Spuyten Duyvel separate Manhattan from the mainland. The rapid growth of the metropolis has expanded it beyond the limits of Manhattan and built populous towns on the opposite shores of all the boundary rivers, Brooklyn and Williamsburg being across East River on Long Island, and Jersey City and its kindred towns on the western bank of the Hudson. Various islands in East River also are utilized for the city's penal and charitable institutions. The capacious harbor, the converging rivers, and the numerous adjacent arms of the sea combine all the requisites of a great port, and they could hardly have been better planned if human hands had fashioned them. There is a vast wharf-frontage, accommodating an almost limitless commerce in and around New York harbor, for it has over fifty miles of shore-line available for shipping. This has attracted the enormous population, there being nearly as many people as live on the island itself housed on the opposite shores or in adjacent towns, who daily pour into New York to engage in its business activity. The southern portion of Manhattan has a low surface, but to the northward it becomes rough and rocky, culminating in high elevations with intervals along the Hudson, rising at Washington Heights to two hundred and thirty-eight feet, where there is a grand outlook. Originally there were ponds and marshes on the southern part of the island, and it was also considerably widened there by reclaiming shallow portions from the rivers. This long and narrow construction of New York puts Broadway longitudinally in the centre of the city, and necessarily throws into it a great traffic. One can hardly make any extended movements in New York without getting into Broadway. Hence that street has its show always on exhibition of the restless rush of life in the modern Babylon, and has become the most famous highway in this country. Its architecture excites admiration, and its perpetual din of traffic and business, with the moving crowds and jams of vehicles, is the type of New York activity. This wonderful street is eighty feet wide between the buildings, and extends for five miles from the Bowling Green to Central Park at Fifty-ninth Street, and from its upper end, beyond this, the "Grand Boulevard," one hundred and fifty feet wide, with pretty little parks in the centre, is prolonged as a favorite drive to the northern suburbs. Broadway in its course diagonally crosses Fifth, Sixth, and Seventh Avenues, and intersects Eighth Avenue at the Park boundary. Here is the "Merchant's Gate," entering Central Park from Broadway, the opposite entrance from Fifth Avenue being known as the "Scholar's Gate," while at Sixth and Seventh Avenues between are respectively the "Artist's Gate" and the "Artisan's Gate." These four entrances admit most visitors to the great park, but it is doubtful if they classify themselves according to these designations.

A STROLL UP BROADWAY.

Let us take a leisurely stroll up Broadway from Trinity Church at Wall Street, for intelligent pedestrianism best displays the town. The street is lined with huge buildings —great office-letting structures reared skyward—and among them little, narrow, crooked streets come in to pour their traffic into the main stream, which carries a vast surging mass of humanity. At Cedar Street is the enormous Equitable Life building, with the Mutual Life building on Nassau Street almost behind it, probably the most capacious of all these aggregations of offices. There are dozens of similar

structures, whose elevators keep constantly moving. The
Western Union building lifts its surmounting tower two
hundred and thirty feet above the pavement. The crowded-
in New Yorker, despairing of lateral expansion, thus seeks
needed relief by going upward. These great houses have
myriads of occupants, and just above them, where Fulton
Street stretches across the island from river to river, the jam
and turmoil from conflicting streams of traffic show the full
tide of human life as developed in lower Broadway. Here
is the office of the New York *Evening Post*, long edited by
William Cullen Bryant. Above is the white marble Park
Bank, and just beyond is the triangular City Hall Park,
with Park Row diagonally entering Broadway. Standing
at this corner, one gets an idea of the rush and restlessness
of New York. Two enormous streams of traffic pour together into lower Broadway, and the policemen in vain try
to effectually regulate the crowds of people, wagons, and
street-cars that get jammed together in horrible confusion.
Upon the left hand is the sombre church of St. Paul with
its towering spire, and upon the right the white marble building of the New York *Herald*. The dark and the white—
the quietness of the one and the airy activity of the other—
are in sharp contrast, and they together look down upon
probably the worst street-crossing in the world.

But we pass this terrible corner with a whole skin, and in
front of us rises, at the lower end of the Park, the magnificent Post-office, which cost the Government seven million
dollars to build, a granite structure in Doric and Renaissance, with a splendid dome and tower that are a landmark
for miles around. The City Hall Park contains the seat of
the New York City government, and may be regarded as
the political and business centre of the city. Around it
and in the many streets radiating from it are a vast labyrinth
of corporate institutions and great buildings whose occupants conduct all kinds of business. This is the region of
newspapers, banks, trusts, insurance companies, railway-

offices, politicians, lawyers, exchanges, etc., with lunch-rooms and restaurants of every degree liberally distributed to feed or stimulate the multitude who rush into lower New York every morning and away again at night. The famous hotel of a past generation, the Astor House, rich in historical associations, stands on the opposite side of Broadway from the Post-office, its severely simple front façade occupying a broad space. Along Park Row many of the horse-car lines come from their terminals, adding to the jam. Stretching back from the *Herald* office are a row of news-paper buildings of wide renown—the *World, News, Times, Tribune,* and *Sun.* For the moment the *Times* in the newest building outtops them all, and the diminutive *Sun* building, a structure of the olden time, looks as if it had been sat down upon very hard. These are on opposite sides of "Printing-House Square," where Franklin's statue adorns the locality, around which a perpetual war of printer's ink rages, for these rival newspapers are always quarrelling about something. The tall and narrow *Tribune* building has its clock-tower reared two hundred and eighty-five feet on high, while beyond there is a huge vacancy from which is to arise the new office of the New York *World.* Park Row runs into Chatham Street, over which the Brooklyn bridge terminal comes down, with elevated and surface rail-roads in ample supply all about. This Chatham Street is the location of cheap shops and concert-halls, and is pro-longed into the Bowery, the avenue of the humbler classes, lined with shops and saloons, always crowded, and having four sets of street-cars running on the surface, besides being liberally roofed over with elevated railroads above. All kinds of cars have unlimited privileges here, and there is not room left for much else.

THE CITY HALL PARK.

This City Hall Park, thus enclosed by Broadway, Park Row, and Chatham Street, is a triangular space which was originally a sort of garden around the City Hall, but is now well occupied by large buildings, for the New Court-house has been built north of the City Hall and the Post-office south of it, with Mail Street opened between. Chambers Street bounds the Park on the north, and upon it faces the New Court-house, a massive Corinthian building of white marble which was a dozen years in progress through the thieving of the notorious "Tweed Ring," who used it to extract fifteen million dollars from the city treasury on fraudulent bills, or more than five times what the work actually cost. This court-house, and the Stewart building on the north side of Chambers Street, occupy the site of an old fort which, in the days of the Revolution, was the British outpost commanding the entrance to the city by the "Northern" or "Bloomingdale" road, now Broadway. The court-house is substantially constructed, and has a large central rotunda, around which are the courts, with the county offices—the Sheriff, Surrogate, Registrar, County Clerk, etc. These are the rich political plums in the local government, and consequently the rotunda, corridors, and stairways are usually crowded by the small-fry "statesmen" who are the dependants of the chieftains holding these fat offices. The entrance on the northern front is impressive—a flight of broad steps flanked by massive marble columns. The New York City Hall is a less pretentious and much older building, constructed in the Italian style of white marble, with brownstone in the rear. Here is the office of the Mayor, and also the meeting-place of that highly-flavored body—the Board of Aldermen. It has a central rotunda also, and the usual copious supply of small politicians, and contains the "Governor's Room," adorned with the portraits of the governors of New York and Revolutionary heroes, and also a fine painting of Columbus. Here are treasured Washington's desk and chair which he used when first President of the United States; but, unfortunately, it must be recorded with sorrow

that some of the occupants of the New York City Hall
have not imitated that illustrious man's example to any
eminent degree.

THE DRY-GOODS DISTRICT.

Upon Broadway, near Chambers Street and just opposite
the northern end of the Park, stands a noted building. It
is a modest brownstone structure, without any pretension,
but it contains the most famous bank in New York, whose
phenomenal success is known in every financial community.
This is the " Chemical Bank," originally started as a chemical manufacturing company with banking privileges. Its
chemistry seems to have been a failure that was soon abandoned, but its banking talents have been so well developed
that its shares of one hundred dollars' par value have sold
for forty-two hundred dollars. The capital of this bank is
only three hundred thousand dollars, but it has amassed a
surplus that is nearly twenty times its capital, and in its
reserves it often holds ten million dollars gold, besides being
usually the strongest bank in New York in its excess of reserves. It has never suspended specie payments, and its
deposits often exceed twenty-five million dollars. Among
its largest stockholders are said to be three New York ladies
who have married foreign titles—the duchess of Marlborough (who was Miss Pine, and afterward Mrs. Hamersley);
the duchesse de Dino (Miss Sampson), and the comtesse
de Trobriand (Miss Jones). Across Chambers Street, and
occupying the entire block to Reade Street above, is the
large white Stewart building, where Alexander T. Stewart
made the most of his fortune in the dry goods trade—an
edifice now converted into a vast caravansary for all sorts
of tenants conducting every kind of business. This building is the outpost of what is known as the "dry-goods district." From the City Hall Park up to Broome and Grand
Streets, stretching over a broad belt of adjacent blocks, this
region deals with all kinds of staple products of the mills

and looms, clothing, and similar goods. Here are located the factors and agents for nearly all of the mills in this country and for many abroad, and the annual money value of the trade they carry on is estimated at seven hundred and fifty to one thousand millions of dollars. Here throbs the pulse of the dry-goods trade of the United States, weakening or strengthening as poor or good crops give the agricultural community a surplus to expend upon dress. Alexander T. Stewart once said that if every woman made up her mind to pass a single season without a new bonnet, it would sufficiently diminish business to bankrupt this whole district. From its centre Leonard Street goes off eastward down to the Tombs prison, standing where once was a swamp—a sombre gray building in the gloomy Egyptian style, which is unfortunately always full of criminals. Canal Street crosses the city through the northern portion of the dry-goods district—a broad highway, formerly a watercourse draining the swamp across Broadway to the Hudson River, but now conducting a busy and valuable trade, which makes its intersection with Broadway usually a lively place. Several large hotels, which were famous in the last generation before the newer houses farther up town eclipsed them, are features of the street beyond. Here are the St. Nicholas Hotel, of white marble, and the Metropolitan Hotel, of brownstone, enclosing the well-known Niblo's Theatre. Beyond, and opposite Bond Street, is the lofty cream-colored marble front of the Grand Central Hotel. It was here that Edward Stokes shot James Fisk, a tragedy that will not soon be forgotten.

IV.

BROADWAY CHARACTERISTICS.

In the leisurely promenade up Broadway we have reached the locality where the wholesale dry-goods trade of the famous street gives place to other trades and also to the retailers. In the neighborhood of Bond Street one encounters the booksellers. This street, with Lafayette Place, Astor Place, and the adjacent parts of Broadway, is the home of much of the bookselling trade of New York. In Lafayette Place is the substantial brick and brownstone building of the Astor Library, one of the benefactions of the Astor family to the metropolis. The Mercantile Library is a very large institution, in Astor Place, between Broadway and Lafayette Place. This brick building was originally Clinton Hall, and in the streets surrounding it occurred the noted "Macready riots" in 1849. In those days it was the "Astor Place Opera-House" and one of the chief theatres of New York. Edwin Forrest and Macready had had a misunderstanding, and when Macready came over here Forrest's friends declared he should not be allowed to play in New York. Macready arrived in 1848, and appeared, without molestation, a number of nights in October, but the next spring, when his farewell engagement was announced, serious opposition was menaced. Upon Monday, May 7, he appeared as Macbeth, but there was so much confusion in and around the house that the curtain had to be rung down before the play ended. He was then inclined to cancel the engagement, but a number of prominent people requested him to remain, promising protection, and he reappeared on the following Thursday. The thorough precautions taken to preserve order within the house enabled him to satisfactorily perform his part, but the Forrest faction outside the theatre, after vainly trying to secure entrance, attacked the building with stones. The police being unable to control them, the troops were called out, and, firing several volleys of musketry along Astor Place, they suppressed the riot and dispersed the mob, but some sixty persons were killed or wounded. The excitement at the time was tremendous, and Macready, declining further invitations to act in New York, soon after went home to England.

At the end of Astor Place stands the Cooper Institute, occupying an entire block—a brownstone building with a fine front, founded and endowed by Peter Cooper for the free education of both men and women in science and art. Opposite is an immense red building also occupying an entire block—the "Bible House," the home of the American Bible Society, where the Scriptures are printed by the million in all languages for distribution throughout the world, and where many religious societies have their offices. Between these two huge buildings the view is of the Third Avenue elevated railway beyond, with its rushing trains. Astor Place is continued diagonally north-east by Stuyvesant Street, originally the lane that led up to old Governor Peter Stuyvesant's country-house. Alongside this street stands St. Mark's Church, in sharp contrast with the modern buildings around it, and here several of his descendants are communicants. Across Second Avenue opposite is the Gothic Baptist Tabernacle and the fine building of the New York Historical Society. When St. Mark's Church was built here in the last century it was a mile out of town and surrounded by country-houses. The quaint little Stuyvesant House then still stood perched on a high bank near the church, and, with its odd-looking overhanging upper story, was built of small yellow bricks brought out from Holland. The whole of this region in the days of "New Amsterdam" was Governor Stuyvesant's "Bowerie" estate, and to it he retired when compelled to surrender to the English in 1664. The road out to the "Bowerie" has since become New York's broadest highway, the well-known Bowery. In this secluded spot Stuyvesant lived for eighteen years, dying in 1682 at the age of eighty, just when Penn came up the Delaware. He was buried in a vault on the site of St. Mark's Church, where a chapel then stood, and his brown gravestone now occupies a place in the church-wall. He was "Peter the Headstrong," the last of the Dutch governors, energetic, aristocratic, and overbearing, and described by Irving as a man "of such immense activity and decision of mind that he never sought nor accepted the advice of others." He was also further described as a "tough, sturdy, valiant, weather-beaten, mettlesome, obstinate, leather-sided, lion-hearted, generous, spirited old governor."

UNION SQUARE.

Returning to Broadway and renewing the northward walk, "Stewart's up-town store," which was his great retail mart, is passed, the huge white iron building stretching back to Fourth Avenue. Hither came many Philadelphians twenty years ago on shopping expeditions, before our own retail merchants had learnt their business as thoroughly as now. There are splendid stores around it, and Broadway for a mile above, with some of the adjacent streets, is now the great shopping-region of New York. A short distance beyond Stewart's is Grace Church, with its rich marble façade and beautiful spire. The parsonage adjoins, with a small enclosure in front, upon which the towering stores encroach as if resenting even that little space reserved from the grasp of trade. Broadway bends slightly to the left, and then at Fourteenth Street circles around Union Square, a pretty park of about four acres, oval in shape, with lawns and shrubbery, and adorned by statues of Washington, Lafayette, and Lincoln. This square is surrounded by grand buildings and stores, among the chief being Tiffany's noted jewelry store, where fashionable New York spends a good deal of money. Fourteenth Street is a wide avenue, having an extensive retail shopping-trade, and this neighborhood is a great locality for theatres, Union Square being a veritable "Rialto" for the actors. To the eastward of Broadway, on Fourteenth Street, is the Academy of Music, a plain, red-brick building of ample proportions. Just beyond is "Tammany Hall," headquarters of the Democratic "bosses" and "sachems" who largely rule the town—also a stone-faced brick structure, but taller and much more pretentious, and surmounted by a statue of the presiding genius of the "Hall," the Indian warrior St. Tammany, who with outstretched hand beneficently looks down upon us. Old Tammany, who has thus been made the presiding genius of the peculiar politics of New York, was a chief of the Lenni Lenapes or Delawares, and was more used to the mild and just methods of William Penn and his Quaker brethren than to the schemes of plunder and trickery over which New York has made him a sort of patron saint. Across the street, and possibly as a warning (though little heeded), the pretty little Grace Chapel is inserted among the rows of drinking-shops and concert-halls with which this section abounds.

MADISON SQUARE.

Again we return to Broadway. Sixteenth Street passes eastward to Stuyvesant Square with its fine St. George's Church. Twentieth Street, also to the east, leads off to the handsome residences of Gramercy Park, where Samuel J. Tilden lived, and where is located that princely gift which Edwin Booth has recently given his profession—the "Players' Club." Beyond, in Broadway, rise like giants three of the noted stores of the street—the carpet warehouse of W. & J. Sloane and the dry-goods stores of Arnold, Constable & Co. and Lord & Taylor. Thus passing one famous establishment after another, with the ceaseless roar of the street-traffic all the while dinning in our ears, we come to

Madison Square. Here is Twenty-third Street, a wide avenue crossing the town, and at their intersection Broadway also diagonally crosses Fifth Avenue. This junction of famous streets has laid out adjoining it an open square covering about six acres, with attractive lawns, trees, and footwalks. It is surrounded by large hotels and noted buildings, and the light stone and general airiness of construction, combined with the trees and grass of the square and the crowds moving in every direction, give the locality an appearance that is decidedly Parisian. Far to the northward Fifth Avenue stretches with its rows of brownstone residences, while Broadway in both directions is the home of business and is a constant and never-ending kaleidoscope from its enormous travel. Both are wide streets, filled from dawn till midnight with thousands of people and vehicles, the brilliancy of the electric illumination in and around the square making the night almost as bright as day. The yellow horse-cars move rapidly and closely together along Broadway upon the road whose franchise was got by Jacob Sharp's bribery of the New York "boodle" Board of Aldermen, several of whom, including Sharp himself, have paid the penalty of their knavery. Yet the construction of this railway, though stoutly resisted for many years, was a great relief to Broadway and a convenience for all New York. The people could not now do without it. The control has passed into the hands of a Philadelphia syndicate, and I understand they contemplate putting a cable motor under the street. The fact that the ordinary New York street-traffic is not carried in vehicles of the same gauge as the railways is of advantage, as it distributes them over the street, instead of putting all on the street-rails, as in Philadelphia. This enables Broadway to carry much more traffic than any of our ordinary streets.

Alongside the intersection of Broadway and Fifth Avenue at Madison Square is the monument to General Worth, a handsome granite shaft erected in memory of that hero of

the Mexican War. The plateau whereon it stands is availed
of as the site for the reviewing stage for processions. Hither
comes the President or the mayor on great occasions, and
when elaborate political or other displays are made Madison Square is an attractive place. In fact, it occupies in
New York much the position of the Place de la Concorde
in Paris or Trafalgar Square in London. It is the great
public assembly-ground, and during many years has seen
New York's greatest outpourings. Bronze statues of Admiral Farragut and William H. Seward adorn the square.
At its north-west corner is Delmonico's famous restaurant,
whose owner, after feeding the *jeunesse dorée* of New York
upon the choicest viands for many years, lost his mind, and
in a fit of aberration wandered over into the wilderness in
New Jersey, and, becoming lost in the woods, actually died
there of starvation. The house still holds its high reputation, and is the great place for balls and banquets. Upon
the west side of the square is a row of stately hotels, the
Fifth Avenue, with its white marble front, being the most
imposing, while just above is the Hoffman House, noted as
containing the most gorgeously appointed drinking-saloon
of New York, where the highest art in rich decorations,
painting, and sculpture is invoked by its proprietor to
attract custom to its bar. Splendid stores and residences,
art-galleries, hotels, and restaurants are in abundance
around this celebrated square, and the adjoining streets
abound in theatres, churches, and popular public resorts.
Upon the east side is the noted Madison Square Garden.
In fact, Madison Square is the social and fashionable centre
of modern New York. Above this famous locality Broadway stretches two miles to Central Park, passing many
hotels and theatres, and also several of the very tall
"French flats," buildings that have been devised for
residences in the crowded city, where the scarcity of land
surface is made up by adopting the methods of the Tower
of Babel and elevating the houses toward the sky. It also

3

passes the new Metropolitan Opera-House, the finest place
of amusement in the city, which the present generation of
wealth and fashion built to eclipse the old Academy of
Music on Fourteenth Street that satisfied their fathers.
But it is a profitless investment as yet. There are theatres
and concert-halls, casinos and other resorts, almost without
number. Beyond the Park, Broadway is prolonged as the
magnificent "Grand Boulevard," and thus it leads to the
remote northern suburbs.

V.

FIFTH AVENUE.

THEY tell us in New York that the main object of working so hard to get rich is to be able to live in a brownstone
mansion upon Fifth Avenue. Here reside most of "the
select four hundred" who are said to be the exclusive
social-status set of Gotham. Their street is a grand one, a
hundred feet wide, extending northward almost in the centre of Manhattan Island. Yet it had a humble beginning,
starting from the original "Potter's Field," where for many
years the outcast and the unknown were buried and over a
hundred thousand bodies were interred. The city spread
beyond this cemetery when it was determined to make the
place a park, and thus was formed Washington Square,
covering about nine acres on Fourth Street, a short distance west of Broadway, from which the famous street is
laid out for six miles in a straight line northward to the
Harlem River. For three miles it is bordered by palatial
homes, and then for over two miles more it is the eastern
boundary of Central Park, while beyond are villas. The
street gives a magnificent display of the best residential
and church architecture of New York, the progress northward into the newer portions showing how time has changed

the styles. At the southern end the older houses are generally of brick, gradually developing into brownstone facings and borders, and then into uniform rows of most elaborate brownstone buildings, with imposing porticos reached by high, broad flights of steps. The more modern structures, as the Park is approached, are of all kinds of materials and designs, thus breaking the monotony of the rich yet gloomy brown. In several places the overflow of business from Broadway has invaded lower Fifth Avenue with stores, but the two miles from Madison Square to Central Park form a street of architectural magnificence which, in its special way, has no equal.

FAMOUS CLUBS, HOTELS, AND CHURCHES.

Attractive residences surround Washington Square, and upon its eastern border is the white marble Gothic building of the University of the City of New York. Adjoining is a fine Methodist church, built of granite. Proceeding northward along Fifth Avenue, the busy shopping-region adjacent to Fourteenth Street spreads some distance, and at Fifteenth Street is a noted corner. Here is the splendid brownstone home of the aristocratic Democrats—the Manhattan Club, where the "swallow-tails" congregate, as the other wing, the "short-hairs," do at Tammany Hall. Behind this club are the buildings and church of the College of St. Francis Xavier, the headquarters of the Jesuits in North America, and not far away is the spacious New York Hospital. The most noted literary and artistic club of New York—the Century—is on Fifteenth Street, east of Fifth Avenue. Farther northward a short distance is Chickering Hall, the chief lecture-hall of the city, and opposite, at the corner of Eighteenth Street, is the residence of August Belmont, the American representative of the Rothschilds. Ivy overruns the mansion, and behind it is a large picture-gallery. At Twenty-first Street is the wealthy and exclusive Union Club, with the Lotus Club in a more modest house across the way. As Madison Square is approached, stores again invade the avenue, while several fine hotels surround the square, and upon leaving it at Twenty-sixth Street the avenue passes between the Hotel Brunswick and Delmonico's, whose great brick building extends to Broadway. Adjoining are the Albemarle and the Victoria, the latter hotel at Twenty-seventh Street also stretching to Broadway. Far to the northward the great street can now be seen stretching up Murray Hill, with its rows of stately buildings, interspersed with stores, art-galleries, and decorative establishments, myriads of carriages rolling over the smooth pavement, and with crowds upon the sidewalks. Parallel to Fifth Avenue, and a short distance east of it is Madison Avenue, also a street of fashionable residences, and second only to the greater highway in magnificence. We pass at Twenty-ninth Street and Fifth Avenue the plain and substantial granite Dutch Reformed church, while at some distance west is seen the giant Gilsey House, towering high on Broadway. To the eastward of Fifth Avenue, also on Twenty-ninth Street, is a little church that has attained a wide reputation. It is a picturesque aggregation of low brick buildings set back in a small enclosure and looking like a quaint mediæval structure. To this church a pompous rector, when asked to say the last prayers over the dead body of an actor, sent his sorrowing friends, saying he could not thus pray for the ungodly, but they might be willing to do it at the little church round the corner. This attractive "Church of the Transfiguration" performed the last rites in presence of an overflowing congregation, and its official title has ever since been sunk in the popular one of " the Little Church Round the Corner."

THE HOMES OF THE ASTORS.

Gradually mounting the gentle ascent of Murray Hill, we come to what a few years ago was the centre of the aristocratic neighborhood at Thirty-fourth Street, on the opposite corner of which are represented the two greatest fortunes amassed in America before the advent of the Vanderbilts. Occupying the block between Thirty-third and Thirty-fourth Streets, on the west side of Fifth Avenue, are two spacious brick houses with brownstone facings, and a large yard between enclosed by a brick wall. These are the homes, respectively, of John Jacob and William Astor, the grandsons of John Jacob Astor, who accumulated the largest fortune known in this country before the Civil War. In Thirty-third Street, near by, lives a great-grandson— John Jacob's only son—William Waldorf Astor, formerly minister to Rome. The Astor estates typify the unexampled early growth of New York and the wealth gained through the advancing value of land as the city expanded. The original Astor was a poor German peasant-boy who came from the village of Waldorf, near Heidelberg, to London, and prior to 1783 worked there for his brother making musical instruments. In that year, being about twenty years old, he sailed to America with five hundred dollars' worth of instruments. Upon the ship he met a furrier, who suggested that he should trade his instruments for American furs. This he did in New York, and, hastening back to London, sold the furs at a large profit. He returned to New York and established a fur-trade, making regular shipments to England, and finally built ships to aid his business as a merchant. He prospered, and at the beginning of this century was worth two hundred and fifty thousand dollars. Then he began buying land and houses in New York, built many buildings, and was so shrewd in his real-estate investments that they often increased a hundredfold. He was liberal and charitable, but of a retiring disposition in later life, and at his death, in 1848, his estate, then the largest in the country, was estimated at twenty-five million dollars. His chief public benefaction was the gift to New York City of the Astor Library, which he bequeathed four hundred thousand dollars to found, and his son, William B. Astor, supplemented this with donations of property and money; so that, besides the buildings, this library now has an endowment fund of about one million eight hundred thousand dollars, and contains some two hundred and fifty thousand volumes: it is maintained almost exclusively as a library of reference. The great Astor estates, now represented by the third and fourth generations, are estimated as aggregating one hundred and sixty million dollars.

THE STEWART PALACE.

Upon the north-west corner of Fifth Avenue and Thirty-fourth Street is the splendid white marble palace built by the late Alexander T. Stewart when at the height of his fame as the leading New York merchant. It was intended to eclipse anything then known in America, and upon the building and its decorations three million dollars were expended, so that this house outshone all other New York dwellings until the Vanderbilt palaces were erected farther out Fifth Avenue. Stewart's fortune was an evidence of the enormous facilities of New York for successful trading, though much of his wealth afterward was invested in large buildings in profitable business localities, notably the great hotels in the Broadway "dry-goods district." Like Astor, Stewart began his career with almost nothing, though at a somewhat later period. He was an Irishman, born at Belfast in 1802, who studied at Trinity College, Dublin, and before taking his degree migrated to New York as a teacher in 1818. He somehow got into the dry-goods trade in a small way near the City Hall Park, and his business grew until he acquired all the adjacent buildings and put up the huge store at Broadway and Chambers Street with which his name is still associated, and afterward established the retail branch farther up town. His business enlarged in every direction until it became the greatest in this country, with branches in the leading cities. Stewart owned the factories making the fabrics he sold, and was also an extensive importer. His business methods were unpopular, though profitable, and involved the remorseless crushing of rivals, so that he had few friends and many enemies. His only trusted adviser, Judge Henry Hilton, lived in a modest brownstone house on Thirty-fourth Street, adjoining the palace. Yet Stewart was charitable. He sent a ship-load of provisions to relieve the Irish famine of 1846, and made large public gifts to aid suffering, while at the time of his death he was building on Fourth Avenue, at Thirty-second Street, an enormous structure intended as a "Home for Working Girls," on which fifteen hundred thousand dollars were expended. It was completed and opened shortly after his death, yet with such stringent rules regulating the "girls' company" and their parrots and cats that a rebellion was soon fomented among the intended beneficiaries, and it had to be closed. A shrewd suspicion has always prevailed that the difficulty was intentional, for the Home, which would have produced no revenue as a charity, was soon afterward reopened as a hotel. Stewart had scarcely moved into his Fifth Avenue palace when he died, and his body was put temporarily into a vault awaiting removal to the magnificent mausoleum being prepared for it at Garden City, Long Island. Then the country was horrified by the news that the corpse had been stolen to revenge business tyranny. Whether it was recovered has never been made known. The childless widow lived in gloomy grandeur in the palace until her death, never seeing visitors, and having watchmen pacing the sidewalk at all hours. The great business that Stewart organized has been broken up and scattered, his enormous fortune is being dissipated in litigation, and, as he left no direct descendants, the estate is rapidly going into strangers' hands.

This empty white marble Stewart palace, which is now for sale, was the first serious innovation made upon the rich brownstone fronts of Fifth Avenue. Thirty years ago the possession of a "brownstone front" was the necessary adjunct of New York social standing. The material came into such extensive use that it gave a distinctive coloring to Gotham. Its sombreness and the general uniformity of architecture have made most of the New York residential streets corridors of gloom. For years, as a competent local authority has described it, "our new houses and blocks were all turned out from the same moulds, and apparently congealed from the same coffee-colored liquid." To break the fashionable monotony required some moral courage, and it was regarded as a startling innovation when the Stewart palace was designed and was found to be slowly growing of marble. Afterward the brownstone was criticised as tending to scale and disintegrate under the extremes of temperature to which it is exposed in this climate. The builders have since made large inroads with other materials, thus giving more individuality to the finer buildings. The Connecticut quarrymen, who once had such a bonanza in their brownstone, are now said to be feeling the change, the demand having declined. The streets adjacent to the palace give evidence of this change. Thirty-fourth Street is a grand highway, and has its uniform rows of brownstone houses, but some distance west of Fifth Avenue is the Institution for the Blind, its extensive white marble buildings being surmounted by turrets and battlements. Near by, on Thirty-fifth Street, is the spacious graystone State Arsenal, the military headquarters of the National Guard. To the eastward, after crossing Madison Avenue, Thirty-fourth Street crosses Fourth Avenue, here widened to one hundred and forty feet, so that the tunnel which takes the street-railways up to the Grand Central Station at Forty-second

Street can go under Murray Hill. The open spaces above this tunnel, giving it light and air, are surrounded by little parks, making this, which is called Park Avenue, one of the pleasant places of New York. Standing here, eastward at Thirty-second Street is seen the enormous pile of buildings forming Stewart's Working Girls' Home, constructed around a spacious courtyard. At Thirty-fourth Street corner is the reddish-brown Gothic Unitarian Church of the Messiah, where Robert Collyer is pastor. The Presbyterian Church of the Covenant is a Lombardo-Gothic graystone building at Thirty-fifth Street. To the northward, over the little parks, the view is closed by the louvre domes of the Grand Central station of the Vanderbilt railroads. All about, in the newer buildings, are seen the architectural inroads made upon the once prevalent brownstone.

VI.

THE VANDERBILTS.

WE continue the walk out Fifth Avenue and approach the top of Murray Hill. At Thirty-seventh Street corner is the "Old Brick Church" of the Presbyterians, standing at about the most elevated portion of the hill, and built solid and substantial, with a tall brick and brownstone spire. The congregation dates from 1767. At No. 425 Fifth Avenue is the double brownstone house which Austin Corbin last winter bought from James Gordon Bennett for three hundred thousand dollars. This price gives a guide to Fifth-Avenue values, and Mr. Corbin says it was a bargain. This was the home of both the elder and the younger Bennett, the former having founded the New York *Herald*. A short distance beyond, at Thirty-ninth Street, is the finest club-house in New York—an elaborate brick-and-brownstone edifice, with a splendid colonnade over the entrance, and having spacious windows that disclose the luxurious apartments within. This is the Republican Union League Club, presided over by the genial Chauncey M. Depew, the president of the Vanderbilt railroads. Just above, on the east side of Fifth Avenue, is the historic Vanderbilt house, No. 459—a wide dwelling of brownstone, evidently built some time ago, and having alongside a carriage entrance into a small courtyard. This was the original home of the Vanderbilts, and is now occupied by one of the old commodore's younger grandsons, Frederick. The fortune of the Vanderbilt family, the greatest yet accumulated in America, represents the financially-expansive facilities of modern New York as manipulated by the machinery of corporation management and the Stock Exchange. It has been piled up by two generations, a father and a son, within the last half century, and is now held by the grandchildren. The old commodore, Cornelius Vanderbilt, who was born on Staten Island in 1794, was an uneducated boatman who traded in a meagre way around New York harbor, and at the age of twenty-three owned a few small vessels, and is said to have then estimated his wealth at nine thousand dollars. He became a steamboat captain and went into the transportation business between New York and Philadelphia, afterward widening his operations. In 1848 he owned most of the profitable steamboat lines leading from New York, and as soon as the California fever began he started ocean steamers in connection with the transit across the Isthmus of Panama. This business grew, and at the height of his steamship career the commodore owned sixty-six vessels, the finest of which, the steamer Vanderbilt, that had cost him eight hundred thousand dollars, he gave the Government for a war-vessel during the Civil War to chase the rebel privateers. The war making American vessel-owning in the foreign trade unprofitable, he determined to abandon it and devote himself to railway management, having already bought largely of railway stocks. At that time he estimated his wealth at forty millions. He got control of the various railroads leading east, north, and west from New York, buying the shares at low figures, and, his excellent methods improving their earning powers, they advanced largely in value. The greatest of these roads is the New York Central and Hudson River Railroad.

When Commodore Vanderbilt died his estate was estimated at seventy-five million dollars, and nearly the whole of it was left to his son William H. Vanderbilt, as he felt the transcendent importance of concentrating wealth when in railway investments to get the full advantage of its power. By its own earning capacity, aided by Stock-Exchange operations, the son saw this colossal fortune still further grow, and when he died suddenly, some four years ago, it had reached an aggregate estimated at two hundred million dollars. At one time William H. Vanderbilt had fifty million dollars invested in United States Fours, and it is no wonder that the comparatively unpretentious dwelling at Fortieth Street and Fifth Avenue became too cramped for the increasing wealth of the modern Crœsus, so that he had to build a row of palaces to house his family farther out toward Central Park. The bulk of his fortune was bequeathed to his two eldest sons, while other sons and daughters were also liberally provided for. The aggregate Vanderbilt fortunes now approximate two hundred and ninety million dollars.

THE CROTON RESERVOIR.

Upon the west side of Fifth Avenue, and diagonally across from the Vanderbilt mansion, is the old Croton distributing reservoir on the summit of Murray Hill, covering four acres, and having the pretty little Bryant Park behind it, extending to Sixth Avenue. This ivy-covered structure looks much like the Tombs prison, being built of granite in the same massive and sombre Egyptian style. The water was first let into it in 1842, and now there is talk of its abandonment, the city having grown far beyond its capabilities. North of this reservoir Forty-second Street stretches across the city, a wide highway, passing at the next block the Grand Central Station. This is the largest railway-station of New York, covering over five acres and having cost two million two hundred and fifty thousand dollars. It is of brick, with stone and iron facings and ornamentation, surmounted by louvre domes, and is an impressive building. Its vast interior halls for the trains is under a semicircular roof supported by arched trusses. Elevated railroads and horse-car lines from "down town" run into this great station, the latter coming up through the Park Avenue tunnel. The surrounding region is animated, abounding with restaurants, hotels, and lodging-houses, and the adjuncts of a railway terminal, including the prosperous Lincoln National Bank, which thrives upon the Vanderbilt patronage. The outgoing railways are laid north from this station through tunnels under Fourth Avenue for a long distance, until in the suburbs they cross the Harlem River and depart north and east. This is the only railway system leading directly from New York City, as all the others have to be reached by ferries crossing the rivers. Returning to Fifth Avenue, at Forty-second Street is a plain and modest residence, No. 503, which is the city home of Vice-President Levi P. Morton, the banker. At Forty-third Street the Jews have built their finest American synagogue, the "Temple Emmanuel," a magnificent specimen of Saracenic architecture, with the interior gorgeous in Oriental decoration. Creeping plants tastefully overrun the lower parts of its two great towers. At Forty-fifth Street is the Universalist "Church of the Divine Paternity," one of the noblest buildings in New York. Just above is the Episcopal "Church of the Heavenly Rest," a curious-looking, narrow-fronted, reddish stone building, apparently squeezed between the adjoining houses, but expanding to large proportions inside the block.

It really looks more like a museum than a church, and is surmounted by statues of brown angels vigorously blowing trumpets toward the various points of the compass. Occupying the whole of the next block, between Forty-sixth and Forty-seventh streets, is the grandest hotel of upper Fifth Avenue—the Windsor, tall and solid-looking, with a comfortable appearance and imposing front. The lobbies within the entrance are spacious, and in times of excitement in the evenings they are filled with the chief men of the city, this being the great resort for gossip and news and stock speculation at night.

THE "LITTLE WIZARD."

Opposite the side of the Windsor Hotel, across Forty-seventh Street, is a square-built and roomy though not large house, with a mansard roof, and an abundance of foliage plants in the rear windows, and having in front an elaborate portico, under which a grand staircase, flanked by evergreens and garden vases, leads up to the hall-door. This is No. 579 Fifth Avenue, the residence of the most mysterious and probably the best-abused person in the United States—a retiring and modest man, who is usually in seclusion, yet manages to communicate with the outer world through the abundance of wires entering his house. The bulls and bears of Wall Street blame upon these radiating wires most of their woes, for Jay Gould is supposed to sit within and constantly manipulate them. This "Little Wizard" has been the greatest speculative power in New York in recent years, and has had a remarkable career, being alike the product, and to a large extent the producer, of modern Wall-Street methods. He was a poor orphan and clerk in a country store, afterward becoming a surveyor and map-maker. He secured an interest in a Pennsylvania tannery, and to sell its leather was the object of his earliest visits to New York. Before long he owned the whole tannery, but his metropolitan visits taught him

there were quicker methods of making money; so he sold
out and removed, being at first too much afraid of New
York to live there, and he made his home in New Jersey.
But it was not long before New York became afraid of
him. His subsequent career is well known. Nobody ever
made such ventures. He was for years the "great bear,"
wrecking, pulling down, ruining—controlling newspapers,
courts, legislatures, and being even accused of trying to
bribe a President. Then, as he became an extensive
investor, he changed, at least so far as his own properties
were concerned, and in his later operations has been a
"bull." His fortune is the largest at present in the hands
of any one man in New York, being mainly in railways
and telegraphs, but its amount is unknown, for Jay Gould
is a sphinx, talking, yet telling nothing. Unostentatious
and modest to an extreme, this wonderful speculator moves
quietly in his work, deeply mourns the recent loss of his
wife, and is training up his sons to take his place. He
makes display only in his grave, having expended one
hundred and twenty-five thousand dollars in building a
miniature of the Pantheon for his mausoleum in Woodlawn Cemetery, in the northern suburbs.

I have written of the old Dutch governor, Peter Minuit,
who bought Manhattan Island from the Indians. About
the time he made that shrewd bargain he founded for his
little colony in 1628 an orthodox Dutch church. After
several removals this church now exists in a costly brownstone structure at Fifth Avenue and Forty-eighth Street.
This magnificent edifice, the inscription tells us, is the
"Collegiate Reformed Protestant Dutch Church of the
City of New York, organized under Peter Minuit, Direc-
tor-General of the New Netherlands, in 1628, chartered
by William, king of England, 1696." The present church
was built in 1872. Filling the entire block above, between
Fiftieth and Fifty-first Streets, is the great Catholic cathedral of St. Patrick, a magnificent white marble structure

in Decorated Gothic, covering a surface of three hundred and thirty-two by one hundred and seventy-four feet. The central gable of the front rises one hundred and fifty-six feet, and the unfinished spires on either side, upon which work slowly progresses, are expected to be three hundred and twenty-eight feet high. This noble church presents a striking resemblance to the great cathedral at Cologne, particularly in the interior, where the softened light unfolds the cloistered arches, the high nave, rich decorations, magnificent windows and splendid altars. Behind the cathedral and fronting upon Madison Avenue is the white marble residence of Archbishop Corrigan, and in an enclosure fronting Fifth Avenue, in the next block northward, is the Catholic Orphan Asylum—a large brick structure, with much of its front made of a continuous series of glass windows. Opposite the archbishop's residence, upon the other side of Madison Avenue and surrounding a courtyard, are the extensive buildings of Columbia College, the old King's College of New York, which was founded in 1754 by a fund started from the proceeds of sundry lotteries, raising in all seventeen thousand two hundred and fifteen dollars. This is now a very wealthy establishment, having other buildings and departments in various parts of the city, and it is famous both as a school of law and of medicine.

THE VANDERBILT PALACES.

The finest portion of Fifth Avenue has now been reached, and, crossing Fifty-first Street, we get into the modern domain of the Vanderbilts. Diagonally across from the cathedral, upon the west side of the avenue, are two elaborate brownstone dwellings with ornamented fronts and having a connecting covered passage containing the entrance-halls for both. They occupy the block, and are the homes of the late William H. Vanderbilt's daughters, being only exceeded in magnificence by his own residence, a drabstone structure of castellated architecture and highly decorated, upon the upper corner of Fifty-second Street. This is now the house of his eldest son, William K. Vanderbilt. The second son, Cornelius Vanderbilt, lives at the corner of Fifty-seventh Street in the fourth Vanderbilt palace, an elaborate brick house with ornamental stone decorations. These palaces were constructed, decorated, and furnished with the intention of outshining any other dwellings in New York, so as to be in keeping with the wealth of their owners and ornaments for the city where it was amassed. Fully fifteen millions of dollars were expended upon them. But, unfortunately, like so many men who have built grand houses, the Crœsus who designed them had barely moved in when he died. It was in the reception-parlor of his new house that William H. Vanderbilt, while talking to Robert Garrett, suddenly fell over from his seat almost into the latter's arms, and instantly expired. Garrett had made a social call after a long estrangement, owing to the railway wars, between the families, Vanderbilt being inclined to reconciliation. The death was unexpected, and knowledge of it was concealed until the Stock Exchange had closed. That night the New York speculators had busy work laying plans to prevent a panic next day. This Vanderbilt mansion is the grandest in New York, and opposite is the tall structure of the elegant Langham Hotel, while on the corner above is St. Thomas's Episcopal church with its beautiful rose windows. Fortunes have been expended upon the decoration of all the dwellings in this costly locality. At Fifty-seventh Street is St. Luke's Hospital, managed by the Episcopal Church. At Fifty-fifth Street is Dr. John Hall's Presbyterian church, of brownstone, the fortunate pastor being said to preach to two hundred and fifty million dollars every Sunday in the largest and wealthiest Presbyterian church in the world. As a guide to the valuation of land on this part of Fifth Avenue, I may mention that twenty years ago Robert Bonner of the

New York *Ledger* bought the east side of the avenue, between Fifty-sixth and Fifty-seventh Streets, two hundred feet front by one hundred and seventy-five feet deep, for two hundred and seventy-five thousand dollars. This land is now valued at one million two hundred thousand dollars without buildings. William Waldorf Astor has just bought the Fifty-sixth Street corner, fifty feet front by one hundred and twenty-five feet deep, for three hundred and twenty-five thousand dollars, and C. P. Huntington the Fifty-seventh Street corner for four hundred and fifty thousand dollars, each intending to build a residence; and the central part has also gone to the Astor family for four hundred and twenty-five thousand dollars. Mr. Astor paid at the rate of forty-seven dollars per square foot, and Mr. Bonner's sons, who were the recent owners, are netting nine hundred and twenty-five thousand dollars' profit on their father's landed investment of two hundred and seventy-five thousand dollars twenty years ago. Along all the cross-streets are displayed elaborate rows of brownstone houses, and as Central Park is approached the enormous "apartment-houses" of French flats that face it rise high above us in various directions. The park is at Fifty-ninth Street, and its dense foliage obliterates much of the view beyond, but Fifth Avenue stretches far northward as the park boundary, with many fine buildings upon it, including the Lenox Library and the Metropolitan Museum of Art. But the travel upon the avenue there is sparse, as its gay equipages generally pass into the park through the "Scholar's Gate."

VII.

THE NEW YORK CENTRAL PARK.

THE pride of New York is its Central Park, the pleasure-ground upon which has been lavished all that art and

4

money could do. The park is a parallelogram in the centre of Manhattan Island, a half mile wide and two and a half miles long, occupying eight hundred and forty-three acres. Much of this space, however, is taken up by the Croton water reservoirs, elevated above the general level, so that the actual park surface is reduced to six hundred and eighty-three acres, or about one-fourth the size of Fairmount Park. This was the first great public park established in this country, the preparation of the ground having begun in 1858. The work opened on the southern portion, and was pushed with vigor, as many as four thousand men being at times employed to make it, in what was then a most unattractive region. The original surface was either marsh or rock, rough and with topography generally the reverse of that needed for a park. The locality for years had been the depository of the town refuse, a desert of coal-ashes and rubbish, the temporary home of colonies of squatters, who built their shanties wherever they thought raking the ash-heaps might yield profit. The removal of this refuse made much of the earlier work, for it had to be excavated to the depth of many feet before the natural surface was uncovered. Enormous labor and prodigious outlay overcame the difficulties ultimately, and then the popularity of the portions of the park that were first opened was so great that plenty of money was afterward granted and the park acquired much celebrity. The long and narrow enclosure is surrounded by a wall, but as this interferes with the cross-town traffic, at about each half mile a street is carried by a subway under the park roads and footwalks, thus giving free passage without access to or interference with the pleasure-grounds. Skilful engineering and landscape gardening have made the most of the unsightly surface dealt with, and attractive features have been produced out of glaring defects. Art, in fact, had to do everything, as the original tract bore neither lawns nor walks, neither lake nor forest. The rocks and débris had to be excavated for the lakes, trees were planted, bridges built, and roads laid out. To many observers its excessive art sometimes becomes oppressive, but this famous pleasure-ground now lacks only the maturing of its trees to become one of the handsomest parks in the world. Its union of art with nature in Italian terraces, many bridges of quaint design, placid waters, towers, rustic houses, nooks and rambles, place it in the front rank among American parks.

Entering from Fifth Avenue at the "Scholar's Gate," the road within the park leads by a gently winding course past vista views and pretty lakes to the Mall, or general promenade. Here on pleasant days many thousands gather to listen to the music. To the westward are broad green surfaces, including a spacious ball-ground, which give a tranquil landscape. Looking northward through the avenue of elms upon the Mall, the little gray stone tower known as the Observatory closes the view far away over another pretty lake. At the end of the Mall the terrace is crossed bordering this lake, the ground sloping to its edges. A fountain plashes upon one side, while on the other is the concert-ground, overlooked by the Pergola, a shaded gallery. Here art has done its best to make magnificence, where gather the "French nurse-maids," usually with a Hibernian accent which the Gallic cap and broad white apron cannot disguise, to indulge in moderate flirtations as they watch the babies. Across the pretty lake, on the Observatory side, is the Ramble, a rocky forest-covered slope, having paths winding through it, and on the highest point a massive structure called the Belvidere. The children have play-grounds, an aviary, and menagerie, and other amusements are provided. Beyond this enchanting region the road winds past statues and ever-changing beauties of landscape and garden, and comes out in a space alongside the smaller reservoir, where stands Cleopatra's Needle, set up near the noble Museum of Art. Then the road passes alongside the larger reservoir with barely enough room for it to get through between the huge bank enclosing the basin and Fifth Avenue, both, however, being admirably masked. In the northern portion the park has another lake and extensive meadows, the artistic decoration here, however, being less elaborate. Gradually the winding road leads to the western side, where it ascends Harlem Heights to a fine lookout. From this elevation far to the north can be seen the tall arches of the " High Bridge," which brings the Croton Aqueduct over the Harlem River into the city, and the tower alongside that makes the reservoir used to force the water to the elevation of the highest buildings. The river's winding banks are steep and picturesquely wooded, and can be traced off toward the Hudson River, across which are the dim and hazy Palisades, marking the New Jersey shore. Just beyond the edge of the park, in the foreground, an elevated railway runs upon its high trestle, here perched upon taller stilts than usual, as it crosses a depression in the surface, beyond which is the noted German picnic-ground, the Lion Brewery. Secluded paths and embowered walks are all about for the solace of the pedestrian, while a flock of contented sheep, who evidently pay no taxes, browse upon the meadows, and are housed at night in a building more magnificent than many upon Fifth Avenue.

THE REGION BEYOND THE PARK.

One-Hundred-and-Tenth Street makes the northern boundary of Central Park, and is about seven and a half miles from the Battery. Beyond this, Manhattan Island has been laid out with broad public roads known as the " Boulevards," and the buildings going up in many places are making it a thickly-inhabited region. The fast trotters of the young bloods of New York speed swiftly upon these superb drives, one hundred and fifty feet wide, for these are their racing-grounds. This is also a land of the squatters, their shanties placed snugly among the rocks. Scarred gray and moss-covered crags thrust up their heads through all this region, with intervening tracts of good soil, where are little market-gardens and hot-beds growing vegetables and berries. The boulevard on which we are driving leads into the King's Bridge road, and, approaching the Harlem River, across it are seen Morrisania and other villages, hazy hills closing the distant view. We go down into the wooded slopes of the valley and across the river by that little old historic bridge whose fame is intertwined with New York's early history and whose timbers mark the political division of New York State. Harrison came to this famous crossing with too big a majority at the last election for New York City and Long Island to overcome it. The Harlem River is a strait whose waters in crooked windings flow with the tide at the bottom of a deep gorge that has the New York Central Railroad on its northern border seeking an outlet along its shore to the Hudson River. Several bridges are thrown across, but the "High Bridge" is the chief, its tall granite piers and graceful arches showing with singular beauty from every point of view, whether seen through the foliage from below or from the distant hilltops.

The Spuyten Duyvel Creek is beyond, the strait connecting the Harlem with the Hudson, and thus making Manhattan an island. It opens out upon that grand river with a magnificent view, having the Palisades for a distant background. The Harlem River, winding between the wooded slopes below the "High Bridge," has on its eastern verge the attractive suburb of Morrisania. Here lived Lewis Morris, one of the signers of the Declaration of Independence, and his brother, Gouverneur Morris, a noted old New Yorker, who bore a striking resemblance to General Washington. The ancient Morris mansion stands near the river, not far away from the bridge. All this section is fast being swallowed up by the spreading streets of New York, of which municipality it now forms a part.

THE GREAT AQUEDUCT.

The Croton Aqueduct, thus brought to the city over the "High Bridge," well described as "a structure worthy of the Roman empire," is over forty miles long from the Croton River to the distributing reservoir on Murray Hill. It originally cost twelve million five hundred thousand dollars, but improvements since have absorbed millions more. The Croton comes down through Westchester county, and falls into the Hudson some twenty-five miles above the city; its head-waters are dammed to make artificial lakes, gathering the supply. Excepting the great storage reservoirs in Central Park, the works were built between 1837 and 1842, and then surpassed all modern constructions of the kind. In its course the aqueduct goes through more than a mile of tunnels bored in gneiss rock, with much of the open cuttings also rockwork. At first, the Croton was dammed by a wall forty feet high, thus making Croton Lake, covering four hundred acres and holding five hundred million gallons. Afterward, across the western branch of the river, a dam seven hundred feet long was built, flooding three hundred acres and making storage for three thousand million gallons. From these lakes, for thirty-three miles to the Harlem River, the aqueduct is built of brick and stone, having a cross-section of about fifty-three and a half square feet and an inclination of about one foot to the mile, or thirty-four feet in the entire distance. There are one hundred and fifteen million gallons flowing through daily, moving a mile and a half per hour. Three huge iron pipes carry the water across the "High Bridge," which is fourteen hundred feet long and rises one hundred and sixteen feet above high-water mark. The arches are eighty feet wide and their openings one hundred feet high, to give free passage for masted vessels. There are eight of these arches in the river-crossing, while seven narrower ones, each of fifty feet span, are on the banks. Standing at the New York end of this picturesque bridge is the solid-looking tall tower

that is a special feature in all the views. Its surmounting
tank is at two hundred and sixty-five feet elevation, and a
portion of the water is pumped up there for the convenient
supply of the highest parts of Manhattan Island. The
greater current, however, flows on to the reservoirs in Central Park, which cover one hundred and thirty-five acres, and
have one thousand two hundred million gallons' capacity,
their elevation being one hundred and nineteen feet. Underground pipe-lines thence convey water to the smaller Fifth
Avenue distributing reservoir on Murray Hill, holding
twenty million gallons. Before long this will be abandoned and the ground put to other uses. Some thirty
million dollars have been expended upon these waterworks,
the large storage reservoirs in connection with the Croton
lakes giving ample opportunity for subsidence, so that the
Croton water is clear, and not ornamented, like ours at
Philadelphia, with all the rainbow hues of the soils of the
Schuylkill watershed. New York's expansive growth has,
however, almost got beyond the capacity even of these
extensive works, so that new enterprises are afoot. At the
Quaker Bridge in the Croton district the most enormous
reservoir in the world is being constructed, intended to
hold forty thousand million gallons, so that no protracted
drouth can imperil the supply. About twenty million dollars will be expended upon this work, and the water will
come to Harlem River by a new aqueduct twelve feet in
diameter tunnelled for twenty-seven miles through the
rocks, and then carried under the river by a tunnel at
about two hundred and fifty feet depth. At One-Hun-
dred-and-Thirty-fifth Street an imposing gate-house is to
admit the new water-supply into the city mains. This
aqueduct is to cost over fifteen million dollars, and its
work through political peculations has recently made
many unsavory scandals. These works are the most enormous ever projected, and in a few years are expected to
give a supply of at least two hundred and fifty million gal-

lons daily—enough for the metropolis for many years to come. Thus New York will have spent altogether over sixty-five million dollars to bring in an adequate water-supply.

THE ELEVATED RAILWAYS.

The Central Park and the extensive region beyond are readily accessible through the lines of the elevated railways stretching from the Battery to Harlem. One cannot stay long in New York without riding upon them. These airy constructions, set up in the streets upon stilts, have solved the rapid-transit problem for the elongated, narrow city. Nowhere have methods of quick transportation been more studied. The character of New York and its surroundings, and the migratory habits of the enormous crowds rushing in from all points in the morning and rushing out again at night, have forced it. A million people cross the Hudson and East Rivers daily, and a half million more move "down town" in the morning, and "up town" again at night. No city anywhere has so many ferries or such vast capacity in the huge boats crossing the rivers, or such gorgeous floating palaces to carry its passengers from its wharves to other cities. Two hundred thousand people daily cross the Brooklyn Bridge, reared high above East River, and a second bridge is projected to cross at Blackwell's Island, so that "up town" may also have an outlet. To secure similar advantages the Hudson River is being tunnelled and a high suspension bridge is also planned across it. Almost every principal street has a horse-car line, and some, like the Bowery, two or three of them. Four lines of elevated railways are overtaxed with traffic, and a scheme has been started to relieve them by tunnelling Broadway, which has the late lamented Jacob Sharp's most lucrative street-railway upon its surface, coining money for Philadelphia owners. As the city could only grow at its distant northern end, the relief for

overcrowded transportation was sought cheaply overhead
that London only got at great cost and serious incon-
venience underground. Yet the new plan was hard to
introduce. When somebody first set up a railway on posts
along Greenwich Street and the "West Side" it had for
years a sickly existence, people being afraid to ride lest it
might topple over. But it grew in favor, and when it paid
there came a rush of capital for investment in more elevated railways, which were speedily built, and for the
present have solved the problem of rapid transit throughout the great length of New York. They have all been
gathered into the "Manhattan Company," ruled by the
"Little Wizard," Jay Gould. Their trains, high up in the
air, rush past the upper windows of the houses, where you
can see the inhabitants eating their meals or doing their
work, or, possibly, going to bed, while the street-traffic
moves slowly and with obstruction beneath. Swiftly and
smoothly gliding through and over the great city, among
the houses and around the corners, now hemmed by tall
buildings within a narrow street, and then quickly given a
broader view upon a wide avenue, this system shows many
New York peculiarities. It is unique, and to most visitors
is as great an attraction as New York can present, giving
more enjoyment at less cost than any other Gotham entertainment. Its convenience is also a charm, and the
admirable system could be copied with advantage wherever rapid transit has become a necessity.

VIII.

THE EAST RIVER.

THE eastern boundary of Manhattan Island is made by
the Harlem and East Rivers. The former flows into the

latter, dividing Manhattan from Ward's Island, that with
Randall's Island to the north and Blackwell's Island to the
south forms the group of " East River islands " upon which
are the penal and charitable institutions of the great city.
The "Commissioners of Charities and Correction" take
charge annually of a large population, sometimes reaching three hundred thousand. The chief buildings are on
Blackwell's Island, the long and narrow strip stretching
nearly two miles in the centre of East River off the upper
city piers, and being barely more than two hundred yards
wide. Upon its one hundred and twenty acres of surface
are the penitentiary, almshouses, workhouses, asylums, and
hospitals, the spacious buildings being of granite quarried
there by the convicts. Over on the city side is Bellevue
Hospital with extensive buildings, also in charge of the
commission, and containing the Morgue and the headquarters of the ambulance corps. In cases of vagrancy and
minor offences the punishment is to be " sent to the Island."
There are insane and inebriate asylums upon Ward's Island,
and also a Soldiers' Home. Randall's Island has the institutions for children and idiots, while upon Hart's Island,
over in Long Island Sound, are the pauper cemetery and
industrial schools. The building and grounds are all upon
the most elaborate scale, and it costs about two million dollars annually for their maintenance. The steamboat ride
along the river, with these extensive establishments and
their attractive, well-kept grounds passing in full review, is
one of the most charming suburban excursions.

To the southward of Ward's Island the shore of Long
Island is thrust out in a way that curves and contracts the
East River passage. Just here, below where the Harlem
joins the East River, the latter turns eastward, and, flowing around the other side of Ward's Island, goes through
the famous Hell Gate to reach Long Island Sound. Formerly, this was a most dangerous pass, through which the
swift tidal current boiled and eddied. Hallett's Point, jut-

ting out from Long Island, narrowed the channel, and Pot
Rock, Flood Rock, the Gridiron, and other reefs obstructed
it, making navigation perilous. Over thirty years ago
desultory operations began for the improvement of this
channel, but a comprehensive plan was not projected until
1866, when General Newton took charge of the work. His
first task was the removal of the reef at Hallett's Point,
where a mass of rock projected about three hundred feet
into the stream and threw the tidal current coming in from
the sound against an opposing rock called the Gridiron.
General Newton sunk a shaft upon the point, and then
excavated the inland side, so that it made a perpendicular
wall, which was curved around and designed for the future
edge of the river. From the shaft tunnels were bored into
the rock under the river in radiating directions, and these
were connected by concentric galleries. The design was to
remove as much rock as possible without letting the water
in from overhead, and then to blow up the rocky roof and
supporting columns, afterward removing the fragments at
leisure. The work began in 1869, the shaft being sunk
thirty-two feet below mean low water, and the tunnels
drilled out under the river through a tough hornblende
gneiss. In 1876 the task was finished, and thousands of
separate blasts had been placed in the roof and supporting
columns ready for the final explosion on Sunday, September 24. There was much trepidation shown in New York,
many people leaving the city, while everywhere the keenest
interest was shown in the result, this being the greatest artificial explosion ever attempted. It was entirely successful, being dislodged by General Newton's little child, who
touched the electric key; and the calculation had been so
accurately made that the great reef was pulverized and the
fragments fell into the spaces excavated beneath without
causing more than a slight tremor in the adjacent region.
By a similar system and more extensive work Flood Rock
was afterward removed from mid-channel, the second great

blast, reducing it to fragments, being discharged in October, 1885. The current still flows swiftly through Hell Gate, but the terrors of the passage are gone.

THE BROOKLYN BRIDGE.

East River below the islands is the locality of the great foreign shipping-trade of the metropolis, the wharves and docks of New York and Brooklyn on either hand being filled with the ships of all nations that come from the most remote quarters of the globe. China and Japan, the Indies, Australia, and the Pacific, all send their products to fill the storehouses everywhere bordering the lines of piers and the extensive basins on the Brooklyn side. High above them rises the huge East River bridge, the tie that binds the twin municipalities. Its massive piers are among the tallest structures about New York, their tops being elevated two hundred and sixty-eight feet above the water. They stand upon caissons sunk into the rocky bed of the stream, which is forty-five feet below the surface on the Brooklyn side and ninety feet below on the New York side. A section of these gigantic piers at the water-line covers a surface one hundred and thirty-four feet long by fifty feet broad. Their towers carry four sixteen-inch wire cables that sustain the bridge, which is built eighty feet wide, so as to give ample passageways for two car-lines, with wagon-roads and footways. The bridge is entirely of iron and steel, and the cables are made of galvanized steel wires, the floor of the bridge at the centre of the river being raised one hundred and thirty-five feet above the water. Between the piers the distance is about sixteen hundred feet, while the entire length of the bridge between the anchorages of the cables is three thousand four hundred and seventy-five feet. These anchorages are enormous masses, each containing about thirty-five thousand cubic yards of solid masonry. The roadway that approaches the bridge on the New York side rises from Chatham Street, opposite the

City Hall Park, while in Brooklyn it comes down upon Fulton Street at some distance from the river, so that the whole length of the bridge and its elaborate approaches is considerably over a mile. It was thirteen years in building, having been opened for traffic in May, 1885, with imposing ceremonies in which both cities joined. The projector of this famous bridge was the late John A. Roebling, and its builder his son, Washington A. Roebling, who caught the dreaded "caisson disease" while superintending the earlier work under water. For years afterward, an invalid, he watched the progress of the later work from his chamber-window on Brooklyn Heights. There were fourteen thousand three hundred and sixty-one miles of wire made to put into the huge cables of the bridge, and their weight is nearly four thousand tons. New York and Brooklyn shared the cost of this enterprise, which was about fourteen million dollars, and its completion, by making Brooklyn free from the risks of East-River ferry transportation, has given that city an impetus which has been increasing its population at a greater rate than any other Atlantic coast city.

THE VIEW FROM THE BRIDGE.

We will cross this famous bridge and enjoy the superb view from its central elevation, which is among the finest that can be got in New York. Its broad roadways rise by an easy gradient from the eastern border of the New York City Hall Park toward the middle of East River. On the outer side of the bridge are the wagon-roads, while between is the promenade for foot-passengers. Between each wagon-road and this footwalk a railroad-track is laid, upon which passenger-cars are run by an endless cable, hauling them rapidly over the bridge in trains of three or four cars, thus greatly facilitating the crossing, there being capacity to carry eight to ten thousand people each way every hour. The tolls are three cents to ride over and one cent to walk, the latter being preferable for the stranger, as the central footway is raised above the outer roads, so that the noble view from the bridge is completely unobstructed. Many pedestrians cross on fair days, and all kinds of vehicles pass and repass in almost unbroken procession. As the ascent rises the grand panorama gradually develops as the house-tops sink below you, until at the centre of the bridge the view spreads out in all its unrivalled glories.

Looking northward, the East River is seen coming down around the sharp bend of Corlaer's Hook on the New York side, opposite which is the deep indentation of Wallabout Bay on the Brooklyn shore, the locality where its earliest settlement was made, and now occupied by the largest navyyard the United States possesses. This yard includes a total area of nearly one hundred and fifty acres, and has over a mile of wharf frontage. Here is the extensive "Cob Dock," where the naval vessels are outfitted, and where last December the grim war-ships that were going out to scare Hayti had to lie several hours in the mud before departure, until the tide rose sufficiently to release them and Admiral Luce received his clothes from Newport. The navyyard proper is an enclosure of forty-five acres, and has a fine granite dry-dock. The Marine Hospital is on the opposite side of Wallabout.

Both shores of the East River are fringed with piers that are crowded with vessels of all kinds, and behind them are vast aggregations of houses on either hand, with myriads of craft in front moving upon the water. The rattle of the railway-cables hauling the cars over and keeping up a merry jingling across their pulleys, and the gentle vibration of the bridge itself caused by the passing traffic, combine with the busy hum of the two great cities and the shrill whistles of the vessels below manœuvring in the crowded channel to add to the life of the scene.

Looking southward, the narrow waterway flows off from beneath us into the broader Hudson River, with Governor's

Island and its fort and round Castle William spread almost across the mouth of the stream. Red Hook Point juts out from the Brooklyn shore toward this island, while far away to the right is seen the colossal French goddess holding up her liberty torch upon Bedloe's Island. Beyond is the broad harbor of the Upper Bay, with many vessels moving and anchored, spreading out for miles to the blue hills of Staten Island, that make an appropriate background. The storehouses and piers accommodating the chief part of the foreign commerce of New York are on both sides of the East River, for to this region come most of the sailing ships from distant countries. Here also is the headquarters of the grain-trade brought down the Hudson in Erie Canal barges, and then sent in lighters all about the harbor. Over by Red Hook, on the left-hand side, is the great Atlantic Dock, where there is an enclosure of fifty acres that can accommodate five hundred vessels and has more than two miles of wharfage, with rows of substantial brick and granite storehouses. It fronts for a half mile on the Buttermilk Channel, having Governor's Island in the foreground. Beyond it, around Red Hook, in Gowanus Bay, are the more extensive Erie and Brooklyn basins, covering a hundred acres. In these localities are accommodated the heavy freight—coal, iron, lumber, corn, sugar, etc.—and over one hundred million dollars' worth of goods of various kinds are often in the stores. This portion of Brooklyn is always a busy place, while behind it rises the aristocratic locality of the "Brooklyn Heights," displaying rows of fine dwellings crowned by church-steeples and spires, and having Gowanus Heights and the foliage and tombs of Prospect Park and Greenwood Cemetery far away in the distance. Turning from this bewitching scene again to the right-hand side, behind the vessels and piers and storehouses is the compact city of New York, the tall buildings and towers of lower Broadway rising up in the background, with the square tower of the Produce Exchange marking

its southern extremity, beyond which is the distant hazy
land of New Jersey. Little puffing, straining tugs draw
huge tall-masted ships under the bridge beneath our feet,
and the crowded boats upon the Fulton ferry, just below
us, move, crab-like, sideways, across the river as they are
swung by the swift-flowing tide. The wind freshly blows
across our high perch, for it far outtops most of the surrounding region. The sensation is much like looking down
from a balloon, and it would be difficult anywhere else in
the world to get a better view of the enormous commerce
and nervous activity of such a great mart of trade.

IX.

THE CITY OF CHURCHES.

WE have crossed the East River bridge to see an unique
municipality. The people of New York are said to go over
to Brooklyn chiefly to sleep or be buried. A large part of
the working population, as well as the merchants of the
metropolis, make it their dormitory, while in the suburbs
are the beautiful cemeteries where dead New Yorkers lay
their bones. Greenwood, which overlooks the harbor from
Gowanus Heights in South Brooklyn, is the finest American cemetery. It is possible that the numerous funeral
processions constantly crossing the East River ferries and
bridge have aided in developing the religious fervor of this
populous suburb, for nowhere else can be found such an
aggregation of sacred edifices, and under the ministry of
a regiment of clergymen, led by such men as Beecher, Talmage, and Storrs, Brooklyn has properly earned her popular sobriquet of the " City of Churches." This place is
entirely the growth of the present century, and its remarkable expansion in recent years is due to the inability of

New York to spread except far northward. Brooklyn stretches several miles along East River and three or four miles inland, and grows so rapidly that next year's census may show a population not much below a million. Yet when this century began it is said to have been hard work to find three thousand people, and, strangely enough, they had to cross over to New York to church. A band of Walloons first settled Brooklyn, just about the time old Peter Minuit was buying Manhattan Island from the Indians. Their descendants used to drive cows across East River to Governor's Island to graze, the river then being in that part—Buttermilk Channel—shallow enough for fording, though now this channel has become scoured out deep enough to float the largest steamers, and the Brooklyn docks and wharves at Red Hook Point and above, where the cows then crossed, now accommodate an enormous commerce. The little ferry at Fulton Street, which first accommodated the straggling village, has grown into more than a dozen steam-ferries of the largest capacity, and a half million people daily cross them at one cent apiece. To see the successful process of packing to perfection an enormous human sardine-box, it is only necessary to look at a Brooklyn ferry-boat going home about sundown. The thousands pouring through the gates do not want seats; they are thankful if there is only standing-room. The ferry is short, as East River is comparatively narrow, being only one-third the width of the Hudson, but its fleet of ferry-boats are the greatest transporters of human beings in the world.

BROOKLYN HEIGHTS.

Fulton ferry leads to Fulton Street, the chief business highway, and the great bridge-approach descends on the Brooklyn shore alongside this street. As various avenues and streets radiate from it, to take Fulton Street becomes, much like Broadway, a necessity in the sister city. It is

5

broad and attractive, stretching five miles to the eastern edge of the town, and at about a mile from the river passes the various city buildings, including the splendid post-office recently erected. From Fulton Street radiate many of the highways leading into the popular residential quarter, Brooklyn Heights, where the tree-bordered avenues are lined with costly dwellings. Orange Street, not far from the bridge, leads off toward the river, and at a short distance, in a quiet spot, is Brooklyn's most famous edifice—a plain, wide, unornamented brick church, bearing the inscription, "Plymouth Church, 1849." Here preached Henry Ward Beecher, the great Puritan, whose family is so noted. His father, Lyman Beecher, like the son, fought slavery and intemperance in Boston and Cincinnati, and was a great pulpit orator. The old man was erratic, however, and after being wrought up by the excitement of preaching is said to have let himself down by playing on the fiddle and dancing a double-shuffle in the parlor. He had thirteen children, who were nearly all famous, and has been described as "the father of more brains than any other man in America." Four sons were clergymen and two daughters noted authoresses. For forty years Henry Ward Beecher ruled Plymouth Church and Brooklyn, but since his death the church has declined. A little beyond Orange Street, Clinton Street leaves Fulton and passes southward through Brooklyn Heights, being the chief avenue of the fashionable district. Embowered in trees, churches and residences border it, and Pierrepont, Remsen, Montague, and other noted streets extend at right angles from it to the edge of the bluff, where the Heights fall sharply off toward the river. Here, at seventy feet elevation and overlooking the lower level of buildings and piers at the water's edge, are the terraces where the finest residences are located, having a magnificent outlook upon the harbor. This region is as highly prized by the Brooklynites as Murray Hill and Fifth Avenue by the New Yorkers. The ships land their cargoes within a stone's throw of the palaces, and the ladies can see the busy cargo-workers from their boudoirs. It is this region that did much to decide the last two Presidential elections, for Brooklyn Heights has ever been the home of the "Mugwumps." Led out of the Republican party in 1884 by Beecher, they elected Cleveland, but their shepherd was stricken down by apoplexy in 1887, and the flock strayed back again the next year to aid in the election of Harrison.

Upon Remsen Street is another noted building, the "Church of the Pilgrims"—a spacious structure of gray cut stone with towers, its most prominent tower and spire being a commanding landmark for vessels sailing up New York Bay. In the lower part of this church, about six feet above the pavement, there is let into the outer wall a small piece of the original "Plymouth Rock" whereon the Pilgrims landed in Massachusetts Bay—a dark, rough-hewn fragment projecting with irregular surface a few inches from the wall. The pastor, Dr. Richard Salter Storrs, is an author, lecturer, and preacher of wide renown. Upon Clinton Street is Brooklyn's finest church—St. Ann's Episcopal— an elegant Pointed Gothic brownstone structure. But everywhere are churches, with miles of rows of comfortable dwellings and every evidence of thrift and wealth, for these descendants of the Puritans are much like other well-to-do Americans. Dr. Talmage's Tabernacle is on Schermerhorn Street, the most spacious Protestant church in this country, having a semicircular auditorium not unlike a theatre, seating over five thousand people.

GREENWOOD CEMETERY.

In the Brooklyn suburbs, and making a border of tombs almost around the town, are the great cemeteries that are the burial-places of both cities. In lovely situations upon the ridges of hills surrounding Brooklyn, Greenwood, Cypress Hills, the Evergreen, the Holy Cross, Calvary, Mount

Olivet, the Citizens' Union, Washington, and other cemeteries cover hundreds of acres. The noted Greenwood
Cemetery occupies about four hundred acres upon Gowanus
Heights, south of the city. This high ridge divides Brooklyn from the lowlands on the south side of Long Island,
and has elevations giving charming views. The way out
to it crosses various railroads that go to Coney Island,
which seems an objective point of most Brooklyn transportation lines. The route leads through a region of flor-
ists and stonemasons with extensive hot-houses and marble-
works—trades that seem to largely thrive upon our sor-
rows. Then a neat lawn-bordered road leads up to the
magnificent cemetery entrance, an elaborate brownstone
structure highly ornamented and rising into a central
pinnacle over one hundred feet high. With the wings
this entrance is one hundred and forty-two feet wide and
covers two gateways, there being over each gate and on
each side *basso-rilievi* representing gospel scenes, the chief
being the Raising of Lazarus and the Resurrection. A more
splendid or appropriate entrance would be hard to find,
and as soon as the gateway is passed the grounds open
in beauty. The ridgy, rounded hills spread in all directions, while through a depression to the right is caught
a bewitching view of New York Bay. The surface is
an alternation of hills and vales, vaults terracing the
hillsides, with noble mausoleums above, and frequent
lakes nestling in the pleasant little valleys. There are
many miles of roads and paths, and vast sums have been
spent on the grander tombs, some being built upon a scale
of magnificence rarely seen. The attractive rural names
of the avenues and walks, the delicious foliage and flowers,
the lakes and valleys, balmy air, and grand views of the
surrounding country constantly presented, make Greenwood a park as well as a cemetery, so that it is without
a peer. A dozen costly pantheons and chapels cover the
remains of well-known people, and one mausoleum is a

large marble church. A three-sided monument of peculiar construction standing on a knoll marks the resting-place of Morse the telegrapher. Horace Greeley's tomb has his bust in bronze on a pedestal. A colossal statue surmounts the grave of the great De Witt Clinton, the governor of New York who built the Erie Canal and thus made the commercial supremacy of the city. The romantic career of Lola Montez ended in Greenwood. Commodore Garrison, who was Vanderbilt's rival in steamship management, is interred in a mosque. The Steinway tomb is a huge granite building. A magnificent marble canopy crowns the Scribner tomb, having beneath it an angel of mercy. The Firemen, the Pilots, and the Soldiers all have grand monuments, the statue sentinels of the latter overlooking the broad waters of the bay. There are so many elaborate sepulchres that it is impossible to particularize, though probably the most splendid of the magnificent tombs of Greenwood is that of Charlotte Canda, who died in early youth, an heiress whose fortune was expended upon her grave. Upon the eastern border of this attractive place is the high lookout, in front of which the flat land at the base of the ridge spreads for miles away to the sea. The hotels of Coney Island, down by the ocean's edge, are dim in the distance, and far over the water the Navesink Highlands in Jersey close the view beyond Sandy Hook. The many railroads leading to Coney Island can be traced as on a map as they cross the level surface. Then, moving from the eastern to the western side of the cemetery through a forest of monuments, another lookout is reached having a broad view over Brooklyn and the intervening harbor to the hills of Staten Island and the Jersey lowlands beyond. This is the western edge of Gowanus Heights, where the busy commerce of the port is spread at our feet. It is this magnificent scene that the marble sentinels overlook who are guarding the Soldiers' Monument erected by New York City, and the declining sun as it sends its rays over the water makes everything beautiful.

PROSPECT PARK.

A short drive leads from Greenwood to Prospect Park, crossing several more railways, all going, like almost every other road, toward Coney Island. Finally, the "Ocean Parkway" is reached, the great Coney Island boulevard, a splendid road, two hundred feet wide and planted with six rows of trees. It is laid in a straight line direct from the south-western corner of the park down to that noted sea-side resort, which is three miles away. Prospect Park, covering nearly a square mile upon an elevated ridge in the south-western part of Brooklyn, is a comparatively recent enterprise. The perfection of elaborate decoration and landscape gardening displayed in the New York Central Park is not seen here, but it has what is better—a good deal more of the perfection of Nature. The attractive undulating surface has scarcely been changed, and the fine old trees that grew many years before the land was thought of for a park are in magnificent maturity. Its woods and meadows, winding roads, lakes, and views combine all the charms of landscape. From Lookout Hill, its most commanding point, there is a view almost entirely around the compass, stretching over land and sea, and including Brooklyn and New York, the Long Island and Jersey shores, Staten Island, the Navesinks, the harbor, and the ocean. Within the park are an enclosure for deer, an extensive lake, and a children's playground much used by the Brooklyn Sunday-schools. Here the concert-grove and promenade are attractive. From this charming place we go away toward the city by the main entrance, which is called the Plaza. This is a large elliptical enclosure, having a splendid fountain in the centre, where the water pours down a huge mound, and as the cataract falls it runs over openings that can be brilliantly illuminated from within. Abraham Lincoln (in bronze) overlooks this Plaza, which leads to Flat-bush Avenue and thence into town. There are many charms of residence in Brooklyn wherein New York is lacking, and they have had much to do with its rapid growth. There is plenty of room, too, for spreading, both for living homes and as a city of the dead, for the back country of Long Island stretches indefinitely toward the rising sun, ready to absorb the millions who may be sent over from Gotham.

X.

GOING TO CONEY ISLAND.

THE visitor to Brooklyn cannot help noticing that nearly all of its railroads lead to Coney Island. This barren strip of white sand clinging to the southern edge of Long Island, about ten miles from New York, is the great objective point of the millions in and around that city when in sweltering summer weather they crave a breath of salt air. There are a dozen ways of going down by both land and water, separately or combined, but when the enormous crowds of the metropolis suddenly take it into their heads to go upon a hot afternoon all the routes are overcrowded. Let us follow the New York and Brooklyn example, and start for Coney Island upon one of the numerous railways, taking the Long Island Railroad to Mr. Austin Corbin's seaside paradise—Manhattan Beach. We are soon trundling mer-rily over the flat land beyond Brooklyn in a train laden with sightseers bound to the races and the ocean, made up of men and women of all nations and all kinds—a human conglomeration such as only cosmopolitan New York can produce. We get past all the cemeteries and their attend-ant monumental yards, and run out among the prolific

potato-fields and cabbage-gardens that furnish staple food
for our numerous Irish and German fellow-countrymen of
these parts. We also cross at grade a half dozen other
railroads, all leading down to the same popular objective
point. We are going through the suburban town of Gravesend, a district of Kings county famous for successful mar-
ket-gardening and practical politics. Its semi-rural and
seacoast population worships always at the shrine of that
noted political chieftain and boss—John Y. McKane.
Gravesend is a township not thickly inhabited by steady
residents, but those it has are gifted beyond most of their
fellows in the practical statesmanship that has always an
eye out for the main chance. It will be interesting to our
Philadelphia friends to know that this region was the ready
absorbent last year of much of the "fund" which the
Quaker City contributed to save the country by electing
President Harrison. McKane on that interesting occasion
was a financial manipulator with telling effect. Gravesend
enjoyed an unexpected and most remarkable political revolution; Harrison's New York majority was made sure,
and Senator Quay, as he found his budget of arguments
(sent from Philadelphia) producing such remarkable results
among the truck-gardeners and clam-gatherers of the district, probably then felt happier than he has at any time
since his candidate became the dispenser of patronage.

SHEEPSHEAD BAY.

As the train rolls briskly across the level surface of this
noted district, we come out from among the corn and cab-
bages to the edge of the great salt-marshes fringing the
Long Island shore. Behind the eastern edge of Coney
Island, Sheepshead Bay puts in, having upon its shore
the ancient fishing-village of that name, which has been
metamorphosed by the march of fashion into a summer-
villa town. The train halts on the outskirts of this village
to land many of its passengers at one of the greatest racing

establishments of the country, the famous race-course of the
"Coney Island Jockey Club." It is one of the chief race-
days of the June meeting, and we enter with the crowds
keenly bent upon the enjoyment of an afternoon's sport.
Passing through the expansive covered ways under the
bordering foliage toward the grand stand and the paddock,
the extensive lawns are found in perfect verdure under the
influence of abundant rains and most careful trimming,
and the flower-beds are charming. The stands are crowded
with thousands of men and women enjoying the races in the
most animated way, and doing not a little speculating upon
the result. The spacious betting-pavilion behind the stands
contains hundreds of excited people, who crowd about the
betting-places, and then wildly rush out to the stand in
front as a bell announces the opening of a heat. Here is
all the mystic and peculiar paraphernalia of the betting-
ring, with placards couched in the special language of
the turf. There are plenty of "mutual machines" for
"straight" and "place" betting, whilst some seventy-five
of those professional sporting individuals known as "book-
makers" have set up business in a long row extending around
the sides of the pavilion, paying one hundred dollars apiece
per day for the privilege. Each has his sign and placards,
making a miniature office where he conducts trade. Here
gather the excited crowds, rushing between the paddock and
the stands, and then to the betting-places, and at times business is brisk.

ON THE RACE-COURSE.

The scene upon the race-course is brilliant and full of
animation, as the people eagerly watch the contests of
speed and training and study with admiration the magnificent movements of the famous animals upon the track. In
the paddock with the horses there gather between the races
the jockeys and the wise men of the turf, who are up on
all points of horseflesh and pedigree and fully posted on

"weights" and all that sort of thing—necessary knowledge
for the accomplished turfman. Out in front is the great
oval race-track, with its distant borders of stables, all the
centre clear of trees and shrubbery, so that nothing ob-
structs the view, and the ground sloping down from the
lawns and stands toward the lower level of the race-track,
keeping every part in full sight as the race proceeds.
Watching the sport from the greensward below or the
stands above—at times wild with excitement or breathless
with hope or despair when some "neck-and-neck" contest
gives an electrical shock to the anxious wagerer as it goes
unexpectedly wrong or otherwise—is a grand mixture of
wealth and fashion with the "lower ten thousand;" for all
manner of men and women love the pleasures and the
chances of the race-track. During the June meeting of
1889 this noted race-course at Sheepshead Bay witnessed
some great contests, among them the "American Derby,"
the "Suburban," run on the 18th—one of the best races
of the season, watched by twenty thousand people, with
nine noted horses contesting for ten-thousand-dollar prizes,
and the estimate being that bets aggregating two million dollars changed hands on the result. This wonderful race, which had been talked about for a half year, as
the vast crowd saw it, was a flying bunch of glossy-coated
horses and little jockeys in bright silk colors passing around
the track in barely two minutes time, the close being a
mighty cheer as the victor rushed under the wire at the
judges' stand and won the race.

In that supreme moment many of the deeply-interested
spectators lived fast, and, as their betting fortunes were
made or marred, their faces told the story. The winner
was August Belmont's Raceland. This race-course is
masked from the railways by a border of foliage which
makes almost the last cluster of thrifty trees on the edge
of the fast land. The racing ended, the crowds moved in
vast procession out to the trains to go down and cool off in

the evening at the Manhattan or Brighton Beach of Coney Island.

THE FAMOUS SAND-STRIP.

It does not take long for the railway-train to cross the salt-meadows from Sheepshead Bay and the little bordering creek, and then to run over the sand behind the great Manhattan Beach Hotel. Here the passengers empty out, and, passing to the front, are in a moment brought in full view of the Atlantic Ocean beating against the protecting bulkhead. The enthusiastic antiquarians of Coney Island insist that this was the earliest portion of these coasts that was discovered, and they tell us how old Verrazani came along in 1529 or thereabouts to find the narrow strip of sand-beach, and how Hendrick Hudson nearly a hundred years later held conferences with the Indians on the island. However that may be, it was not settled until comparatively recently, being used for grazing cattle, while the present wonderful development as a summer resort has been a matter of the last fifteen or twenty years. The hard and gently-sloping beach faces the Atlantic Ocean and gives excellent facilities for bathing. The place can be so easily reached and in so many ways, both by land and water, and at such a small cost, that it is no wonder on hot afternoons and holidays the people of New York and Brooklyn go down by hundreds of thousands. Coney Island is separated from the mainland only by a little crooked creek, and it has two deep bays indented behind it—Gravesend Bay on the west and Sheepshead Bay on the east. The name is said to come from Cooney Island, meaning the "Rabbit Island," rabbits having been among its chief inhabitants in the earlier days. At present, during probably one hundred days from June until September, the Coney Island season is an almost uninterrupted festival, and no French fête-day can exceed the jollity on these beaches when a hot summer sun drives the people down to the seashore to seek relief and have a good time. They spread over the four or five miles of sand-strip, with scores of bands of music of various grades of merit in full blast; countless vehicles moving; all the minstrel shows, miniature theatres, Punch-and-Judy enterprises, carrousels and merry-go-rounds, big snakes, fat women, giant, dwarf, and midget exhibitions, circuses and menageries, shooting-galleries, concerts, swings, flying horses, and fortune-telling shops open; with oceans of beer "on tap," not to speak of liquids of greater strength; and everywhere a dense, good-humored crowd sight-seeing, drinking, and swallowing "clam chowder."

THE UNIVERSALITY OF THE CLAM.

The only country approaching this place in similar scenes is France, and there is nothing like Coney Island elsewhere on the American continent. Our French cousins, however, while they may drink wine and beer, can hardly be accused of consuming "clam chowder" to any appreciable extent. The clam is universal, and is the bivalve to which Coney Island and its visitors pay special tribute. This famous bivalve is the *Mya arenaria* of the New England coast, which is said to have been the chief food of the Pilgrim Fathers for years after they landed on Plymouth Rock. Hence the devotion of New England and New York to the mysteries of "clam chowder," which, like the "baked beans" of Boston and the "scrapple" of Pennsylvania, has become a national dish. Being found in abundance in all the neighboring waters, Coney Island naturally serves up the clam as its most popular food, and it can be got in every style according to taste, amid the unlimited magnificence (including the bill) of the gorgeous hotels and restaurants of the Manhattan and Brighton beaches, or of varying quality and surroundings at the cheaper shops farther westward toward Norton's Point. At one establishment of renown the visitor, besides his "chowder," also gets a copy of the "Song of the Clam," the following being the most thrilling stanzas:

"Oh, who would not be a clam like me,
By maiden's lips embraced?
And men stand by with jealous eye
While I grip the fair one's waist.

"Who better than I? in chowder or pie,
Baked, roasted, raw, or fried?
I hold the key to society,
And am always welcome inside."

The crowds going to Coney Island on a summer afternoon or evening usually rush back home again the same night, although the lodging and hotel accommodations are upon a vast scale. The aggregation of buildings here, some being of magnificent proportions and decorations, represents, I am told, with the elaborate general improvements and the extensive means of getting to them, an investment of over thirty million dollars. A season at Coney Island is said to be poor indeed that does not have ten millions of visitors, who will leave behind as many dollars, besides paying fifty cents fare to get here and return, making five millions more. Thus an enormous fortune is expended on one brief watering-place season, and with the preparations for gathering this golden harvest it can be readily believed that some of the huge hotels lose money unless they take in an average of five thousand dollars a day. When the season is in full movement five thousand waiters are said to be employed in the hotels and restaurants, besides the necessary regiments of other help. These are huge figures for a watering-place, but they are the outgrowth of its enormous business. No other summer resort has such an aggregation of near-by population to draw upon, for it is estimated that over three millions of people are within a brief ride of this wonderful sand-strip, and hence its great popularity among the masses around New York harbor.

XI.

THE AMERICAN BRIGHTON.

CONEY ISLAND stands pre-eminent as the greatest water-ing-place in the world. There are often poured into it, by the dozens of railway and steamboat lines leading from New York and Brooklyn, half a million people in a few hours when the idea gets possession of them to go down. The long and narrow sand-strip may be divided into four sec-tions, being a succession of villages chiefly composed of restaurants and hotels, built along the edge of the beach and a single road behind it. As best known to the New York rough of a past generation, the original Coney Island was the western end or Norton's Point. The better classes of visitors do not now go to this end, which has been a resort of long standing and occupies a considerable por-tion. The middle of the island is a locality of higher grade and is known as West Brighton Beach. Here are the great iron piers projecting into the ocean for steamboat-landings, being surmounted by pavilions used for restau-rants, while beneath are bathing-houses. Music, electric lights, and fireworks are displayed on these piers, and many visitors thus get access by water. At West Bright-on is also the Observatory, moved here from Philadelphia after the Centennial Exhibition, and rearing its tall frame-work high in the air. Here also are the "Big Elephant," and the "Sea Beach Palace," another Centennial building, used for a hotel and a railway-station. It must not be for-gotten that every hotel of pretensions in this lively place has its own railway, and that the competition to get possession of visitors really begins at the ferry-houses and railway-wharves of New York. The grand "Ocean Parkway," the wide boulevard leading from Prospect Park on the edge of Brooklyn, terminates at West Brighton Beach. East of this is a space nearly a mile in width which is partially vacant between West Brighton and Brighton Beaches. An elevated railway connects them and also a fine driveway called the Concourse, but the eastern part of the latter has been washed away, and carriages have to take another route farther inland. Brighton Beach is the third section, and about a half mile farther east is the fourth and most exclusive section, Manhattan Beach, the two beaches being connected by a steam narrow-gauge railroad called the " Marine Railway," which also has been washed away, and has had to retreat to another more inland route.* Manhattan Beach is Mr. Austin Corbin's enterprise, containing the most elaborate and costly of the Coney Island hotels, the Manhattan and the Oriental, the latter an immense establishment of over five hundred rooms.

CONEY ISLAND WRECKAGE.

Nothing is more impressive on these beaches than the evidence given of the great power of the sea as shown in recent storms. There have been established here by human ingenuity the most extensive attractions for the public entertainment in grand hotels, delicious green lawns, and splendid promenades, with music-pavilions, theatres, and bathing-houses. During two or three past seasons, however, old Neptune has had a spite against Coney, especially against the costlier portions. Suddenly taking a freak during a wild storm, he has attacked and destroyed in a few hours what has taken years to construct. Upon the lowlands and marshes between Brighton and Manhattan

* This Marine Railway was again washed away by the great storm of September, 1889, which also did serious damage to the bulkheads in front of Manhattan and Brighton Beaches.

Beaches the sea has made the latest serious inroads, having washed out a deeply-indented semicircular bay, around which are the wrecks of buildings and the demolished splendor of bygone days. At the east end of Brighton Beach the scene at the opening of this season was like a piece cut out of the ruins of Johnstown, with everywhere smashed houses and wreckage, which were being gathered into piles and burnt. The huge Brighton Hotel, to secure safety, had been hauled a thousand feet back from its original site, this being skilfully accomplished by putting a number of railway-trains under the building and hauling them with locomotives, which were simultaneously and successfully moved at a given signal. Much of the place where the hotel formerly stood is now covered by the sea, the waves washing over it and beating against a new border of earth, piles, and sand-bags which has been put up to protect the lawns, which have been again laid out in most artistic manner in front of the hotel. A skilful gardener has restored all the beauty of the greensward and flowers, but alongside, to the eastward, when I saw it, were the battered ruins of the bathing-pavilion, while beyond stood up the half-destroyed trestle of the "Marine Railway," an abandoned skeleton with the waves playing all around it.

Manhattan Beach in front of its hotel stretches far into the sea, eastward of this wreckage, to the original water-line, being protected beyond the great music pavilion and lawns by a ponderous bulkhead constructed of repeated rows of piles filled in between with huge stones. This bulkhead is over thirty feet thick, and outside it there stretch into the ocean several long narrow piers of stout timbers that break up the cross-currents of the sea, and thus aid in holding the sand-deposits in front. This stout bulkhead has thus far been a complete protection for the extensive Manhattan Hotel, but as I sit and write at the window the waves are dashing against it, driven before a strong southerly wind with terrific force, booming with a solemn sound

that can be heard far away, while the angry waters splash
high above and over the broad walks upon the edge.   Old
Ocean at times makes terrific attacks upon this stubborn
sea-wall, and the angry blow and seething rush betoken an
energy threatening to break the barrier, for this ancient
and untiring enemy generally conquers.   It is curious to
note some of the freaks of his foaming majesty along this
threatened shore.   The sands washed from the eastern
parts of the island are all moved westward, and piled up
to make new land in front of West Brighton.   Here the
shore-line has made outwardly under the great iron piers,
so that for more than half their length there is now dry
land, and the merry-go-rounds and cheap shows of all
kinds are in full blast where the sea had complete sway
but a short time ago.   These changes are constantly making along the front of this popular sand-strip, every great
storm producing alterations in the contour of the shore, so
that while the public spend much money at Coney Island,
it takes nearly all the profits of the show to maintain the
costly establishments and provide protection and needed
improvements.

THE CONEY ISLAND CONSTANT FÊTE.

The vast crowds emptied out of the railway-trains arriv-
ing every few minutes are poured into the great hotels and
swarm out upon the grounds fronting them, where the bands
play.   Here are the finest musicians and orchestras giving
afternoon and evening concerts to enormous audiences.   The
renowned Patrick Sarsfield Gilmore wields the baton at
Manhattan, while Herr Seidl of Metropolitan Opera-House
fame is the maestro at the Brighton, each having a magnificent band.   Where favorite cornet-players get five hundred dollars weekly the price of board and victuals may
be expected to be high.   The scene in front of these great
hotels on a summer evening will not soon be forgotten.
Not a tree will grow, and the breezes blow briskly over the

6

water. The piazzas are filled with supper- and dinner-parties, the music amphitheatres have their crowded audiences, and thousands saunter over the lawns. The blaze of illumination and brilliancy of fireworks are added to the glare of electric lights, and the bustling crowds, music, and general hilarity give the air of a great festival. Vast bathing-establishments adjoin, with hundreds of private dressing-rooms and wooden pathways down to the sea, lighted by electricity, where poles and ropes enclose the bathing-grounds to guard against danger. These houses also have restaurants, with open-air exhibition-halls, where thousands sip their beer and listen to the performance, much the same as upon the Parisian Champs Élysées. Out in front is the pathway of the ocean commerce into New York harbor, with the twinkling lights of Sandy Hook and its attendant lightships beyond. All kinds of side-scenes abound—fortune-tellers and silhouette-profile-cutters—and after having filled yourself up with beer and "clam chowder," which is so liberally placarded in all quarters, you can get yourself accurately "weighed for one cent," the only cheap thing at Coney Island. Everywhere the most extensive preparations are made for serving meals, as the vast crowds must be fed. Beer is served without stint, and the laws elsewhere provided for Sunday observance do not seem to reach this extraordinary island, where the atmosphere appears to inspire a thirst of consuming character. It is at West Brighton that the maze of hotels, restaurants, and shows blooms in chief luxuriance, and its main highway, Surf Avenue, is a great sight, the excitement, crowds, and general intensity being usually greatest on Sundays. Yet the multitudes are all orderly and good-humored, requiring but slight police supervision, and the clangor of dozens of bands distracts if it does not entertain. Rows of places have their flags flying and their signs out, showing devotion to the popular Coney Island luxury, the clam—one enthusiast who cooks them in full view calling his place the " Hôtel de Clam." At the headquarters of the "Louisiana Sere-naders" one can see the show for a quarter and have "a genuine old style Coney Island clam-roast" into the bar-gain. Photographers take pictures, and "safe-deposit com-panies" are established that take charge of lunch-baskets and parcels for a small fee. The style of the place degen-erates the farther westward one wanders, while the crowds do not diminish, and the universal charge for almost every-thing at the "West End" is a "nickel."

It is noteworthy that at Coney Island the development of the place is progressive as one goes from the west toward the east end. The scale of the buildings, the prices, and the character of entertainment gradually advance, until at the east end, or Manhattan Beach, a condition of magnificence has been reached enabling a careful man to manage to exist at the rate of about ten or twelve dollars a day. It is in this financially aristocratic region that they say the smiling hotel-cashier takes a close survey of the guest and endeavors to size up the bill proportionately to the supposed plethora of the pocket-book. Once, however, I am told, one of these keen hotel-cashiers made a mistake. He charged what might have been regarded as a stiff price, but the guest, after look-ing at the bill a moment, shoved it back with the contempt-uous remark, "Guess again, young fellow; I've got more money than that."

THE OBSERVATORY.

The great Observatory, which was brought here from George's Hill in Fairmount Park, its light iron frame-work rising three hundred feet, having elevators con-stantly running, supports a broad platform giving an excellent view. When the journey to the top is accom-plished the first impression made is by the dissonant clangor of the scores of bands of music below, heard with singular clearness and much more intensity of sound than on the ground. This unanimous noise ascends from all sorts of structures of many shapes and styles, and generally having flat pitch-and-gravel roofs, making a variegated carpet far below us. From this high perch Coney Island is seen spread out, the long sand-strip upon the edge of the ocean, with the foaming lines of surf slowly and regularly rolling in upon it. Toward the eastward, at Brighton and Manhattan Beaches, it bends backward like a bow, with a semicircle notched into it where the sea has made its inroads beyond the Brighton Hotel. To the westward the curve of the beach is reversed, and the extreme point of the island ends in a knob, having a hook bent around on the northern side. The "Concourse," covered with moving vehicles, curves around parallel to and just inside the surf-line, suddenly ending where the sea has destroyed it, the carriages passing inland to another road. Far away beyond are the big hotels of Manhattan Beach. Behind this long and narrow strip of sand there are patches of grass and much marsh and meadow stretching away to the northward, and through the marsh can be traced the crooked little stream and series of lagoons separating Coney Island from the mainland. Far off over these level meadows runs the broad and tree-bordered "Ocean Parkway" toward Prospect Park and Brooklyn, with the hills of the park and the tombs and foliage of Greenwood Cemetery closing the view at the distant horizon. Other wagon-roads and a half dozen steam-railways stretch in the same direction, some crossing the bogs on extended trestle-bridges. There are thousands of people walking about on the streets and open spaces beneath us, while upon the ocean side the piers extend out in front, with their processions of steamboats sailing to or from the Narrows to the northward, around the knob and hook at Norton's Point. To the southward, over the water, are the distant Navesink Highlands behind Sandy Hook, and the adjacent New Jersey coast gradually blending into the Staten Island hills to the westward. Haze covers the open sea, and far to the eastward, seen across the deeply-indented Jamaica Bay, are the distant sand-beaches of "Far Rockaway," which has witnessed the most recent colossal failure in financing a mammoth seaside hotel.

The night follows the day, and as a glorious sunset pales the artificial lights come out and sparkle all over the place, gas and electricity aiding innumerable colored lanterns to make an illumination. The universal music renews its strongest if not its sweetest strains, and gorgeous displays of fireworks burst out of the great hotels. The festival proceeds with uninterrupted pleasure and hilarity through-out the evening, until the crowds get an idea that the time has come to start home; and then comes one of the chief Coney Island sights, the stampede to the railways and steamboats. Over land and water the vast human current then sets toward Brooklyn and New York. The crowds that have been so orderly are still well-behaved, for the sea air is a sedative, and they stream through the ticket-gates in an almost resistless tide, the trains and steamers being loaded and despatched as fast as possible. It is when the time arrives for going home, and these swelling torrents of humanity flow out upon station and pier, that the vast magnitude of a Coney-Island summer Sunday crowd can best be measured. It is something almost beyond de-scription.

XII.

NEW YORK HARBOR.

THE finest view in New York is from the tall tower of Mr. Cyrus W. Field's Washington Building, which is one of the sentinels standing at the foot of Broadway. This tower upon the outpost at the lower end of Manhattan

Island rises nearly three hundred feet above the pavement. The wind whistles sharply as we peer out from this great elevation, and beneath us the green grass of the Battery Park spreads out past the low red-roofed buildings of the Castle Garden emigrant dépôt, just in front, until it reaches the water's edge, where the Hudson and East Rivers mingle their currents together to form the harbor. The shining rails of the snake-like elevated railways curve across the park from either side until they come together at the South Ferry. Out in the harbor a little way is Governor's Island, nestling cozily upon the water, with its little Castle William upon its western verge and the flag of the army headquarters waving from its staff. Beyond the island, Red Hook juts out from Brooklyn, with the Buttermilk Channel between. Upon the right hand the goddess holds her torch on high as a guardian to the mariner, and in front, as she looks toward the sea, expands the great harbor, its widely-extended shores rising into the enclosing hills, seen far away over the water, that come almost together at the Narrows, where the sunlight glints on the surface. Such is the enchanting scene as we look southward over the Upper Bay and through the distant narrow opening to the broad expanse of the Lower Bay beyond. Moving or at anchor, everywhere are seen myriads of the vessels that make the commerce of New York. Great steamers, puffing tugs, stately steamboats, ships, barges, schooners, ark-like ferryboats, yachts, skiffs, lighters, and the multiform craft of rivers and sea are everywhere making kaleidoscopic changes of position. All about the borders of the harbor are fringed the busy towns and villages that have gathered for satellites to New York. Here, on the right, are the great railway terminals of Jersey City, and beyond, its shipping-wharves and coal-ports and oil-tanks spread far up the Kill until lost in the distance. Over there, at the left, are the vast storehouses, docks, and piers of Brooklyn, with Gowanus Bay glistening behind the jutting Red Hook Point, and Gowanus

Heights rising beyond, while far away over these can be traced the spider-like threads that are interwoven to make the distant elevator standing out against the horizon at Coney Island. Such is the outlook given from our high perch on the southern point of New York over a harbor and commerce that are excelled nowhere in the world.

Then, turning about to get the northward view back over the great city, on either hand the two rivers can be traced, one wide, the other narrow, as they go away, one north, the other north-east. Within their watery embrace is the broadening surface of the town, while its populous suburbs stretch far back from the opposite shores. Thousands of buildings of all conceivable kinds are crowded together, a mass of curious roofs, through the centre of which is cut down the deep, straight fissure of Broadway. Far below, between its bordering rows of tall buildings, the street-cars and wagons and many busy people crowd along, and above rise the huge houses and spires, making the line of the famous street, some of them yet unfinished and having nimble workmen perilously climbing about them to push their structure still farther skyward. Off over the East River the graceful curving cables of the Brooklyn bridge are thrown across, high above all the surroundings, with the solid towers rising above and the vessels moving on the water in full view far below. Steeples, domes, chimneys, turrets, roofs, and steamjets are seen everywhere; and thus stretches northward the vast city until lost in the haze of the horizon, bordered away up the western bank of the Hudson by the distant wall of the Palisades. The elevated trains rattle upon their long lines of rails that can be traced for miles among the mazy labyrinths of houses. The deeply-cut and crooked, narrow streets curve off from our feet through the masses of buildings like trenches, down in the bottom of which the ant-like inhabitants are creeping. Thus, standing upon the highest elevation in lower New York, and with the whistling wind creaking and rattling the strong iron stays of the tall little tower, yet having its foundations firmly built into the solid rock beneath the level of the river-bed, the varying noises of the traffic and the countless whistles of the river-craft come up to us from all sides to tell of the restless, tireless energy seething below. It is a superb outlook, never to be forgotten, over the greatest city and harbor of the New World.

SAILING DOWN THE BAY.

Let us descend and take a closer view of the harbor that has been thus grandly scanned. On one of the many steamers a brief and pleasant journey can be made down through the Narrows toward Sandy Hook. With a fresh wind blowing in our faces we head for that little opening between the hills making the harbor entrance, and apparently leading only to vacancy. The wake of the vessel is a line of bubbling foam among the watercraft as we pass away from the Battery and behind the lovely foliage of its park see Broadway stretching back through New York. Ahead of us the Narrows seem apparently filled by the yachts that spread their white wings across the distant expanse of the Lower Bay. Gaining speed, we pass upon the one hand the old castle and forts of Governor's Island, and upon the other grandly rises the colossal Statue of Liberty, gaining in grandeur upon the nearer view. Soon we cross below the entrance to East River, spanned above by the great bridge, and then skirt the lines of stores and shipping in front of Brooklyn, which stretches off into Gowanus Bay with its beautiful background of Greenwood Cemetery. We are gliding smoothly over the inner harbor, an irregular, oval-shaped body of water about five miles broad and eight miles long, and ahead of us the pretty hills of Staten Island gradually approach those of Long Island to make the Narrows, each bold shore being covered with villas. We pass the Quarantine Station at Clifton, where the yellow flag warns incoming vessels to anchor and await the inspection of the health authorities before they go up to the city. The landing is rather dilapidated, but it has a pleasant background in the garden-environed residence of the doctors, whose certificates give entrance to New York after their brimstone buckets have often gone aboard to provide fumigation as a partial recompense for their fees. The bold bluff stretching southward from the Quarantine rises to the frowning ramparts of Fort Wadsworth, overlooking the Narrows, where the Hudson River has forced a passage through the broken-down mountain-range to the sea. These same ramparts give a glorious view over both the lower and the inner bays that spread from the city down to the distant sand-streak of Sandy Hook. Fort Lafayette rears its deserted red brick walls upon an island in the Narrows, and behind it rise the batteries of Fort Hamilton on the Long Island shore. Thus the fortifications frown from the hill-slopes, and the guns expose their little black muzzles, and, were it not that everything is overrun with weeds and soldiers are scarce, one would suppose that the entrance was effectually guarded.

THE LOWER NEW YORK BAY.

From the Battery down through the Narrows to Sandy Hook is about eighteen miles. With accelerated speed the vessel goes through the attractive pass and enters the Lower Bay. This is a grand harbor—a triangular sheet of water measuring nine to twelve miles on each side and almost completely landlocked. The New Jersey shore makes its southern boundary, stretching westward into Raritan Bay, thrust up into the land between Jersey and Staten Island. The green hills of the island, crowned with villas, make the north-western boundary of the bay. Long Island and the ocean, with the projection of Sandy Hook, are on the eastern side. This magnificent Lower Bay has an anchorage-ground covering eighty-eight square miles. With the inner harbor and the rivers about one hundred and fifteen square miles of available anchorage are provided—a most admirable roadstead. As we move along, Coney Island gradually unfolds across the waters of Gravesend Bay, outside the Narrows, its huge hotels and elevator and mammoth elephant being in full view. This long strip of sand, with its curious hooked end, is a guard to the Lower Bay, and we approach it from behind. On both sides as the bay broadens the shores recede, and amid the fleets of yachts and vessels of all kinds the steamer heads for Sandy Hook. The freshening wind gives a foretaste of Old Ocean as lingering looks go back toward the receding Narrows. Quickly passing the jutting end of Coney Island and moving out in front of it, the panorama enlarges as the shore spreads away past Brighton and Manhattan Beaches, with their great hotels, and Far Rockaway, which looms in the distance. The elephant, with his surmounting howdah, as we get out in front shows his enormous head in ponderous majesty. But soon Coney Island gradually fades as the route is followed southward toward the Hook.

The Navesink Highlands that come up from the westward partly cross the view ahead, and seem to be suddenly cut down as the land falls away to make the low point running out to form the Hook. The steamers that have gone down ahead of us one after another as they get in behind Sandy Hook turn sharply around with the channel, as its red bordering buoys guide them from the south to the east, and then they begin the long journey over the ocean, each leaving a streak of black smoke carried off before the wind. Looking back beyond the vessel's wake, the dim outline of Coney Island can be traced, with the distant Narrows seeming almost closed and apparently alongside. We have reached the Hook, and find that, though noted, it in reality is not much of a place. A green fringe borders the yellow sandbank, as the end hooks around backward and makes a little harbor, while beyond are the white lighthouse and the lower beacon-light on the point. There are a few houses and the ruins of an extensive though abandoned fort, partially built upon a plan that was costly, but is now obsolete. The sandy surface is strewn with bursted guns that have been tried at the Government testing-station, which has for many years been located here. Far southward from the Hook the Navesink Highlands stand boldly up, bearing their twin lighthouses that are the first guide to the distant mariner seeking the harbor entrance. The low shores of Long Island are dimly seen as they recede to the north-east. Beyond is the broad Atlantic.

XIII.

STATEN ISLAND.

THE fair island of Aquahonga, as our aboriginal ancestors, the Mohicans, called Staten Island, is always admired by the voyager on New York harbor, but is rarely visited. Its pleasant hill-slopes border the Upper and Lower Bays upon their western side. It has long been a land of seclusion, of sylvan homes, and of lovely views. Recently, however, the restless spirit of Erastus Wiman broke through the bucolic fetters that had bound up its burghers for a century, and, capturing its railways and ferries from the Vanderbilts, he is opening it to the world, and by bringing in the Baltimore and Ohio and Lehigh Valley railroads he intends to develop a vast terminal trade from the West that will fringe its harbor shores with docks and storehouses. They say that, by rights, this ancient island of Aquahonga belongs to New Jersey, but that it was captured by New York. The narrow "kills," stretching for nearly twenty miles from St. George down to Perth Amboy, make the boundary, and that robust Jerseyman, Mr. Cortlandt

Parker, has often declared a big swindle was perpetrated when New Jersey was robbed of this fair island, over which the myriads of summer musicians from the prolific Jersey bordering marshes around Newark Bay still enjoy their sovereign right to revel amid the pleasant hills and vales and to interrupt the dreams of her people by their insinuating addresses. I have already told of the first coming of the English to New York harbor in 1664, which was under a grant of King Charles to his brother the duke of York of all the country from Canada down to Virginia. Subsequently, the duke granted to Berkeley and Carteret the portion lying between the Hudson and the Delaware Rivers. This grant grieved the New Yorkers much, and they complained that it gave away the best lands around their harbor; so they tried hard to get it all back, and in practice they did get back Staten Island. Some sharp fellows invented the fiction on which they insisted that the Arthur Kill was the Hudson River, and, taking possession of the island, they never gave it up. A legal contest was fought for over one hundred and fifty years, and it was not until 1833 that a treaty between the States declared the Kills to be their boundary.

This pleasant island is shaped somewhat like a leaf, hung, as it were, upon the long projecting peninsula between Newark Bay and New York harbor, the Kill von Kull stretching westward to divide the island from this peninsula, which at that part is the town of Bayonne, running off into Bergen Point. From Elizabethport on the western side of Newark Bay the Arthur Kill stretches, a narrow strait, far southward, broadening somewhat into Staten Island Sound, and debouching at Perth Amboy into the western end of Raritan Bay. The island is about sixteen miles long, and from its eastern slopes has a noble outlook over the Lower New York Bay toward the ocean. Pretty beaches line these coasts, which rise sharply into hills inland, and most of the points of vantage have been availed of for villas.

The "Staten Island Rapid Transit" system is rapidly developing the capabilities of this elysium. Its ferry is established at Whitehall Slip, the lower point of the Battery in New York, with all the elevated railways running into the capacious ferry-house. The biggest ferry-boats in the world cross this five-mile ferry southward to St. George on the northern point of the island. The approach down the harbor is very fine, the hills rising abruptly behind the landing, terraced with the pleasant houses of the village. To the left, a short distance away, is the Narrows, beneath which the company hopes some day to bore a tunnel connecting with Long Island and Brooklyn, so as to give them the benefit of freight and passenger direct interchange—a work that can be done, it is said, for six millions of dollars. To the right the narrow strait of the Kill von Kull stretches off westward, gathering on its crowded Jersey shores a commerce exceeding that of Boston, Philadelphia, and Baltimore combined in the immense trade which it supplies from the great trunk-line terminals.

THE "RAPID-TRANSIT" BOOM.

The "Staten Island Rapid Transit Company," and I know not how many other kindred enterprises, are the outgrowth of the energy of Erastus Wiman, who with his associates managed to get possession of pretty much everything worth having on this island. The idea he has been working out is that its shores are the best and only place left for the expansion of the commerce of New York harbor, and their adaptation for the receipt, storage, and shipment of freight is of incalculable future value. At the same time, the island itself is regarded as the nearest outlet for New York's surplus population, which at some time must largely occupy it. There have been acquired two miles of water-frontage for docks and stores along the Kill and the harbor, with the best facilities and ample depth. Bringing in the Baltimore and Ohio Railroad over its Arthur

Kill bridge will make this frontage available for a vast traffic. The heavy terminal charges for freight, lighterage, and handling that are universal around New York harbor can here be reduced. The ferry and railway take passengers from New York for ten cents to any part of the island, while commutation rates reduce this to five cents for the residents. The insular population is, consequently, rapidly increasing, being now estimated as beyond sixty thousand. There is plenty of room for expansion, for in its widest portion the island is eight miles broad and it covers some fifty-eight square miles. The railway has three branches—two going from the ferry-landing at St. George, one each way along the shore behind the docks and villages at the waterside, while the third branch stretches southward completely through the island to Tottenville, opposite Perth Amboy. The abrupt hill-slopes run at some places into elevations three hundred feet high, thus diversifying the surface and giving superb building-sites. Down these hills more "kills" of greater or less magnitude run off to the surrounding waters, while as the island spreads southward toward Raritan Bay the land flattens out to the monotonous level of the adjacent Jerseys.

For a brief survey of this "Rapid-Transit" development it is necessary to begin by a walk about St. George, a name wherein the projector shows his loyalty to his British origin. Here is shown the enormous establishment necessary for the sporting and amusement facilities of the metropolis. It has the finest baseball and entertainment grounds and grandstands near that city, drawing many thousands of visitors, and most admirably appointed and located closely to the ferry. This of itself is a largely paying institution. The surface of St. George rises somewhat steeply into the eminence of Fort Hill behind the village, where Lord Howe had his camp when the British troops occupied Staten Island during the Revolution. Part way up this hill-slope, and at an elevation of about one hundred feet above the harbor, is the projector's pleasant villa of Tantallen, where there is a gorgeous view over the great harbor and back northward to the city of New York, five miles away. In the centre of this magnificent picture is the distant foliage of the Battery Park, with the maze of buildings and steeples of the city rising behind it. To the left hand stands the Liberty statue, dwarfed by the broad intervening space, and having the Hudson River coming in between; while down in the foreground is the little lighthouse, standing on its stilts, that warns the mariner off Robbins's Reef. To the right the tall and massive Brooklyn bridge, with its graceful cables hanging apparently like the thinnest spider's web in mid-air, spreads broadly across the scene, stretching into Brooklyn town, and then Gowanus Heights, and, finally, the bold promontory of Fort Hamilton at the Narrows. The water plays with light and shadow, and the vast commerce and myriads of moving vessels are all mapped out almost at our feet, making a scene of which the eye can never tire.

A "RAPID-TRANSIT" JOURNEY.

We enter the cars of the railway, which are built like those of the elevated roads in New York, and for a hasty visit take first the line along the shore at the eastward, passing behind and through the villages of Tompkinsville, Stapleton, Clifton, the Quarantine, and Fort Wadsworth, beyond the Narrows. After a few miles' ride the railroad brings us out to its end, at Arrocher, almost at the water's edge of the Lower Bay, where the sea rolls in upon a splendid beach that is five miles long, while beyond there is a magnificent outlook over the blue and dancing water to the far-off Navesink range and the long, low point of Sandy Hook. Upon this route are passed the extensive storehouses of the American Cotton Dock Company, an enterprise under the management of a leading warehouseman, Bostwick, which has demonstrated the storage-cheapening capabilities of the place. They now store more cotton than all the other stores around the harbor, and save that trade thirty thousand dollars monthly by reductions in terminal charges, the cost of storage being diminished from thirty cents to ten cents monthly per bale. Enormous advances in land prices have been made along these shores, quadrupling within a few years, and the new buildings everywhere going up show how the new inhabitants are coming in. In fact, the growth is much like the Aladdin magical expansion of a Western town when first touched by a railroad.

We return to St. George and take the western line of rails along the bank of the Kill von Kull. Across its waters are the active commerce and busy terminals of Bayonne, the forest of vessel-masts at the petroleum wharves and the adjacent coal-shipping piers. These fringe the whole Jersey shore, with populous towns behind them and a green background in the Bergen Hill. Here are the Standard Oil-Works and the terminals of the Tidewater Pipe Line, recently beguiled away from Philadelphia by the magnetic attractions of that vast monopoly. The train swiftly passes extensive plaster-mills and zinc-works, and glides along in front of the Sailors' Snug Harbor, where some seven hundred old salts are spending their declining years as they look out upon the enormous commerce of the strait in front of their attractive home. Moving through village after village, this great trade is displayed, ending at the coal-piers of Port Johnson and the town of Bergen Point, beyond which the waters of Newark Bay stretch far back into the broad expanse of the Jersey lowland meadows. This busy Kill, thus heading in the bay, is about a half mile wide, but the powerful tidal current moving in and out of the bay scours it out deeply. We pass the Starin ship-yard, the headquarters of J. H. Starin, the chief New York steamboatman, and through the town of Richmond, the county-seat of Richmond county, and said to be the best town on Staten Island, having a goodly population of well-to-do working people living in comfortable frame houses and favored with two great blessings in these degenerate days—good roads and moderate taxes. Off the shore is the little oblong Shooter's Island, set in the mouth of Newark Bay, a sort of small attendant satellite upon its bigger neighbor. Through the thickly-settled region to the westward we move rapidly to Erastina, where is another grand pleasure-ground, used for athletic sports and "Buffalo Bill" enterprises. Here beams down upon us the imposing sign of the "Wild West Hotel," showing the sportive temper of the place. This is five miles from St. George, and beyond it the railway is laid two miles farther to the new Baltimore and Ohio bridge over the Arthur Kill, just south of Newark Bay. The route soon exhausts the fast land, and over a mile of trestles lead out to the bridge, which is seen across the marshes, the huge trusses of its great draw rising high above the stream. All the land hereabouts is a vast salt-marsh, through which the Kill wanders southward, having highly-scented fertilizer-factories and oil-refineries on its banks. These, of course, are useful in their way, but their perfumes do not seem to be effective in limiting the mosquito crop, for which these marshes are chiefly known to fame. The bridge is about eight hundred feet long, and it has an enormous draw, over three hundred feet long, with a passage-way one hundred and fifty feet wide on each side of the central pivot pier. In fact, the massive structure seems to be almost all draw. Beyond, the incomplete railroad goes westward some five miles into the New Jersey Central tracks, west of Elizabeth. As we stand at the bridge and look across the monotonous flats, this town makes their background, spreading like a low fringe of trees and buildings, with a square church-tower and a spire or two rising against the sky, while from it, through the marshes, the little Elizabeth River flows out to the Kill.

Again returning to St. George, we start out upon the third branch of this wonderful little railroad, laid between the others and running completely down the leaf-shaped island to its end. This, like the others, is extensively ballasted with ship-ballast brought from all parts of the world and cheaply landed here. The enterprising president has thus absorbed historic stones from Pompeii, gravel from China, and the varied rocks and soils of Italy, Britain, France, Germany, and the Indies, making a remarkable aggregation. The route climbs a grade of ninety feet to the mile till it gets upon the elevated plateau making the larger part of the island, which has many pretty lakes nestling among its higher hills, with fine country-houses in all directions. Here is a place of wonderful rural beauty, the railway running along a plateau with the harbor in full view, while inland the surface rises into a range of higher hills whose wooded tops are elevated three hundred feet. Their slopes fall off abruptly, as if they had once formed a border for the harbor, but, the waters receding, the dry bed was left, whereon the railway is now laid. Upon this almost level surface of excellent farming land is the village of New Dorp, the original settlement of the Vanderbilts, a farm of about four hundred acres. We halt at the station and look over the place with the little church on the hill-slope that guards it. This is an ancient Moravian foundation, a plainly built, square white wooden structure, with an inscription announcing it to be the "Protestant Episcopal Church of the United Brethren, founded 1763; the present edifice built 1844." Tombs and gravestones are all about, and from the front portico we can overlook the entire farm to which the old commodore came early in life, and where William H. Vanderbilt was born and lived an agricultural laborer for forty years. He was evidently of little account in those days, but fame found him through the road of enormous wealth afterward. The old farmhouse still exists, but a more modern one has been built near by. Far away in front spreads the magnificent harbor, and as we look northward across the water we see the little red houses out on the Romers Islands, used for the Lower Quarantine, with the hotels and buildings of Coney Island spread out in the distance beyond, and Far Rockaway looming up at the horizon.

We turn our backs upon this beautiful scene, and, looking westward, past the churchyard and its tombs and up the terraced hill behind, with its fringes of forest, see between two wooded slopes the round-topped hill within which rest the two great millionaires, father and son. This hill upon the highest part of the island rises steeply, and into its front is built their spacious gray granite mausoleum. It is an imposing yet not funereal structure, with a wall in front to prevent intrusion, while in a little house alongside live the watchmen who are constantly on duty to prevent any desecration of the tomb. Here repose all that is left of the two wealthiest Americans—a peaceful spot, overlooking their home before their gilded lives began, and a sentinel at the gateway of New York. To the southward, a short distance down the range of hills, stands a lighthouse guiding the mariner up the harbor-channel into Sandy Hook. In the old churchyard the graves of many Vanderbilts and their collaterals are scattered about like the outpost pickets around the great mausoleum where the chieftains of the family are laid to rest.

XIV.

THE NEW YORK ANNEXED DISTRICT.

THE metropolis, as already noted, has during recent years in its expansion northward been absorbing considerable portions of Westchester county. These are known as the "Annexed District," and they embrace some of the most beautiful environs of New York beyond the borders of Manhattan Island. There is no prettier place than the little winding, tortuous valley, with its Hudson River Railroad border curving around the northern part of the island, made by the narrow Spuyten Duyvel Creek. It comes out through a deep gorge to the great river, making a sheltering cove where Hendrick Hudson, when he first discovered it, anchored his ship, the Half Moon, in his voyage up the river in 1609. The shores were then peopled by warlike Mohegans, who were proof even against the seductive aroma of the explorer's schnapps, for they attacked him with arrows from the shore and forbade a landing. This creek was historic in its subsequent naming. The redoubtable old Governor Stuyvesant had a wonderful trumpeter, Anthony von Corlaer, who lost his life in attempting to swim the stream during a violent storm. Irving tells the tale, and how his death named the creek. "The wind was high," he writes, "the elements were in an uproar, and no Charon could be found to ferry the adventurous sounder of brass across the water. For a short time he vapored like an impatient ghost upon the brink, and then, bethinking himself of the urgency of his errand (to arouse the people to arms), he took a hearty embrace of his stone bottle, swore most valorously that he would swim across in spite of the devil (*en spyt den duyvel*), and daringly plunged into the stream. Luckless Anthony! Scarcely had he buffeted halfway over when he was observed to struggle violently, as if battling with the spirit of the waters. Instinctively he put his trumpet to his mouth, and, giving a vehement blast, sank for ever to the bottom. The clangor of his trumpet, like that of the ivory horn of the renowned Paladin Orlando when expiring on the glorious field of Roncesvalles, rang far and wide through the country, alarming the neighbors around, who hurried in amazement to the spot. There an old Dutch burgher famed for his veracity, and who had been a witness to the fact, related to them the melancholy affair, with the fearful addition (to which I am slow in giving belief) that he saw the Duyvel, in the shape of a huge mossbunker (a species of inferior fish), seize the sturdy Anthony by the leg and drag him beneath the waves. Certain it is the place, with the adjoining promontory which projects into the Hudson, has been called *Spyt den Duyvel* ever since."

EXTENSIVE SUBURBAN PARKS.

Much of the "Annexed District" beyond this historic stream is yet in its primitive condition, having been maintained in the old estates that come down from the days of the Knickerbockers. While New York has in Central Park all that art can furnish, yet its excessive artificiality, recognized especially since the opening of Fairmount Park, and its comparatively small size, have led the metropolis to seek new, larger, and more natural parks in this northern region. Six years ago the legislature of New York created a commission to select lands for the purpose, and it has about completed its labors, locating three large parks and a number of smaller ones in this new region, the whole including some thirty-eight hundred acres, which have cost nearly ten millions of dollars, and it contemplates spending many millions more upon their improvement. The three larger parks are "Van Cortlandt," near the Hudson River and about four miles north of the High Bridge over Harlem River, comprising nearly twelve hundred acres; "Pelham Bay Park," on the Long Island Sound shore, about nine miles from Harlem River, including seventeen hundred and fifty acres; and the "Bronx Park," between the two, having six hundred and fifty acres. These three great pleasure-grounds, which can have almost limitless development, will be connected with each other by magnificent tree-lined avenues six hundred feet wide. The

Van Cortlandt Park, whose western verge overlooks the Hudson, is accessible by three railways. Its diversified and picturesque landscape is to be availed of largely for military purposes. There is a level parade-ground covering about one hundred and twenty acres, and a long and level field which can be easily adapted for a rifle-range fifteen hundred yards in length. There is also a lake, and the quaint old stone mansion where lived the Van Cortlandts, whose successive generations have owned the estate, will be carefully preserved. The hill elevations give magnificent views of the Palisades and along the Hudson for miles.

THE LOVELY BRONX.

A shallow and almost aimless little stream, flowing from above White Plains down to Long Island Sound, with many pools and rapids, and occasionally broadening into quiet, mirror-like lakes, is the Bronx River, which makes the eastern boundary of northern New York City. It comes down through a green and well-watered and shaded valley a half to three-quarters of a mile wide, and it is a considerable portion of this bewitching region that makes the Bronx Park,

> " Where gentle Bronx, clear, winding, flows
> The shadowy banks between ;
> Where blossomed bell or wilding rose
> Adorns the brightest green."

A brief drive from Harlem River along the newly-opened boulevard leads to this lovely park, which stretches from the ancient village of West Farms northward to Williamsbridge, making a constant succession of attractive landscapes. The region is hilly, and in places the little river has carved its winding channel at the foot of huge gray rocks rising in perpendicular walls fifty feet high. Giant trees flourish in all their native dignity, many of them much over a century old. The wildness and seclusion of the place, its natural charms and romantic character, make one almost believe that New York cannot possibly be near such an attractive wilderness. In fact it was designed by Nature's handicraft for a park, and human hands cannot improve it. Yet it is less known to the average New Yorker than Central Africa. The Delanceys were once the owners here, and the huge Delancey pine, one hundred and fifty feet high and straight as an arrow, stands in a prominent position, having a large branch reaching upward upon one side with interlacing boughs, making it appear not unlike a gigantic harp. The "balanced boulder" is near by, weighing hundreds of tons, yet easily rocked to and fro. In one portion the Bronx flows deep down between high walls of rock, where the thin-armed white birches wave their slender limbs a hundred feet above the water. Having broken through this gorge, the stream meanders amid stretches of green lawn and meadow scattered over with thickets. Here was an early home of the Lorillards, which the Park officials propose to now make a botanical garden. In portions of the upper Bronx one is reminded of the scenery of our Wissahickon.

THE GLORIES OF PELHAM BAY.

At the entrance of East River into Long Island Sound the peninsula of Throgg's Neck is the northern headland. Beyond this the waters of the sound have deeply indented the New York shore, and there is thrust out the green peninsula of Pelham Neck. All this is some distance east of the Bronx in Westchester county, but it is a region soon to be "annexed." Eastchester Bay is on the southern side of the neck, and Pelham Bay beyond it, while immediately in front is City Island, reached by a long drawbridge. To the north is Hunter's Island, to which another bridge gives access. This Hunter's Island, and more than two square miles of the hills and meadows adjoining on the mainland, make the park of Pelham Bay. Many old mansions are scattered over this domain, which belonged to the Hunters, the Lorillards, Potters, and other families. The island belonged to many generations of the Hunters, and near the bridge a large gateway keeps out intruders, having on one of the marble gate-posts "Hunter's Island" carved in plain characters. Years ago another wealthy man bought this island, and, these words offending him, he brought up a marble-cutter from New York who chiselled them off, and carved instead the words "Higgins's Island." But Higgins was ultimately gathered unto his fathers, and the next owner, revering him less than the antiquity of the place, had "Higgins" eliminated, and "Hunter's Island" again stands out in bold relief. The gate-post has become very thin under this treatment, but the city of New York will probably now spare it. The western edge of Pelham Bay Park is Hutchinson's River, which flows down into East-chester Bay and recalls the days of the Salem witchcraft. Poor Anne Hutchinson fled here to escape burning as a witch, and on City Island built a hut on a little cape known to this day as Anne Hook. She lived there peace-fully for a year, harming nobody and declining every in-vitation of the islanders to stir from her home. One morn-ing a young girl went to visit Anne, but found the hut in ashes, and before the door lay the poor woman where she had been tomahawked and scalped by the Indians. No one has dared to build a house on Anne Hook since, for many are the tales of how on bleak and rainy nights the phantom Indians sneak through the underbrush and shriek a ghostly requiem as they dance around the site of the burning hovel.

Just beyond this park is the famous Glen Island, where John H. Starin on his excursion-steamers takes nearly a million people every summer, showing the popularity of all the resorts on these pleasant shores. Fishing, boating, and bathing are provided on the waters, and the sinuosities of the shores of islands and mainland provide many cozy nooks, so that villas are dotted in most favorable localities. From the hills forming the higher portions of the park the view over the sound for miles in both directions, and upon the hazy land beyond, is very fine. Magnificent old oaks and elms adorn the forests that were thrifty young trees before the Dutch came to New York. Most of the estates have been well kept, so that landscapes have been preserved and improved for generations. There is every variety of scenery—hill and woodland, meadow and plain, and splendid water-views bordered with the delicious green that clings around the myriad bays and coves of the sound and its pleasant islands. Thus the metropolis expands, and having learnt, with growing wealth, the charms and benefits of bringing the country into the town, it makes these parks before the rows of city buildings reach them. Such is the grand environment of Nature's loveliness that is being developed around and in the steadily-expanding domain of northern New York City.

XV.

ENTERING NEW ENGLAND.

WE reluctantly leave the attractive environment of the metropolis to extend our journey toward the rising sun. From the Grand Central Station of the Vanderbilt lines, on Forty-second Street in New York City, the New Haven Railroad carries us into New England. The line runs out of town through long tunnels, and then, skirting Central Park, turns north-east across the Harlem River, through Morrisania, Fordham, and a succession of attractive villages among the hills and rocks, until it runs along and finally crosses the pretty little Bronx River on the northern border of Bronx Park. Swiftly rolls the train along the edge of Woodlawn Cemetery, where Jay Gould has built the magnificent mausoleum for his final home. Traversing a region of market-gardens and patches of forest, sprinkled with outcragging rocks and dotted over with villas, the line passes New Rochelle, where the French Huguenot refugees settled two centuries ago after Richelieu had driven them out of La Rochelle. Here in his declining years lived the noted Tom Paine upon an estate given him by the New York State Government. The most prolific crop borne in the country hereabout is rocks, and the few patient husbandmen who still remain here to battle with Nature have gathered the loose stones into piles for fences, which cross the land in all directions. This rocky development is most profuse at the village of Mamaroneck, which in the Indian tongue means "the place of rolling stones." Once in a while a serious effort is made to till this stony land. Over the mazy lines of stone fences and rocks of all kinds, a hundred yards away may be seen a man with a yoke of oxen trying to plough, but scarcely moving, for he has to go slow lest the plough strike a sunken crag and cause a catastrophe. The farther we go the greater the development of rocks, the bright foliage of the trees springing up among them making a pleasing contrast. Thus moving, about twenty-five miles from New York the train crosses Byram River, and we are in New England, which the old saying announces as stretching "from Quoddy Head to Byram River." This original Yankee-land, although the smallest section of the United States, has made the deepest impress upon the American character, and has carried the banner of enterprise and colonization throughout the entire Western country. In ideas and thought, as well as in migration, the New Englanders are usually our leaders, being the people of most advanced views in politics and religion, and usually the pioneers of radicalism. They have not enjoyed the agricultural advantages of other sections, the bleak climate, poor soil, and generous distribution of rocks and sterility making farming hard work with meagre results, so that the chief Yankee energies have been devoted to developing vast manufacturing industries, literature, commerce, and the fisheries; in short, the Yankees have had to live by their wits, and have most admirably succeeded. All the six New England States are not much larger than New York in surface, while their population is much less; but the indomitable spirit of the Pilgrims and other religious enthusiasts who were the earliest settlers implanted the untiring energy that has carried New-England ideas, methods, and population all over New York and the great West.

THE LAND OF STEADY HABITS.

We have crossed the little Byram River into Connecticut, and in the intervals of rocks the train goes over inlet after inlet thrust up into the land from Long Island Sound, each having its galaxy of little rounded islets set in the entrance, and its sloping shores studded with attractive villas embosomed in foliage. The glimpse along each inlet gives pretty though brief views over the distant waters of the sound, with the sun shining on the white-winged yachts beyond. Sharp is the contrast between Connecticut and New York City, so recently left behind us. With a population scarcely one-fourth the millions of souls clustering around New York harbor, yet this "Land of Steady Habits" has always made the deeper impress upon the character and policy of the country. The guiding hands and ingenious brains ruling New York business affairs are largely transplants from Connecticut and New England. De Tocqueville pointedly illustrated this subtle influence in a little speech he made after his American visit at a Fourth-of-July dinner in Paris. In his quaint broken English he said:

"Von day I vos in the gallery of the House of Representatives. I held in my hand a map of the Confederation.

Dere vos von leetle yellow spot called Connect-de-coot. I
found by de Constitution he was entitled to six of his boys
to represent him on dat floor. But when I make the acquaintance personel with the member, I find dat more than
thirty (30) of the Representative on dat floor was born in
Connect-de-coot. And den ven I vos in de gallery of the
House of the Senate, I find de Constitution permit dis State
to send two of his boys to represent him in dat legislature.
But once there, ven I make de acquaintance personel of
the Senator, I find nine of the Senator was born in Connect-de-coot.

"And now for my grand sentiment: Connect-de-coot—de
leetle yellow spot dat make de clock-peddler, de schoolmas-
ter, and de Senator; de first give you time, de second tell
you what to do with him, and de third make your law and
civilization."

This wonderful little State covers only four thousand
seven hundred square miles, and, excepting Rhode Island
and Delaware, is the smallest in the Union. It is the special land of "Yankee notions." It gave the country the
original personation of "Brother Jonathan" in Governor
Jonathan Trumbull, who was so useful a coadjutor to
Washington. Consulting him in many emergencies, Washington was wont to remark, "Let us hear what Brother
Jonathan says"—a phrase finally popularly adopted and
making him the national impersonation. It has the great
Puritan college of the country—Yale—ruled by the Con-
gregationalists. It has more varied and more productive
manufactures than any other people of similar means. Its
abundant water-powers contribute to this, and nearly all its
inhabitants are engaged in manufacturing of one kind or
another. Its machinery and methods are largely the inven-
tions or improvements of its own people, among whom three
stand out prominently: Eli Whitney, of the cotton-gin;
Samuel Colt, of the revolver; and Charles Goodyear, of
India-rubber fame. The inventive talent of the State is

such that its people proportionately get more patents than those of any other, one to every eight hundred inhabitants being annually granted. Such is the diversified genius that has made Connecticut the "Wooden Nutmeg State," and De Tocqueville rightly called it the "leetle yellow spot dat make de clock-peddler," for Connecticut has almost monopolized clock-making for all the world. It leads in the production of India-rubber and elastic goods, in hardware and in myriads of ingenious "Yankee notions," and is also very near the front rank in making sewing-machines and arms and war material. Its name comes from the chief New England river—Connecticut meaning the "Long River"—flowing down from the White Mountains to the sound. Its rugged surface is diversified by long ridges of hills and deep valleys, generally running from north to south, the prolongation of mountain-ranges beyond the northern border. Through the western counties the picturesque Housatonic comes down from the Massachusetts Berkshire hills; the centre is crossed by the Connecticut Valley, a region of beautiful scenery and great fertility; while in Eastern Connecticut the Quinnebaug makes a deep valley, and, finally flowing into the Thames, seeks the sea at New London. The many hills make many streams, and wherever one is large enough to make a water-power, there clusters a nest of busy factories.

SOME ATTRACTIVE CONNECTICUT TOWNS.

Our train glides through Greenwich, the south-western town of New England, and as we enter the Yankee-land on a high hill stands the Puritan outpost—the stately graystone Congregational church with its tall spire. The town stretches up to the wooded slopes north of the railway and away to the edge of the sound on the south. It was here that General Putnam in 1779, to get away from the British dragoons, swiftly galloped down the rude rocky stairway leading from the old church, while their bullets rattled around him. "Old Put's Hill" is there, looking much as it did in his day. The train rolls along past attractive inlets and harbors, one of the prettiest being Mianus River, with Cos Cob on its bank just beyond Greenwich. The railway winds among more rocky regions with their brilliant adornments of foliage, and soon passes picturesque Stamford, where twelve thousand people are gathered upon the hills and vales covered with the homes of New York business-men who come out to this lovely place to live. Their dwellings show good taste in architecture and embellishment, and the busy factories reflect the prevalent phase of Connecticut life. Here in the last century lived Colonel Davenport, whom the poet Whittier immortalized. He was a legislator and described as "a man of stern integrity and generous benevolence." When, in 1780, the memorable "Dark Day" came in New England, some one, fearing it was the day of judgment, proposed that the House adjourn. He opposed it, saying, "The day of judgment is either approaching or it is not; if it is, I choose to be found doing my duty. I wish, therefore, that candles may be brought." South Norwalk is another nest of busy mills, within an outer setting of wooden houses that spreads up into Norwalk beyond. The thrifty settlers hereabout originally bought a tract which extended one day's "north walk" from the sound, and hence the name. Fine oysters are gathered in its spacious bay, and the white sails of the pungies add charms to the harbor view. There are ten thousand people in these twin factory-towns, who make shoes and hats and door-knobs and locks, and when the day's labor is ended enjoy the attractive land- and water-views that are all about. On the lowlands to the eastward the noted Pequot Indian nation, once ruling this region, was finally overpowered by the colonial troops, and the Sasco Swamp, in which they were captured, now has cattle grazing and oxen plodding upon almost the only good land seen on the route. Thus we come to tranquil old Fairfield, introduced by a rubber-factory and embowered in trees. Its green-bordered streets are lined with cottages, and the church-spires rise among the groves, while along the shore it has the finest beach on Long Island Sound.

The Pequannock River is crossed a few miles farther on, with the busy city of Bridgeport on its banks. The train runs in among the enormous mills that have gathered forty thousand people here—a hive containing some of the greatest establishments in the world for making sewing-machines and firearms. Here are the huge factories of the Wheeler & Wilson and Howe Sewing-Machine Companies, Sharp's Rifle Company, and the Union Metallic Cartridge Company, with some of the greatest carriage-building shops in the country. Cutlery and corsets, carpets, organs, and soap also occupy attention. The esplanade of Seaside Park over-looks the harbor and sound beyond, and toward the north the city stretches up the slopes into Golden Hill, named from its glittering mica deposits, where magnificent streets display splendid dwellings. But the lion of Bridgeport is P. T. Barnum, who is passing his ripe old age in the stately villa of Waldemere. The veteran showman first developed the financial advantages of amusing, and possibly humbug-ging, the public on a great scale, and also (with Jenny Lind) started the American fashion of paying extravagant sums to opera-singers, giving her one thousand dollars for each of one hundred and fifty nights of concert-singing. He introduced Tom Thumb, who was born in Bridgeport, to an admiring world, and his " great moral shows " are familiar travelling caravans through the country. But Bridgeport is left behind, and then in quiet old Stratford, in marked contrast, it is seen that the new and active order of things has not yet wholly disturbed the old, and that neither hotel nor factory encumbers the greensward or en-croaches upon its sleepy houses, where one may dream away a sweet twilight under the shade of grand trees even more ancient than the village. Beyond we cross the broad bosom of the placid Housatonic, and over patches of marshland come to Milford, with its long stretch of village green neatly enclosed, and its houses upon the bank of the silvery Wap-o-wang, back of which spread the wide streets lined by rows of overarching elms. A colony from Milford in England settled this place two hundred and fifty years ago, and, managing to crowd the Indians off the land, established the primitive church, this being the usual beginning of all New England settlements. Then, true to the American instinct, they at once proceeded to hold a convention, the result being the unanimous adoption of the following:

"Voted, That the earth is the Lord's, and the fulness thereof.

"Voted, That the earth is given to the saints.

"Voted, That we are the saints."

The descendants of these pioneer saints of Milford now make straw hats for the country. Beyond the town the railway crosses a broad expanse of salt-marshes, and the train soon halts at New Haven.

XVI.

THE CITY OF ELMS.

THE magnificent elms of the city of New Haven, arching over the streets and the Public Green and grandly rising in stately rows, make the earliest and the deepest impression upon the visitor. In one of his most eloquent passages the late Henry Ward Beecher said the elms of New England are as much a part of her beauty as the columns of the Parthenon were the glory of its architecture. Sharing this feeling, one goes about the Academic City, and can readily appreciate the admiration all true New Englanders have for their favorite tree. The grand foliage-arched avenues of New Haven are unsurpassed elsewhere, so that they are the crowning glory as well as the constant care of the town. Among the finest of these avenues is the one separating the grounds of Yale College from the beautiful Public Green of the city—a magnificent Gothic aisle of rich green foliage-covered interlacing boughs. While these trees contribute so much to the beauty and notoriety of New Haven, its greatest fame comes from the possession of Yale College, one of the most extensive and comprehensive universities in the world. For almost two centuries this noble foundation has exerted a widely-diffused and advantageous influence upon the American intellectual character, and around it and its multitude of buildings of every kind now clusters New Haven town. This college began in a very small way at Saybrook, at the mouth of the Connecticut River, in 1701, and had only one student during its first year. Subsequently, for a more convenient location, it was removed to New Haven, the first commencement there being in 1718, and its first college building was then named Yale College—a name afterward adopted in the incorporation of the university, and given in honor of Elihu Yale, a native of the town, who went abroad and afterward became governor of the East India Company. He made at different times gifts of books and money amounting to about five hundred pounds sterling, his benefactions being of much greater value on account of their timeliness.

Yale is the orthodox Congregationalist college of New England, usually having over one hundred instructors in the various departments, and about eleven hundred students. Its buildings are of various ages and styles of architecture, the original ones being the plain-looking "Old Brick Row," north-west of the New Haven Public Green, behind which what was formerly an open space has become gradually covered with more modern structures, while various others, such as the Peabody Museum, the Sheffield Scientific School, and the Divinity Halls, are located on

8

adjacent grounds. The line of ancient college buildings in the "Old Brick Row" facing the Public Green has quite a venerable and scholarly aspect, one of the best of them, "Connecticut Hall," having been built with money raised by a lottery and from the proceeds of a French prize-ship captured in the colonial wars antedating the Revolution, when Connecticut aided King George by equipping a frigate. This row stretches broadly across the greensward, fronted by stately arching elms arranged in quadruple lines. Besides the great value of its lands and buildings, Yale College has an invested fund of some one million seven hundred thousand dollars, and its annual income, including the tuition fees, is about three hundred thousand dollars. The Peabody Museum contains one of the best collections of curiosities in the country, and the Yale Library is extensive. There are scores of buildings of all kinds—from the grand academic halls down to the windowless and mysterious mausoleum that I am told entombs the "Skull-and-Bones Society"—occupying the spacious grounds of this famous college.

THE LAND OF QUINNEPIACK.

The Indian name for the region round about New Haven was Quinnepiack, and to this day the placid Quinnepiack River flows through a deep valley past the noted "East Rock" into the harbor. Old John Davenport was the leader and first pastor of the infant colony that settled here—an earnest preacher, revered by the Indians as "so big study man," who delivered the original sermon on founding the town from the text: "Wisdom hath builded her house; she hath hewn out her seven pillars." From this came the original scheme of government for the colony by the seven leading church members, who were known as the "seven pillars." It has since greatly grown, probably in some other things than in the quality of its piety, and, like all these Connecticut towns, is a busy hive of industry. Its many mills make agricultural machinery, corsets, scales, carriages, organs, and pianos, with a vast amount of "Yankee notions" of various kinds and miscellaneous hardware. There is also some commerce, chiefly with the West Indies and along the coast, and numerous railways fetch in the trade of the surrounding country. New Haven has tastefully adorned suburbs, where the hills and elevated roadways afford charming prospects. In the outlying regions, however, the great attractions are the two bold and striking promontories known as the East and West Rocks, which are high buttresses of trap rock lifting themselves from the plain upon which New Haven is chiefly built, one on each side of the town, in a magnificent array of opposition, and each rising over four hundred feet. Some of the inhabitants think these grim precipices in remote ages may have sentinelled the outflow of the Connecticut River between their broad and solid bases to the sound. Each of these tremendous cliffs is the termination of a long ridge or mountain-range that comes down from the far North. The Green Mountain outcropping, stretching southward from Vermont, is represented in the West Rock, while the East Rock terminates what is known as the Mount Tom range, through which the Connecticut River breaks a passage up in Massachusetts, and part of which rises a thousand feet in the "Blue Hills of Southington," making the most elevated lands in the State of Connecticut. The summits of these two great rocks, thus projected out toward Long Island Sound, afford grand views. In a cave upon the West Rock the three regicides, Goffe, Whalley, and Dixwell, were in hiding, and the three avenues leading to this rock from the city are named after them. Dixwell's bones repose upon the Public Green at the back of the "Centre Church," which stands in the row of three churches occupying the middle of the green, which was the common graveyard of colonial New Haven. The approach to the East Rock, going out Orange Street, is grand. The

rock is elevated high above the marshy valley of Mill
River winding about its base, and reared upon the topmost
crag is a noble monument erected by New Haven in memory of the soldiers who fell in the Civil War—a magnificent
shaft overlooking the town and valley that is seen from
afar. The whole surface of the East Rock is reserved as a
public park. Upon the face of the cliff the perpendicular
strata of reddish-brown trap stand bolt upright. There are
well-laid roads of easy gradient gradually rising through
the bordering ravines and amid the forest until the top is
reached, where from this elevated outpost there is a charming view. Far over the flat plain to the southward spreads
the town, with its little harbor stretching out into the
sound, and beyond, across the silvery waters, there can be
seen the distant hazy shores of Long Island, twenty-five
miles away. The numerous wooden houses nestle among
the trees, and the two little crooked rivers coming out of
the deep valleys on either side of the great rock wind onward to mingle their waters in the harbor. Smoke ascends
from the numerous factory-chimneys down by the water-
side, while all around the country is dotted with flourishing
villages. This is the noble outlook over the " City of Elms "
and its pleasant surroundings as seen from this grand outpost rising high above the plain upon which the Academic
City is built.

FROM NEW HAVEN TO HARTFORD.

Almost under the shadow of the towering East Rock is
laid the railway connecting New Haven with Hartford, and
thence it passes northward along the valley of Quinnepiack
River over flat meadow-land bordered by blue hills. Brick-
making seems to be the chief industry on these meadows, and
they are prolific grass-growers, judging by the hundreds of
little haystacks dotted over them. Soon, however, sterility
is developed, for vast sand-deposits overlie the soil, and
farming here must be a discouraging occupation. These

moors, with their sands and sloughs and scrub timber, demonstrate the plight of the average Connecticut settler, for, being unable to wrest a living out of the land, he either has to go to making "Yankee notions" or emigrate or starve. Wallingford is passed, its church-towers crowning the hill to the eastward of the railway and watching over a population largely made up of German-silver and plated-ware manufacturers. When this town was founded John Davenport was invited to come out from New Haven and conduct the religious services. He came and preached the initial sermon from a text regarded as appropriate to the locality: "My beloved hath a vineyard on a very fruitful hill." Beyond, and nestling under the shadow of the "Blue Hills of Southington," is Meriden. These hills rise high above its western and northern borders in the West Peak and Mount Lamentation. Here is another active hive of factories fringed around with the neat wooden dwellings of their operatives, while the villas of their owners are scattered about in pleasant places upon the steep declivities of the adjacent hills. These people are industrious workers in iron and steel, in bronze and brass, in making tin, Britannia, and electro-plated silverware. The chief establishment of the place is the well-known Meriden Britannia Company, its enormous mills being spread for a long distance along the railway and making the greatest manufactory of its kind in the world, sending out over five million dollars' worth of its wares in a year.

Meriden and Berlin, a short distance northward, are the headquarters of the peripatetic Connecticut tin-peddler, who starts out laden with all kinds of tin pans and pots and other bright and useful utensils to wander over the country and charm the rural housewife with his bargains. Berlin began the first American manufacture of tinware in the last century. While it bears an ambitious German name, it was started by a colony of shrewd Yankees. These New England villages—and there are hundreds like them—all

seem to be cast in the same mould and to have similar characteristics. There are in each the beautiful central public
green shaded by rows of stately elms; the tall-spired churches;
the village graveyard, usually sloping down a hillside,
with the lines of white gravestones supplemented in the
modern interments by more elaborate monuments; the
attractive wooden houses nestling amid foliage and surrounded by gardens and flower-beds, the homes of the
people; and the big factories that give them employment. Some of these villages, being larger than others,
may show a greater development in various ways, but,
excepting in size, all are substantially alike. The ox-
team slowly plods along the road, and the scanty crop
in the field shows how the sand and stones have choked
the efforts of the husbandman. And, thus gliding along
past village and mill, there soon comes into view the distant gilded dome of the Connecticut State Capitol, and
finally the broad fronts of the buildings of Trinity College surmounting Rocky Hill. The train runs among a
labyrinth of factories down upon the edge of the little
Park River, and soon halts at the station, under the
shadow of the Capitol, in the centre of the city of
Hartford, on the Connecticut River.

XVII.

THE CONNECTICUT VALLEY.

THE noted Adraien Block, the Dutch navigator, built at
the Battery in New York in 1614 the first ship ever constructed in New York harbor. The four little huts he put
up to house his crew and builders were among the first
structures of the early colony. His blunt-pointed Knicker-
bocker yacht of sixteen tons he named the " Onrest," and

in her started on a voyage of discovery through Hellgate into Long Island Sound. To him belongs the honor of discovering on this important voyage the principal river of New England, and after his explorations he rested on the land that still bears his name—Block Island. The sources of the Connecticut River are in the highlands bordering Canada at an elevation of more than sixteen hundred feet above the sea, and it flows south-west over four hundred miles to Long Island Sound. The Indians called it " Quonektakat," or the " Long River," and hence the name and that of the " Nutmeg State " wherein it finds its mouth. The river has always been noted for beautiful scenery, and has many cataracts, among them South Hadley in Massachusetts and Enfield in Connecticut, furnishing abundant water-power to the mills lining the banks. It flows into the sound thirty-three miles east of New Haven, at Saybrook. The first English patent for lands on these coasts was granted to Lord Saye and Sele and Lord Brooke, and, this being the earliest settlement under their auspices, it bears their double name. The original colony was planned with great care, as the place was expected to become the home of distinguished men, and a fort was built on a hill at the river's mouth. According to the story told by the historian, it was to Saybrook that Cromwell, Pym, Hampden, and Haselrig, with their party of malcontent colonists, intended to emigrate when they were stopped by King Charles. Had this movement been consummated it might have greatly changed the subsequent momentous events in England. A little west of the old fort there was a public square laid out, where, according to the town plan, their houses were to have been built. I have already mentioned that Yale College began in Saybrook, its first building being a long, narrow, one-story structure looking much like a ropewalk ; and this house was afterward removed with the college to New Haven. The founders of this great educational establishment were pious men, who in 1708 drew up the "Saybrook Platform," with a declaration that "the churches must have a public profession of faith, agreeable to which the instruction of the college shall be conducted."

The ancient Saybrook fort stood upon a steep and solitary knoll known as "Tomb Hill," which a few years ago was carried off bodily by a railroad to make embankments across the adjacent lowlands—an act of vandalism strongly criticised at the time, one of the critics bitterly remarking, "It is fortunate that the Acropolis and the temples of Baalbek are not in America." The earliest governor of the colony, Colonel Fenwick, was afterward one of the regicide judges, and his memory is preserved by the village hotel—Fenwick Hall. Old Saybrook is a languid sort of town, however, chiefly spread along one handsome wide street, canopied over by the arching branches of its stately trees, under which the distant vista view looks almost like a scene through a veritable foliage tunnel. This sedate and historic settlement gives to-day an exhibition of the original Connecticut in the serene dignity it enjoyed before the great impetus of manufacturing industry came. The quietness and placidity are just the opposite of the present pushing, busy Connecticut as shown in its many hives of industry, where the modern Yankee race is striving how to do most work in the shortest time. The broad Connecticut River flows back and forth in front with the tide in rather tame and uninteresting fashion, and presents an additional scene of restfulness in keeping with the ancient colony upon its shores. The Saybrook fort only saw warfare once, and that was during the early boundary disputes with New York. On this occasion, we are told, the Dutch from Manhattan marched against it "brimful of wrath and cabbage," but, seeing it would be stoutly defended, the chronicler testifies to their prudence by adding, "they thought best to desist before attacking." The lower Connecticut flows through a prolific agricultural region, with lands enriched by copious dressings of fish-manures got from the river. It passes picturesque shores and sundry farming-villages below Middletown, amid scenes that in a diminished sort of way are reminders of the hills along the Hudson. Another nest of active mills is at Middletown, making plated wares, pumps, and webbing, sewing-machines and tapes. Its shaded streets lead up the hill-slopes here enclosing the river that have within their recesses valuable quarries of Portland stone. The court-house is a quaint little miniature of the Parthenon. The Wesleyan Methodist College is located here, Memorial and Judd Halls being grand buildings. North of Middletown, green, level, and exceedingly fertile meadows adjoin the river, their great yield being the noted onion crops of Wethersfield. This was the earliest Connecticut settlement, and its onions permeate the whole country. It is historic, too, for here convened the first Connecticut legislature to declare war against the Pequots in 1636, while one of the old mansions of the town is pointed out as the place where Washington and the French officers prepared the plans which ended the Revolution by the great victory at Yorktown.

THE QUEEN CITY OF NEW ENGLAND.

We have ascended the Connecticut River to the State Capital, the noted city which repeats in this newer land the name in the mother-country of the ancient Saxon village at the " Ford of Harts," whence some of its first settlers came. It was the brave and pious Thomas Hooker who led his flock from the sea-coast through the wilderness to Hartford to establish an English settlement at the Indian post of Suckiang, where the Dutch had previously built a fort and trading-station at the bend of the river. That quaint historian of early New England, Cotton Mather, afterward described Hooker as " the renowned minister of Hartford and pillar of Connecticut, and the light of the Western churches." This lovely and most substantial city

well deserves its favorite title of "The Queen." Its centre
is a beautiful park, in front of which the narrow and winding stream known as Park River flows down to the Connecticut. From the railway-station a light bridge leads
over this little river to the triumphal brownstone arch with
surmounting conical towers which is the tasteful entrance
to the park. This arch honors the men sent out from the
city who served and fell during the Civil War. A grand
highway then continues up the hill to the Capitol building,
the finest structure in New England, an imposing Gothic
edifice of white marble three hundred feet long, all its
fronts being elaborately ornamented with statuary and
artistic decoration, while the high surmounting gilded dome
rises two hundred and fifty feet. The interior is well
lighted, and seems to be thoroughly adapted to the purposes of the State Government and the halls of the legislature of the "Nutmeg State." Rugged and famous old
General Israel Putnam, the idol of this land of steady
habits, has his statue in the Capitol grounds; he died here
in 1790. "The Putnam Phalanx" is the crack military
company of Hartford, a body dressing in an antique Continental uniform and having a membership of about one
hundred and twenty-five of the wealthiest townsmen.
Within the Capitol is the bronze statue of Nathan Hale
of Connecticut, whom the British during the Revolution
executed as a spy. It is one of the most striking master-
pieces of sculpture. The almost living figure seems animated with the full vigor of earnest youth, and with outstretched hands actually appears to speak his memorable
words: "I only regret that I have but one life to lose for
my country." The battered and weather-worn gravestone
that originally covered Putnam's grave is also kept as a
precious relic, and alongside of it are cases containing the
battered battle-flags of the Connecticut regiments. Within
the gorgeous Assembly Chamber, which is the gem of this
magnificent building, the law-makers, it is hoped, now en-

act milder legislation than the rigorous "Connecticut blue laws" of the olden time, when the iron rule of the stern Puritan pastors, then governing the colony, created a Draconian code inflicting death-penalties for the crimes of idolatry, unchastity, blasphemy, witchcraft, murder, man-stealing, smiting parents, and some others, while savage laws also punished Sabbath-breaking and the use of tobacco.

THE CHARTER OAK.

Much of Hartford clusters around the "Charter Oak," although that famous tree is now only a memory revered by the townspeople. Thirty-two years ago it was blown down in a storm, and its remains were made into many precious relics. Our old friend "Mark Twain," who lives in Hartford, and therefore knows much of the matter, says he has seen all conceivable articles made out of this precious timber, there being, among others, "a walking-stick, dog-collar, needle-case, three-legged stool, bootjack, dinner-table, ten-pin alley, toothpick, and enough Charter Oak to build a plank road from Hartford to Great Salt Lake City." This ancient tree concealed the original royal charter of the colony when, in 1687, the tyrannical governor Andros demanded its surrender. While the subject was being discussed in the legislature the lights were put out, and in the darkness a bold colonist seized it, and, running out, hid the precious document in the hollow of the oak. A marble slab now marks the place on "Charter Oak Hill" where the tree stood alongside "Charter Oak Place," and "Charter Oak Avenue" leads up to it. The fine statue surmounting the Capitol dome and representing the female genius of Connecticut, which overlooks the city with outstretched hand, is crowning the municipality with a wreath of Charter Oak leaves. The oak leaf is repeated in many ways in the gorgeous decoration within and upon the Capitol building, and also upon many structures throughout the city. The name of "Charter Oak" is given to a bank, a life-insurance company, and many other institutions of the solid community which is blessed with this honored memory.

Hartford, in proportion to its population, is the wealthiest American city. It is financially great, particularly in insurance, there being no less than twenty-one fire and life companies, some of them of great strength and doing business in all parts of the world. Its Charter Oak Insurance Company dwells in a granite palace on Main Street, and some others, such as the Hartford, the Ætna, the Connecticut Mutual, and the Phœnix, also have fine buildings. These companies have a widespread business, and some of them enormous capitals and assets. The city also has many strong banks, and is renowned for its numerous charitable institutions, its extensive book-publishing houses, and its educational foundations, the most noted being Trinity College. From the elevated position of this college there is a grand view across the intervening valley to the hills of Farmington and westward to Talcott Mountain. The vast wealth of the Hartford people has enabled them to enrich its picturesque suburbs, so that an extensive district around it is covered with magnificent villas, making a semi-rural residential section that is unsurpassed by any other New England city. Arching elms, as everywhere else, embower here the lawn-bordered avenues that stretch for long distances, and in many localities the superb hedges impart quite an English air. Some of the splendid suburban homes of the "Queen City" are perfect gems of artistic construction and attractive decoration, the evidences of the wealth of the people being shown on all sides. There is also a devotion to art, the galleries of the Wadsworth Atheneum having a fine collection. Among the relics kept here are General Putnam's sword and the old Indian king Philip's club.

But the citizen whom Hartford seems to hold in highest esteem is the late Colonel Samuel Colt, who invented the revolving pistol. He was a native of Hartford, and his remains rest under a noble monument in Cedar Hill Cemetery. A beautiful little brownstone Gothic chapel, the "Church of the Good Shepherd," has been built in his memory. Colt when a boy ran away from home and went to sea, and is said to have there conceived the idea of his great invention. During several years he sought with indifferent success to establish an arms manufactory. He did not prosper until 1852, when he started a factory in Hartford, and with the great demand for small-arms then stimulated by the opening of the California gold-mines and the exploration of the Western Plains, and afterward vastly expanded by the necessities created by the Civil War, his factory grew into an enormous business. "The Colt Arms Company," which was for many years managed by General Franklin, is the chief industrial establishment of Hartford, having very large buildings adjacent to the Connecticut River that are filled with the latest appliances and machinery for making the most approved arms of all kinds. These mills, however, thrive only on war, and it may gratify our Peace Society to know that they are now running very light, though still making a goodly number to supply a demand for pistols and rifles that is constant. They employ a small army of very intelligent-looking workmen, who appear to be in advance of the average in intellectuality. Throughout these vast works there is everywhere seen a reminder of the great Hartford inventor in the representation of his family coat-of-arms, the heraldic " colt rampant," which is stamped upon all the arms and impressed and reproduced upon all the adornments of this greatest Hartford establishment.

XVIII.

THE CONNECTICUT INTERVALES.

A SHORT distance north of Hartford is the imaginary
line that marks the Massachusetts southern boundary. We
follow up the Connecticut Valley, which is here a broad and
comparatively level region of good land, with the placid
river flowing through it. We have temporarily left the
region of sand and stones so well developed in the " Nutmeg State," and come into the rich meadows of Mattaneag,
a fertile intervale, where the fences are built of wood, as
stones seem scarce. Its entrepôt is Windsor, an agricultural
colony started by John Worham, who, the local historian
says, was the first New England pastor who used notes in
preaching. Whether he defied the " blue laws " by using
tobacco we are not told, but his colony is to-day a great
tobacco-growing section, through which the Farmington
River flows down from the western hills. The Enfield
Rapids of the Connecticut are here, and a canal formerly
used to take the river-craft around the obstruction now
gives ample water-power to many paper and other mills
that make the town of Windsor Locks. The river flows
swiftly over its pebbly bed, being dammed above to divert
some of the water into the canal. The Hazardville Powder-
Works are not far away, the greatest gunpowder-factory in
America, and Thompsonville is adjacent, a maker of carpets
to a prodigious extent. Then we cross the boundary into
the " Old Bay State," the chief New England commonwealth, also largely a nest of factories, and the leading
State of the Union in the manufacture of cotton and
woollen goods, boots and shoes, leather and paper. Massachusetts, like Connecticut, has, it is true, in the Housatonic
and Connecticut Valleys some productive soils, but the
greater portion of the more elevated lands, as well as the

long sandy coasts, gives no encouragement to the agriculturist. Its surface is diversified, the Vermont Green Mountains coming down through the western portion in the Taghkanic and Hoosac ranges of Berkshire county, that are parallel, and form the famous Berkshire Hills. In the north-west corner the most elevated summit, " Old Graylock," rises nearly thirty-six hundred feet, while in the south-west Mount Everett exceeds twenty-six hundred feet. The foothills from the eastern verge of the Hoosacs slope into the beautiful Connecticut Valley, while near the centre of the State that river forces a passage below Northampton between two detached ridges, the Mount Tom range on its western bank rising thirteen hundred feet in one place, and Mount Holyoke on the eastern bank, eleven hundred and twenty feet. These are the southern outposts of the White Mountains of New Hampshire. Farther eastward are detached peaks, the chief being Mount Wachusett.

SPRINGFIELD AND ITS ARMORY.

Just north of the Massachusetts boundary the river sweeps grandly around in approaching the town of Springfield, built on the eastern bank and spreading for a long distance up the slopes of the adjacent hills. This is one of the busiest and most prosperous cities of Massachusetts, being an important railway-junction, where the lines along the Connecticut Valley cross the route from Boston to Albany and the West, and being also a huge factory, especially for the making of arms. The Puritan missionary shepherd, William Pynchon, led his hardy flock to this Indian land of Agawam in 1636, and the statue of Miles Morgan, a noted soldier of that early time, stands, matchlock in hand, in heroic bronze on the public square. Heretofore I have referred to the great amount of firearms-making that is conducted in New England, where all kinds of arms are made, and literally for all the world. Springfield has among its numerous factories two enormous military establishments. I have noticed for a good while past that in shooting affrays and suicides, as well as in those unfortunate cases where somebody " didn't know it was loaded," the weapon is usually a " Smith and Wesson." It is at Springfield that the " Smith and Wesson Company" makes its pistols, in works that seem big enough to provide the means of speedily annihilating a good deal of the surplus population of the globe. At Springfield also is established the United States National Armory. This enormous factory, which makes the arms for the United States army, occupies an extensive enclosure on Armory Hill, up to which the surface gradually slopes from the river, so that it gives an admirable view over the town. The chief buildings stand around a quadrangle, making a pleasant stretch of lawn with regular rows of trees crossing it. A few cannon are scattered about and point toward the entrance-gates, to give it a military air, and hundreds of men in the shops are making the Springfield breech-loading rifle, the standard weapon of the army. All the parts are constructed by automatic machines, some of which are most ingenious mechanisms. Very intelligent workmen are employed, and many an old man is here who has grown gray in the service, " rotation in office" not being fashionable in the armory. These Springfield rifles are packed twenty in a case, and most of them are forwarded to the arsenal at Rock Island on the Mississippi River, which is the base of supplies for the Indian country and the Western frontier, where most of the army is stationed. The laboring day in this establishment is eight hours, from 8 A. M. to 5 P. M., with an hour's rest at noon, but all wages are paid by the piece. The prosperity of the town largely depends upon the armory, which employs so many of its people, and has been in active operation almost all the time since the colonial days. It was here that most of the arms were made for the Revolutionary army and the cannon were cast that helped defeat Burgoyne at Saratoga. The armory as seen

now was mainly the product of the late war, when it ran
day and night during four years, and at times employed
over three thousand men.   It made nearly eight hundred
thousand rifles for the Union armies.   The arsenal, a large
building on the western side of the quadrangle, has been
thus described by Longfellow :

> " This is the arsenal.   From floor to ceiling,
>   Like a huge organ, rise the burnished arms ;
> But from their silent pipes no anthem pealing
>   Startles the villages with strange alarms.
>
> " Ah ! what a sound will rise—how wild and dreary !—
>   When the death-angel touches those swift keys !
> What loud lament and dismal Miserere
>   Will mingle with their awful symphonies !"

From the arsenal tower a fine view is had over the busy
town, with the smoke from its factory chimneys and the
roar of its many moving railway-trains, and far away the
rich farms of its bordering meadows and the hills enclosing
them studded with villas and hamlets.

HOLYOKE AND THE HADLEY FALLS.

At Springfield and Holyoke, not far away, are made
three-fourths of the fine papers manufactured in the United
States.   The valley of the Connecticut north of Springfield is another hive of industry, repeated in town after
town, whose mills are located amid some of the finest
scenery in New England.   Winding among the hills in
wayward fashion, the river receives its tributaries, and all
the water-courses teem with factories.   From the eastern
hills the Chicopee flows in, the falls making an admirable
water-power that turns many wheels, giving employment
to a population of thirteen thousand, chiefly workers in
cotton and wool, brass and bronze.   Just above, in the
Connecticut River, are the Hadley Falls, the greatest
water-power of New England and the creator of the town

9

of Holyoke. In a distance of little over a mile the river descends in falls and rapids for sixty feet, and by a system of canals the water is led for three miles along the banks, serving paper-mills and other factories. There are twenty-six paper-mills, employing more than four thousand people, and these, producing the finest qualities, are at the same time the most extensive paper-makers in the world. There are also other factories. A better situation could not have been devised for this industrious town of over thirty thousand people, whose manufacturing abilities are multiplied by the advantage of having the river wind around them on three sides. Yet they use even more power than the water gives, judging by the belching smoke from the tall chimney-stacks. Thus for miles along this picturesque valley are the beauties of Nature combined with the strongest practical demonstration of human industry. Approaching Holyoke, the railway on which we are travelling crosses the river directly into the centre of the hive, and then, one after another, spans the network of canals leading the water to the mill-wheels, and at frequent intervals displaying their foaming outfalls. The great descent that is available enables the water to be used over and over again. The main fall in the river has a descent of thirty feet, and to prevent erosion is covered with an inclined apron of stout timbers sheathed with boiler iron and spiked securely to the rock-ledges beneath. Down this smooth surface the surplus waters gracefully glide. The stratified layers of rock protrude in great masses below the fall, while above the character of the scene is quickly changed by a huge boom set across the river for catching logs, of which millions are thrown into the upper waters of the Connecticut.

THE LAND OF NONOTUCK.

We advance above Holyoke into scenery growing ever more charming. The hills have come nearer the river and abruptly rise into the dignity of mountains. The river winds about their bases, and after flowing to the westward along the foot of a ridge it abruptly turns, and, passing between the great peaks, winds about the ridge to the eastward. The first is the Mount Tom range, and the other Mount Holyoke, having between them the Connecticut, which passes out through the notch from the extensive valley above. Within the gorge the stratified rocks thrust up their long thin edges in diagonal dip where the water has worn them away, and the scarred faces of the bordering cliff show that the passage had been rent in some remote age by a mighty convulsion of nature. Above this gorge a vast alluvial plain stretches across the broad valley, and far away to the northward ridge after ridge crosses the country as the distant hills gradually rise into higher elevations beyond Massachusetts. This is the fertile land of Nonotuck, which was bought from its Indian owners in 1653 for "one hundred fathoms of wampum and ten coats." Here is built Northampton, one of the most beautiful villages of the Connecticut Valley. The fairest fields surround it, with thrifty farmers cultivating their rich bottomlands, and the splendid outlook these people have in front of their doors is the glorious panorama of the noble heights of Holyoke and Nonotuck in the Mount Tom range, with the river flowing away between them. Solomon Stoddart was the sturdy Puritan pastor who ruled the flock at Nonotuck for fifty-six years, the village being surrounded for protection by a palisade and wall. The little church in which he preached measured eighteen by twenty-six feet, and was built in 1655 at a cost of seventy dollars, the congregation being called to meeting armed and by the blasts of a trumpet:

> "Each man equipped on Sunday morn
> With psalm-book, shot, and powder-horn,
> And looked in form, as all must grant,
> Like th' ancient, true Church militant."

This renowned pastor was a man of majestic appearance, and as good a fighter as he was preacher. He never hesitated to lead his people in their Indian wars, and once he rode into an ambush, but the awestruck savages, impressed by his noble bearing, hesitated to shoot him, saying to their French allies, "That is the Englishmen's god." The present stone church is the fifth that has been built on the original site. During nearly a quarter century the noted Jonathan Edwards—the greatest preacher and metaphysician of his time—was the Northampton pastor, but he was dismissed in 1750 because, owing to the growing laxity of the Church, he insisted upon "a higher and purer standard of admission to the communion-table." Even in lovely Northampton factories appear, as in the other towns along the romantic Connecticut.

The level land of Nonotuck, stretching to the northward, raises much tobacco, for among the strange mutations of advancing time is that which makes the descendants of the framers of the savage "blue laws" against tobacco now get their livelihood by its cultivation. It is here a profitable crop usually, but the growers say its development is risky and uncertain, the sale being subject to the whim of the market, which, whenever there comes a good yield of Connecticut tobacco (a light leaf), is generally made by the dealers to prefer a dark leaf. The Connecticut River winds in wide, circular sweeps among the fields and meadows of this prolific valley, but seems to make little progress as it goes around great curves of miles in circuit. Upon an isthmus thus formed, with the huge loop of the river stretching far to the westward, stands "Old Hadley." The Connecticut has made a five-mile circuit to accomplish barely one mile of distance, and across the level isthmus from the river above to the river below, stretching through the village, is the noted "Hadley Street," the handsomest highway of New England in natural adornments. Over three hundred feet wide, this street is lined by two double

rows of noble elms, with a broad expanse of greenest lawn
between, and nearly a thousand ancient trees arching their
graceful branches above it. This quiet street has a perfection of greensward, for it is almost untravelled. Its inhabitants grow tobacco and make brooms. Hadley was the
final home and burying-place of Goffe and Whalley, the
regicides, who fled here from New Haven. When their
house was pulled down, it is said the bones of Whalley were
found entombed just outside the cellar-wall. It was the
house of the pastor, and they were concealed in it fifteen
years, their presence being known to only three persons.
It is said that once during their hiding Indians attacked
the town, and after a sharp fight the people gave way, when
there suddenly appeared " an ancient man, with hoary locks,
of a most venerable and dignified aspect," who rallied them
to a fresh onslaught and scattered the Indians in all directions. He then disappeared, and the inhabitants attributed
their deliverance to "a militant angel." This was Goffe,
and the tale is "Old Hadley's" chief legend. "Fighting
Joe Hooker" was a native of Hadley, and he probably
had his first day-dreams of war and battle under the magnificent elms of Old Hadley's famous street.

XIX.

MOUNT HOLYOKE.

THE famous "Mount Holyoke Seminary" is the most
noted institution of Central Massachusetts. This female
collegiate school is at South Hadley, almost under the
shadow of the mountain amid magnificent scenery, and
has been in existence more than half a century. It has
educated many missionary women for their labors in distant lands, and continues its successful career with a fame

that is far-reaching. But we have not time to linger, and start to make the ascent of the mountain. Through quiet Old Hadley and past its magnificent, but silent and almost deserted, street, and across the tobacco-plantations and meadows of the broad intervale, rounding a bend of the swiftly-flowing river, we go along toward the abrupt face of Mount Holyoke, its notched and round-topped crags stretching far off in the range to the eastward. An inclined-plane railway ascends the steep mountain-side to the top of the highest peak. Across the river to the westward is the twin range of Mount Tom, with the peak of Nonotuck forming its eastern buttress where the river flows out of the valley. Tradition says this broad and fertile plain, spreading almost to the northern Massachusetts boundary, was once a lake, with the outlet toward the west behind the Mount Tom range, until the waters broke a passage through the ridge and thus made the present Connecticut-River route to the sea. These guardian peaks of Tom and Holyoke bear the names of two pioneers of the valley who are said to have first discovered the pass. The origin of Mount Holyoke has evidently been volcanic, and it is built up of trap rock, lifting its columned masses abruptly from the level floor of the valley, and being without foothills to dwarf its great elevation. There is, consequently, given from the summit a grand and unobstructed view entirely around the horizon, for the peak is isolated. This view, spreading almost from Long Island Sound northward to the White Mountains of New Hampshire, and from the Berkshire Hills in the west to the cloud-capped mountains Monadnock and Wachusett fifty miles to the eastward, is regarded as the finest in New England. The broad and highly cultivated valley of the Connecticut, with its winding, wayward stream flowing apparently in all directions over the rich bottom-lands that are cut up into such diminutive farms and fields like so many "plaided meadows," gives a charm that is lacking in most other mountain-views.

To the southward are the towns of Holyoke and Spring-field, through which we have come, and beyond them, in the distance, the gilded dome of the Hartford Capitol glistening under the sunlight, with far away the dim gray outlines of the New Haven East and West Rocks down alongside the sound. Moving around toward the west, the view gradually rises from the Connecticut River Valley into the high hills of Berkshire crossing the western horizon.

Spreading off toward the north-west is the broadening intervale, displaying many miles of level land, with charming Northampton nestling amid its foliage, while beyond the expanse of garden-land is a hilly region terminating finally in the Hoosacs, and behind them the misty height of Old Graylock, over forty miles away. Almost beneath our feet, in the foreground, is the great "ox-bow" of the Connecticut, where the river used to flow around a circuit of nearly four miles and accomplished only one hundred and fifty yards of actual distance, until an ice-freshet recently broke through the narrow isthmus and made a straight channel across it. But nearly all the romance is taken out of this liquid "ox-bow" by its being crammed full of floating logs awaiting a market. To the northward the river sweeps around more curves, also well supplied with logs, and here, almost beneath us, is "Old Hadley," with its wide and noble elm-bordered street, looking like a half dozen green and golden-hued streaks across the narrow level neck of land beyond which the river makes its wide and graceful loop. Farther northward can be traced the repeated river-reaches, with intervening ridges of hills partly hiding them, and the abrupt Sugarloaf Mountain rising in solitary grandeur over Deerfield. This portion of the valley was the theatre of some of the bloodiest tragedies of the remorseless "King Philip's War," of which we learnt much in our school days. That implacable chief of the Narragansetts in his attack upon the settlers made the tall Sugarloaf his lookout station, whence he directed the movements of his warriors, and a crag on the top is yet called " King Philip's Chair." In the north-east rises cloud-capped Monadnock, with the distant Green and White Mountains of Vermont and New Hampshire showing up in rows of peaks all about the northern horizon. The eastern view is mainly over successive ranges of forest-clad, rough-looking hills, making a wilderness almost without habitation, dissolving finally into more farm-land to the south-east and into the river valley again to the south, where the glistening stream flows in placid beauty onward toward the sea. Such is the glorious view from this magnificent mountain-top, standing almost in the centre of Massachusetts and giving an outlook over four New England States.

PENETRATING THE HOOSACS.

On its eastern slopes the Hoosac range sends down various streams through wild and romantic gorges into the Connecticut Valley, and one of these is Deerfield River, debouching some distance north of Mount Holyoke. Here is the village of Old Deerfield, whose streets often ran with blood in the Indian wars, and whose young men were then described by the quaint Puritan chronicler as " the very flower of Essex county, none of whome were ashamed to speak with the enemy in the gate." The Sugarloaf and Mount Toby are its guardian peaks, and the Fitchburg Railroad from Boston, coming across the valley and through the village, takes advantage of the wild and winding cañon of its mountain-torrent to ascend the grade westward to the wall of the Hoosac Mountain, which for years obstructed its farther journey. This railway is laid high upon the side of the bold and charming Deerfield gorge, spanning its tributaries, and following a sinuous path carved out of the rocks, while here and there pretty cascades tumble down the mountain-side to the wildly-rushing stream below.

The line is constructed in this way through the most
romantic portion of the picturesque defile, beyond which
the valley somewhat broadens, and then the stream-bed
rises more nearly to the level of the railway, the foaming
waters being of the dark and transparent amber color made
by the pines and hemlocks, while the torrent rushes over a
succession of rocky ledges set on edge, sprinkled with
myriads of rounded boulders that have been brought
down by freshets. Frowning peaks and ridges rise high
above us in this complete wilderness. Within the heart
of the defile, however, is a pleasant village, where the
stream darts down a series of cataracts and rapids with a
descent of one hundred and fifty feet, this being Shelburne
Falls. The river roars through a channel worn deeply into
the rocks, and plunges down successive falls like an irregular
and badly broken stairway. Here, amid all this natural
magnificence, are planted more prosaic mills, making cutlery, locks, and gimlets, while the neighbors tend their
sheep and "tap" the numerous maple trees for sugar.
We ascend the gorge farther, and find in each brief broadening expanse of valley, the little hamlet and church-spire
among the trees, with towering mountains looking down
upon them. One of these sequestered villages, Buckland,
was the birthplace, in 1797, of Mary Lyon, the devout
and noted teacher who founded Mount Holyoke Seminary.
Onward among the savage peaks, the line crossing the rapid
winding torrent to seek the best route amid hills that rise
two thousand feet above the water, the train swiftly rolls
until it reaches a place where the mountain-wall stands up
directly across the passage. The Deerfield River, coming
down from the north, sweeps grandly around a loop; the
railway crosses high above it, where the sloping banks are
covered with the broken rocks cast out from tunnel-borings,
and suddenly the car rushes into the famous "Hoosac Tunnel," the longest on this continent. It took twenty years to
bore this tunnel, which was made by the State Government

of Massachusetts to secure the shortest route and easiest gradients, and also a competitive line between Boston and the West; and the work cost sixteen million dollars: it is nearly five miles in length.

NORTH ADAMS AND PITTSFIELD.

There is a ten minutes' interval of swift movement through the great tunnel, the darkness dissipated by hundreds of electric lights, and then the train emerges on the western side of the mountain, running down the slope into the valley of the little Hoosac River, with the towering Taghkanic range beyond. This latter to the northward rises into the double peaks of Old Graylock, the monarch of the Berkshire Hills, overlooking the town of North Adams. The scarred surfaces, exposed in huge, bare places far up their sides, show the white-marble formation of these hills. North Adams is noted as having been the first place on the Atlantic seaboard where " Chinese cheap labor " was employed, these Celestials having been imported to work in its shoe-shops in consequence of a troublesome strike. It is a wealthy manufacturing village, and the chief settlement of Northern Berkshire. The busy Hoosac turns the mill-wheels, and at the head of the main street is its group of churches, with the memorial statue of a soldier standing among them, recalling the late war. About a mile west of North Adams, down the Hoosac, at a road-crossing, was the site of old Fort Massachusetts, the "Thermopylæ of New England " in the French War, where, in 1746, its garrison of twenty-two men held the fort two days against an attacking force of nine hundred: they killed forty-seven, wounded many more, and only yielded when every grain of powder was gone. We turn southward along the Hoosac through this picturesque valley, and journey up the narrow, crooked stream with its frequent dams, the mills working the waters for all they are worth. On either hand the higher ridges enclose the view—that to the westward

being the barrier separating from the Hudson Valley in
New York, while "Old Graylock, cloud-girdled on his purple throne," stands guardian at the northern entrance. The
journey passes many mills, and it seems difficult to imagine
how the villages have managed to find room enough to stand
amid the encroaching hills. These settlements are picturesque, but seem in a sort of decadence, the migration of
their people to the West having curtailed growth. The
town of Adams is passed, having a few hundred population,
the most famous of its inhabitants being Miss Susan B.
Anthony. At times the valley broadens, with the Hoosac
meandering among the fields, but the mills have chimney-
stacks and coal-piles, showing that steam has to supplement
the water-power. Sheep and cattle graze and villas abound,
and here is Cheshire, noted for its cheeses, while not far
away the late lamented humorist "Josh Billings" was born,
then named H. W. Shaw before he wandered away to become an auctioneer and lecturer under his popular sobriquet. Soon we lose the narrow, wayward Hoosac in the
reservoir made of its head-waters that they may better
serve the many mills below.

Almost embracing the sources of the diminutive Hoosac,
with its branching head-streams coming out of many pretty
lakes and springs, originates the Housatonic River, its Indian name meaning the "flowing, winding waters." It
flows south, as the other does north, and this part of the
valley is an elevated region of sloughs and lakes, from
which the watershed tapers off in both directions. Upon
this high plateau, more than a thousand feet above the sea-
level, is located Pittsfield, the county-seat of Berkshire,
thus named in honor of William Pitt the elder in 1761.
The centre of the town, as throughout New England, is
the public green, here called the "Heart of Berkshire."
Upon it stands Launt Thompson's famous bronze statue
of the "Color-bearer," cast from cannon given by Congress
—a spirited young soldier in fatigue uniform holding aloft

the flag. This statue, which is so much admired, has been
reproduced upon the Gettysburg battle-field to mark the
position of the Massachusetts troops. It is the monument of
five officers and ninety men of Pittsfield killed in the war,
and at the dedication appropriate to it were read Whittier's
eloquent lines:

"A voice from lips whereon the coal from Freedom's shrine hath
    been
 Thrilled as but yesterday the breasts of Berkshire's mountain-men;
 The echoes of that solemn voice are sadly lingering still
 In all our sunny valleys, on every wind-swept hill.

"And sandy Barnstable rose up, wet with the salt sea-spray;
 And Bristol sent her answering shout down Narragansett Bay;
 Along the broad Connecticut old Hampden felt the thrill,
 And the cheer of Hampshire's woodmen swept down from Holyoke
    Hill:

"'No slave-hunt in our borders—no pirate on our strand!
 No fetters in the Bay State—no slave upon our land!'"*

Around this celebrated green are the churches and public buildings of the town, while not far away a spacious and
comfortable mansion is pointed out that was for many years
the summer home of Longfellow and the place where he
found "The Old Clock on the Stairs." Upon one of the
buildings near this green a modest, weather-beaten sign
bears the well-known name of Henry L. Dawes, the Massachusetts Senator, who lives at Pittsfield in one of its
most unpretentious houses, showing that his statesmanship has not produced him great wealth. As everywhere
else, mills make much of the trade of Pittsfield, and the
trains of the Boston and Albany Railroad roll through

* Whittier's lyric "Massachusetts to Virginia," inspired by the
Latimer fugitive-slave case in 1842, when an owner from Norfolk
claimed the fugitive in Boston, and was awarded him by the courts;
but so much excitement was created that the slave's emancipation
was purchased for four hundred dollars, the owner gladly taking
the money rather than pursue the case.

it on their journeys. Its highways in every direction lead
out to lovely scenes upon mountain-slopes or the banks of
lakes. This region was the Indian domain of Pontoosuc, "the
haunt of the winter deer," and this is the name of one of
the prettiest of the adjacent lakes. Onota is another of
exquisite contour, a romantic lakelet elevated eighteen hundred feet which gives Pittsfield its water-supply. Berry
Pond is here with its margin of silvery sand strewn with
delicate fibrous mica and snowy quartz. Here are the
"Opes," as the beautiful vista views are called along the
vales opening into the adjacent hills. One of these to the
southward overlooks the lakelet of the "Lily Bowl." Here
lived Herman Melville, the rover of the seas, when he wrote
his sea-novels. The chief of these vales, however, is north-
west of Pittsfield, the "Ope of Promise," giving a view
over the "Promised Land." This tract, we are told, was
named with grim Yankee humor, because the original
grant of the title was "long promised, yet longer de-
layed."

XX.

THE BERKSHIRE HILLS.

WE have come into the "Heart of Berkshire," the region
of exquisite loveliness that has no peer in New England.
Berkshire is the western county of Massachusetts, covering a surface about fifty miles long, extending entirely
across the State and about twenty miles wide. Two mountain-ranges bound its intermediate valley, and these make
the noted "Berkshire Hills" that have been the theme
of warmest praises from the greatest American poets and
authors. Their song and story have been sung and written by Longfellow, Whittier, Bryant, Hawthorne, Beecher,

and many others, and are interwoven with the best American literature. It is a region of myriad lakes and mountain-peaks, of lovely vales and delicious views, and its pure waters and exhilarating air, combined with the exquisite scenery, have made it most attractive to tourists. Beecher wrote that it "is yet to be as celebrated as the Lake District of England or the hill-country of Palestine." One writer described the Berkshire "holiday hills lifting their wreathed and crowned heads in the resplendent days of autumn." Another says it is "a region of hill and valley, mountain and lake, beautiful rivers and laughing brooks." Miss Sedgwick writes of the "rich valleys and smiling hillsides, and deep set in their hollows lovely lakes sparkle like gems." Fanny Kemble long lived at Lenox in the most beautiful part of this region, and she wished to be buried in its churchyard on the hill, saying, "I will not rise to trouble any one if they will let me sleep here. I will only ask to be permitted once in a while to raise my head and look out upon the glorious scene." It is to the Berkshire Hills that visitors go to see the autumnal tints of the forests in their greatest perfection. The abundant rains of last season made the foliage unusually luxuriant, and much of it remained vigorous after parts had turned by ripening rather than by frosts. This placed an unusual proportion of green in the picture to enhance the olives of the birch, the grayish pinks of the ash, the scarlets of the maple, the deep reds of the oak, and the bright yellows of the poplar. These in combination made a magnificent contrast of brilliant leaf-coloring, and while it lasted the mantle of purple and gold, of brilliant flame and resplendent green, with the almost dazzling yellows that covered the mountain-slopes, gave one of the richest feasts of color ever seen. Of this Berkshire magnificence of autumn Beecher writes: "Have the evening clouds, suffused with sunset, dropped down and become fixed into solid forms? Have the rainbows that followed autumn storms faded upon the mountains and left their mantles there? What a mighty chorus of colors do the trees roll down the valleys, up the hillsides, and over the mountains!"

LENOX.

In the midst of all this natural grandeur is Lenox, eight miles south of Pittsfield—the "gem among the mountains," as Silliman called it—standing upon a high ridge at twelve hundred feet elevation, and rising far above the general floor of the valley, the mountain-ridges bounding it upon either hand, here about five miles apart, having pleasant intervales between. Summer and autumn sojourners greatly enlarge the population when hundreds of happy pilgrims come hither from the large cities, most of them having their own villas. The slopes and crests of all the hills round about Lenox are crowned by mansions, many of them costly and imposing, adding to the charms of the pleasant landscape. At the head of the chief street, the highest point of the village, stands the old Puritan Congregational church, with its white wooden belfry and a view all around the compass. It brings back many memories of the good old times before fashion sought Lenox and worshipped at its shrine:

"They had rigid manners and homespun breeches
    In the good old times;
They hunted Indians and hung up witches
    In the good old times;
They toiled and moiled from sun to sun,
And they counted sinful all kinds of fun,
And they went to meeting armed with a gun,
    In the good old times."

To the northward, seen from this famous old church beyond many swelling knolls and ridges, rises Old Graylock, looking like a recumbent elephant as the clouds overhang its twin rounded peaks thirty miles away. From the church-door, facing the south, there is such a panorama that even without the devotion of the inspired Psalmist one might prefer to stand in the door of the Lord's house rather than dwell in tent, tabernacle, or mansion. This glorious view is over the two valleys, one on either hand, their bordering ridges covered with the fairest foliage. To the distant south-west, where the Housatonic Valley stretches away in winding courses, the stream flowing at times in wayward fashion across the view, there are many ridges of hills, finally fading into the horizon beyond the Connecticut boundary. The hillside is covered with the churchyard graves, and then slopes down toward the village with its galaxy of villas, among which little lakes glint in the sunlight of a bright morning. It is no wonder that Fanny Kemble desired to be buried here, for she could not have found a fairer resting-place on earth, though Beecher in his enthusiasm hoped that in her life to come she would "behold one so much fairer that this scenic beauty shall fade to a shadow."

THE STOCKBRIDGE BOWL.

The broad grass-bordered main street of Lenox, under its rows of stately overarching elms, leads southward down the hill among the villas that give the place its greatest charm. The "boom" in the picturesque has put up land-prices here to twenty thousand dollars an acre in some cases, and the deep valleys around the village, with their knolls and slopes, give such grand outlooks that buildings can be placed almost anywhere with advantage. Some are very costly, and all are named, the Yankee ingenuity reproducing some of the exhilarating air of Lenox in these names. Thus we have "Breezy Corner," "Windyside" and "Gusty Gables," with "Cozy Nook" and "Nestledown." "Glad Hill" overlooks a charming lake. Southward of Lenox one comes upon the outer elevated rim of the "Stockbridge Bowl," and can look down within this

grand amphitheatre upon Lake Mahkeenac nestling there,
with Monument Mountain closing the distant view beyond.
Villas perch upon all the terraces and knolls surrounding
this famous "Bowl," and one modest and older mansion
overlooks it among so much modern magnificence—Hawthorne's "House of the Seven Gables." Here he lived for
many years in a quaint little red wooden house, looking as
if built in bits, and having a glorious view for miles away
across the lake. Over the hills we go, up and down the
terraces that widely encircle the "Bowl," now under arching canopies of elms, then through the forest, past little
lakelets, enjoying fascinating views in all directions, around
the broad basin formed by the hills as we encircle the placid lake. Red-topped and white-topped villas occupy all
the points of vantage. Here live the New York bankers
and merchants in palaces that have cost princely sums, and
to this enchanting place hie the wealthy to rest after the
seashore and Saratoga seasons. From one of the most
noted of these villas, on "Lanier Hill" high above the
"Bowl" and its surrounding vales, we can overlook several lakes and study the rock-ribbed structure of this
charming region, thrust up in crags and layers of white
marble, while the walls and stone-work of the buildings
are also mostly white, contrasting prettily with the green
sward and foliage. Here is scanned the Laurel Lake, and
the village of Lee beyond nestling in the deep valley along
the winding Housatonic. Its tall white church-spire rises
among the trees as we descend steeply upon it. The surrounding slopes, as elsewhere, are covered with villas, and
the marble-quarries and paper-mills have made the fortune
of the town. These paper-mills do a great work, but the
Lee quarries are the most noted in America. The pure
white marble, cut out of deep fissures alongside the Housatonic, has built some of our most famous structures, including the Capitol at Washington, our Philadelphia City Hall,
and the Drexel Building.

10

The Stockbridge village is across an intervening ridge beyond the "Bowl." The wayward Housatonic encircles Lee and flows athwart the valley toward the west, thus making a meadow on which this pretty hamlet stands. Turkeys walk about and pumpkins lie in the fields preparing for the feast of turkey and pumpkin pie at the autumn Thanksgiving—the great Yankee holiday that has spread all over the country. Monument Mountain and Bear Mountain guard the smaller "bowl," into which we now come, with Stockbridge scattered through it upon the winding river-banks. "Field's Hill" overlooks the town, where Cyrus W. Field and his brothers were born and still have villas on the paternal estate. The quiet town seems almost asleep beneath its embowering elms under the rim of the hills upon the river-bordered plain. It was the Indian village of "Housatonnuc" in colonial days, and upon its green street stands a solid square stone tower, with a clock and chimes, bearing the inscription, "This memorial marks the spot where stood the little church in which John Sergeant preached to the Indians in 1739." It was the gift of David Dudley Field to his birthplace. The "Muhhekanew" tribe, or "the people of the great moving waters," afterward called the Stockbridge Indians, were early discovered by the Puritans, and Sergeant was sent a missionary among them, laboring fifteen years. Jonathan Edwards, the renowned metaphysician, succeeded him after the differences with the church at Northampton, and came out into the Berkshire wilderness, living among these Indians six years and preaching by the help of interpreters. The modern clergy may be surprised to learn that this great pastor labored here for an annual salary of thirty-five dollars, with ten dollars extra paid in fuel. But he lived happily at Stockbridge, which the late Governor Andrew called one of "the delicious surprises of Berk-

shire," and in one of the oldest houses in the village wrote
his celebrated work on *The Freedom of the Will.* He left
in 1757 to become president of Princeton College, and died
the next year. His Indian flock hold a wonderful tradition. A great people, they said, crossed deep waters from
a far distant continent in the north-west, and by many pil-
grimages marched to the seashore and the valley of the
Hudson. Here they built cities and lived until a famine
scattered them and many died. Wandering for years in
quest of a precarious living, they lost their arts and manners, and part of them settled on the Housatonic, where
the Puritans afterward found them. In these later days
they are dispersed, whither no one can tell, but on the slope
of a hill adjoining the river remains their old graveyard,
with a rugged, weather-worn shaft surmounting a stone pile
to mark it. The memory of Edwards is preserved by a
granite obelisk in front of his little wooden house.

These are all gems set in mosaic among the elms along
the village street, and, including a beautiful memorial
church, they have been given by sons and daughters of
Stockbridge who have gone elsewhere, but have not forgotten their nativity. To us in Philadelphia a memory of
Stockbridge is the fact that it was the birthplace of John
S. Hart, long the principal of the Central High School in
its best days.

GREAT BARRINGTON.

Through the gorges we follow down the Housatonic
River, the mountain-ridges pressing closely. The stream
feeds more mills, but its sharp curves that make such
pretty views have given a difficult task to the railway-
builder. The water pours down frequent white-marble
dams and bubbles over rapids, with steep tree-clad slopes
hemming in the banks, while the jagged sides and rough
crags of Monument Mountain rise high to the eastward.
This was the "Fisher's Nest" of the Stockbridge tribe,

and as Hawthorne, from his seven-gabled home, looked out
upon its gnarled and forest-covered walls of rocks, he described its full autumnal glories as "a headless sphinx
wrapped in a rich Persian shawl." A cairn found on the
summit gave the mountain its name, the tradition telling of
a mythical Indian maiden who jumped from the top, and
her tribe when they passed by, throwing stones on the spot,
thus built the cairn. Some one has certainly thrown many
stones all around this rugged mountain piled up with
marble crags in a region having abrupt peaks starting out
over the whole surface about it. Monument Mountain's
long ridge finally falls off, and then the lowlands broaden
to the southward as the Housatonic winds in wider channel
to Great Barrington. Here stands another typical New England village spreading along its broad elm-embowered street,
with Mount Everett grandly rising over its south-western
border and another galaxy of peaks encircling the basin
wherein the place is built. Less attractive only than
Lenox and Stockbridge, it possesses the finest country-
house in Berkshire—a mansion illustrating the affection
the New England emigrant always bears the home of
youth. Mark Hopkins went from here to California to
make a fortune and die. His childless widow, also from
this village, with thirty million dollars at her disposal, determined to rear a memorial on the farm where she spent
her childhood days. On the meadow, almost at the riverside, she has built a home of the native marbles of the
Berkshire Hills exceeding in costliness and magnificence
any other private dwelling in this country. As the building grew she became so enamored of it that she finally
took the architect for a second husband. She regularly
travels across the continent between her winter California
home and her summer home here. High above the noble
house rises the special Berkshire hill of Great Barrington, and to its summit we are taken to be shown the
view beyond. The solid sides of broad Mount Everett stand

up a few miles away, the sentinel guarding the south-western corner of Massachusetts, and to the westward are stretched the lands of New York beyond the Taghkanic range to the distant Catskills across the valley of the Hudson. A little way southward is the Connecticut boundary with successive ranges of hills. Productive valleys have herds grazing along the river almost beneath our feet, and the pleasant villages of Egremont and Sheffield nestle under the shadow of Everett. The marble of the Sheffield quarries built our Girard College. Thus have we followed the picturesque Housatonic from its sources near Pittsfield among these glorious Berkshire Hills, and from this elevated perch can still trace it far from us as it flows away through the winding vales into Connecticut, to be ultimately swallowed by Long Island Sound beyond the peaceful plain of Old Stratford.

XXI.

TRAVERSING THE OLD BAY STATE.

THE Boston and Albany Railroad is one of the main routes of travel between the Atlantic seaboard and the West, and is a prominent " Vanderbilt line." It crosses Massachusetts from Berkshire to the coast, going through the chief interior cities of the " Old Bay State." It was one of the earliest railways built, being in progress from 1833 to 1842, when the line was opened to Albany, and the project was derided as chimerical. A leading Boston newspaper of that day, the *Courier*, said it could only be built at " an expense of little less than the market value of the whole territory of Massachusetts, and, if practicable, every person of common sense knows it would be as useless as a railroad from Boston to the moon." Yet it was built and prospered, and the great Commonwealth, to break its profitable monopoly, had afterward to undertake the prodigious task of boring the Hoosac tunnel, so as to provide a competing line. Coming up from the Hudson River at Albany, this great railway crosses the Taghkanic range to Pittsfield, and then gets out of the Berkshire Valley by climbing over the Hoosacs. It crosses this latter flat-topped ridge amid grand scenery at an elevation of about fourteen hundred and fifty feet, and then, descending into the Connecticut Valley, gets down almost to the tide-water level. Almost from the summit of the Hoosacs it seeks a route by the wild defile through which a mountain-brook goes down, and for a dozen miles or so has steep gradients and a crooked course along this torrent. The brook flows into the Westfield River, and that, in turn, into the Agawam, which enters the Connecticut River opposite Springfield. Within these deep defiles, which seem to have been fashioned especially to provide a railway-route, the scenery is very fine; but their contracted bottom-lands bear a plentiful crop of stones, which the people have gathered to form many fences, and it is evidently hard scratching for any of them to extract a living from the soil.

In its lower portions the Westfield Valley occasionally broadens into the level meadows of rich land so generally seen in these New England vales, and thus from under the shadow of towering peaks and frowning ridges the railway leads us out of the Berkshire Hills toward a more promising if less picturesque region for the herdsman and farmer. Thus we come through the fertile Indian domain of Woronoco to the pleasant town of Westfield, noted for its whips and cigars, as its factories have long since outstripped its agriculture. The train then glides along the pretty reaches of the Agawam, winding over the extensive plain of the Connecticut Valley, past more paper-mills, and finally crosses that river into Springfield. The different streams around Springfield, like so many of the limpid waters elsewhere in Massachusetts, are chiefly devoted to paper-making, so that when we ascend another valley with its swift-flowing rivulet, east of Springfield, the route again leads us among the paper-makers. Few can imagine the extent of this industry in Central and Western Massachusetts, or conceive of the enormous amounts of paper of all kinds that are now made, not only for printing, but also for consumption in various arts and manufactures. This region is certainly devoted to the interests of the paper-makers. But, steadily rolling along through one thriving manufacturing village after another, we get away from the purer waters and out of the paper district, though still continuing among many mills, and find the industries changing to the making of cotton, woollen, and leather goods. Thus at Brookfield the apple-orchards divide the honors with shoe-factories in the town that was the birthplace of the celebrated female agitator, Lucy Stone. The waters of the Quaboag Pond turn some of its wheels, and then flow off by Sashaway River through Podunk meadows to seek the Connecticut through the Chicopee. Shoemaking villages are all about, and at Spencer was born the inventor of the sewing-machine, Elias Howe. Crags and boulders are plentiful in scenery at times picturesque, but the hills have lost their grandeur, so that eastward from Brookfield they become gradually subdued, and the railway traverses a region of ponds and streams and stones, where every water-power is fully availed of. While there are comparatively level stretches, yet most of the surface seems untillable, and it is quite evident the people had to seek other means of livelihood.*

* It is difficult to say where New England has its most sterile region, but in Massachusetts it is generally agreed that the town of Ware, on the Ware River, some distance north-west of Worcester, is hard to beat in this respect. It is a picturesquely located mill-village, but its soil is hard and sterile. The original grant of its land was made to soldiers after King Philip's War as a reward for bravery. They thankfully accepted the gift and went there, but after examination they left and sold all their title at the rate of

Thus we come to Worcester, whose chief newspaper, the *Massachusetts Spy*, started as a spy upon the Royalists in the exciting times preceding the Revolutionary War, is still a prosperous publication. It was at a Worcester banquet in 1776 that the "Sons of Freedom" drank the noted toast: "May the freedom and independence of America endure till the sun grows dim with age and this earth returns to chaos: perpetual itching without the benefit of scratching to the enemies of America!" This is the second city of Massachusetts, about forty-four miles west of Boston, but it has almost ceased to be a Yankee town from the steady migration of the native-born population westward, they being replaced in the numerous mills largely by French Canadians, Swedes, and Irish, the latter element being in strong development. Worcester has little to show beyond its extensive factories, its railway-station—which is the finest in New England—and the noble soldiers' monument on the Common. It possesses the splendid buildings of the Massachusetts Lunatic Asylum, standing on the highest hill in the suburbs, where the patients can overlook, at a distance, the greatest attraction of the neighborhood, Lake Quinsigamond, a long, deep, and narrow loch nestling among the hills and stretching four miles away, with its

about two cents an acre. Somebody wrote a poem describing the creation of the place, from which I quote a specimen stanza:

> "Dame Nature once, while making land,
> Had refuse left of stone and sand.
> She viewed it well, then threw it down
> Between Coy's Hill and Belchertown,
> And said, 'You paltry stuff, lie there,
> And make a town and call it Ware.'"

President Dwight once rode through the town, but he never wanted to see it again, and said regretfully, in describing the land: "It is like self-righteousness; the more a man has of it, the poorer he is."

little gems of islands and villa-bordered shores. Beyond it, scattered over the distant rim of enclosing hills, are several villages of Yankee homes, with their church-spires set against the horizon. This lake is a noted regatta-course. The venerable historian George Bancroft was born in Worcester. The town had a checkered colonial career, the Indians repeatedly driving out the early settlers, until they built a fortress-like church on the Common, where each man attended on the Sabbath, carrying his musket and six rounds of ammunition. These resolute colonists, as may be supposed, were Puritans bent on having their own way, for when a few Scotch Presbyterians came along in 1720 and built a church of their creed, it was declared a "cradle of heresy" and demolished. The mills that have attracted a population of eighty thousand are numerous in Worcester and make its prosperity.

Among the adjacent hills there appears a little stream, flowing off toward the south-east, with many curves and constantly enlarging current, until it falls into Narragansett Bay, about forty-five miles distant. When the recluse Anglican clergyman, William Blackstone, who first settled Boston about 1625, learned, after a brief experience, that he could not get on with the Puritan colonists, he sold out for about one hundred and fifty dollars and "retired into the wilderness." He went some forty miles into the interior, and during over forty years made his home on the banks of this stream among the Indians, so that it was named after him. The valley of this Blackstone River is the seat of some of the greatest manufacturing industries of New England, chiefly in fabrics of cotton and wool. In its brief course it descends more than five hundred feet, giving a valuable water-power that is availed of to the utmost; and as the mills have grown vastly beyond the capacity of the river, steam-power is used also to a large extent. Upon its upper waters this stream has only comparatively small establishments, but the lower half of its course displays an array of enormous factories that is something astonishing in its convincing demonstration of the methods by which New England secures not only subsistence, but wealth, despite the inability of the Yankee husbandmen to extract much from the soil. This rapid stream, winding among its enclosing hills in very crooked course, must have been a picturesque torrent in the colonial days. But now it is much changed. Numerous ponds and reservoirs, with other feeders, accumulate a vast amount of water for the Blackstone River in the southern part of Massachusetts, and it has largely become a succession of dams and canals that for more than twenty miles are lined by mills, the water no sooner having turned one set of wheels than it is sent along for use by another. More than half a million people live in this short but busy valley stretching through Massachusetts and Rhode Island. The operatives, as at Worcester, are composed chiefly of the French Canadians, Swedes, and the various British races, and in some of the towns the French preponderate. The Yankees long ago left this region in droves to build up the West, and have thus been replaced by other races of less restless ambition, who are content to work in the mills. This teeming mill-country appears to have plenty to do, and the work-people are well clad and seem comfortably well off, living in rows of neat dwellings, generally, like most of the smaller New England homes, built of wood, though some are of brick.

THE VAST INDUSTRIAL HIVE.

From Worcester we turned down this Blackstone Valley, which is one of the greatest mill-regions of the United States. Frequent settlements nestle among the hills enclosing the river, which make a rather narrow valley, the slopes being well wooded, but rarely rising over one hundred feet high. The chief industries begin at the Rhode Island boundary, at the towns of Waterford and Black-

stone, gradually spreading into the larger town of Woonsocket. Canals conduct the water from the frequent dams
to the mill-wheels, while the tall chimney-stacks and steamjets show that much power is added. At Woonsocket the
stream goes around circuitous bends in admirable style for
conducting its waters through the mills, and here thirty
thousand people make cotton and woollen cloth. The
noted " Harris cassimere " is the chief manufacture, and
Mr. Harris lives in a pleasant house overlooking the town
and his Social Mills. The entire river-current is drawn
under the mill-wheels as the stream winds among the rocks
which are bared below the dam, and upon the surrounding
hills the operatives live in many rows of attractive frame
houses. The rush of waters and the rattle of looms are
Woonsocket's steadfast lullaby, while on the outskirts rises
Woonsocket Hill, the highest mountain in Rhode Island,
and having, in the curious hydraulic arrangements of this
region, a pond on its summit. Below this the Blackstone
River is a succession of manufacturing villages—Manville,
Albion, Ashton, Lonsdale, Valley Falls, Central Falls, and
Pawtucket—each with its great dams and reservoirs holding the waters that pour out in steady streams to turn the
wheels. The banks are lined with enormous factories, some
being buildings four and five stories high and a thousand
feet long, with hundreds of windows and ponderous stair-
way-towers separately constructed as fire-escapes. These
mills are usually built of brick, and some are quite ornamental. All have auxiliary steam-power, and in most cases
the steady growth of the establishment can be traced from
the first small mill, usually of stone or plaster, extended by
additional larger buildings as profits accumulated.

Rarely do these huge establishments bear either sign or
name, and it is said that many of the operatives actually
do not know who they are working for. Most of the mills
are owned by wealthy corporations having their head-offices
in Boston or Providence. The railway runs among them

near the river, crossing from one side to the other as bends make necessary. The country has picturesque features, but does not seem very inviting, so far as can be seen from the valley, for rocks abound in profusion on the enclosing hill-slopes. Few localities, however, can rival this industrial development. Here gathers an army of Rhode Island operatives whose labors have made the State rich, and given it, small as it is, pre-eminence as a textile manufacturer. The Blackstone waters, which are doing such good service, become steadily greater in volume, but are more and more polluted as they descend, so that in its lower course it is a dark-colored and most malodorous stream. The railway runs among the dams, and sometimes over them, and as the hills protrude it boldly cuts them through, piercing in one of those cuttings through Study Hill, where Blackstone lived in his hermit home among his books, the river rushing swiftly along its base. At Pawtucket there are twenty-five thousand people, the town extending up into the villages of Central and Valley Falls, and here are the greatest thread-factories in the country; and the river, having a descent of fifty feet, gives enormous power, which is drawn upon at different levels from several dams. Pawtucket makes all sorts of textiles and muslins, and calicoes are turned out in large amounts. The slopes running up from the valley, with much surface on the elevated lands above, are covered with operatives' houses. As night falls upon this busy river ten thousand lights dance in the factory-windows and are reflected in the black waters below. This town has the most attractive situation on the Blackstone, which here has its name changed to the Pawtucket River; and it is famous as the place where cotton manufacturing first began in New England in 1790. The noted Samuel Slater, who was born at Belper in Derbyshire, England, had worked there for both Strutt and Arkwright, and learning that American bounties had been offered for the introduction of Arkwright's patents in cotton-spinning, he crossed the ocean and landed at Newport in 1789.   Here he learned that Moses Brown had attempted cotton-spinning by machinery in Rhode Island.   He wrote to Brown, telling what he could do, and received a reply in which Brown said his attempt had been unsuccessful, and added, "If thou canst do this thing I invite thee to come to Rhode Island and have the credit and the profit of introducing cotton manufacture into America."   Slater went to Pawtucket, and on December 21, 1790, he started three carding-machines and spinning-frames of seventy-two spindles.   He afterward became a prominent manufacturer, building large mills there and elsewhere; and the impetus he thus gave Pawtucket made it the leading American manufacturing town for nearly half a century.

XXII.

THE LAND OF THE NARRAGANSETTS.

WE have come down the busy Blackstone River through Pawtucket, and find it dissolving gradually into a region of more mills and frame houses toward Providence.   The river, which for a brief space is known as the Pawtucket, finally, at its mouth just below, becomes the Seeconk River, making part of Providence harbor and one of the heads of Narragansett Bay.   The industrial operatives to-day swarming the banks of this remarkable stream are somewhat changed, however, from those who peopled its shores in earlier times.   They were not then much as textile workers or Quaker and Baptist cotton-spinners, but when provoked they made good fighters.   The bloodiest Indian war in which the New England colonists ever engaged was "King Philip's War," much of which was fought in this neighborhood, though it also extended to the then remote western settlements of the Connecticut Valley. This famous chieftain had been brought up by his father, Massasoit, as a friend of the white man, but bad treatment made his love turn to hatred, and, preaching a crusade among all the New England tribes, he began a war of extermination. In the end the Puritans were too much for him, and after his forces had been almost annihilated he was slain. Philip was the grand sachem of the Wampanoags or Narragansetts, and his people occupied all the country around Narragansett Bay, to which they gave the name. They were a numerous and powerful Algonquin tribe, and Canonicus and Canonchet, also Narragansett chiefs, have their names preserved in islands in the bay, but, unfortunately, to-day nothing is left of this noble Indian nation but a handful of weak and neglected half-breeds. All around Narragansett Bay, which extends inland from the Atlantic Ocean for thirty miles to Providence, are memorials of the race. The shores, once their domain, now make the little State of "Rhode Island and Providence Plantations," which still keeps the title thus written in King Charles II.'s original charter. It is the smallest State of the Union, being less than fifty miles long and only forty miles wide, having a land-and-water area, including the bay and its shores and islands, of barely thirteen hundred square miles. Yet this diminutive sovereign State has two capitals, which come down from its origin—Providence and Newport—one for each set of plantations combined in the charter, Newport being on Rhode Island. The bay divides it into unequal portions, the western shore having the largest surface. The hills on the eastern shore run up into Mount Hope, near the town of Bristol, which was King Philip's home and the scene of his death. Were the old Indian now alive he could from his eyrie look down upon another busy manufacturing settlement bordering the bay, making muslins and prints and large amounts of India-rubber goods. Rhode Island is densely populated, but half the people live in Providence, the second city of New England. These Rhode Islanders labor in their mills with prodigious result, the State ranking first in the Union in the proportion of product to population. They turn out more textiles than any other State excepting Pennsylvania and Massachusetts.

"WHAT CHEER, NOTOP?"

Nine hundred years ago the Northmen discovered Vinland, which has since been demonstrated by industrious investigators to have been this busy region around Narragansett Bay. Acting upon this belief, the Scandinavians in various parts of New England held celebrations two or three years ago and set up a commemorative statue in Boston. While, however, we are not so sure about the first discovery, we do know all about the first settlement by the brave and pious Welshman Roger Williams, the heretical Salem preacher whom the Puritans banished from Massachusetts in 1635. He went afoot to the Seeconk plains along the lower Blackstone River, and, halting there, lived with the Narragansetts, who were always his firm friends. But the wrathful Puritans would not tolerate this, and ordered him to move on, so that in the next spring, with five companions, he embarked in a log canoe and floated down the Seeconk River, his movements being watched by groups of Indians on the banks. He crossed over the stream and landed on what has since been called "What Cheer Rock," on the eastern edge of Providence, thus named because when Williams stepped ashore some of the Indians pleasantly saluted him with the friendly greeting, "What cheer, Notop?" (friend)—words still carefully preserved throughout the city and State in the names of banks, buildings, and various associations. Regarding this a good omen, he forthwith started a settlement, naming it Providence, "in grateful acknowledgment of God's merciful providence to him in his distress." The old gentleman's exalted piety

was beyond question, and not only is the religious spirit in
which the city was founded indicated in its name, but even
in the titles of the highways are incorporated the cardinal
virtues and the higher emotions, as in Joy Street, Faith
Street, Happy Street, Hope Street, Friendship Street, Benefit Street, Benevolent Street, and others. He became a
Baptist, and the "Society of the First Baptist Church,"
which he founded, claims to be the oldest Baptist organization on the continent. But Roger Williams was somewhat
unstable, and only remained with this church as pastor four
years, as he then withdrew, having grave doubts of the
validity of his own baptism. It appears that when the
church was started a layman, Ezekiel Holliman, first baptized Williams, and then Williams baptized Holliman and
the others. When he withdrew it was not only from the
pastoral relation, but he also ceased worshipping any longer
with his brethren, and his conscientious scruples finally
brought him to the conclusion that there is "no regularly
constituted church on earth, nor any person authorized to
administer any church ordinance, nor could there be until
new apostles were sent by the great Head of the Church,
for whose coming he was seeking." His meetings during
many years thereafter were held in a grove. A new church
was built in 1726 by this venerable Baptist society which he
founded, and in its honor they had "a grand dinner." The
elaborate banquet of those primitive days consisted of the
whole congregation dining upon one sheep, one pound of
butter, two loaves of bread, and a half-peck of peas, at a
cost of twenty-seven shillings. To-day their white painted
wooden church, with its surmounting steeple, overlooks the
city from a slope rising above Providence River.

THE CITY OF PROVIDENCE.

Upon a semicircular line laid around the "Cove" in the
centre of the city the railway-train enters Providence. This
circular body of water, having rows of trees planted around

it, is a broadening of a water-way and a vile-smelling place
—it receives so much sewage—but it is to be covered in and
made an attractive railway-terminal. Adjoining is the
massive City Hall, the handsomest public building in
Rhode Island, a structure of granite that cost one million
five hundred thousand dollars. In high relief upon its
front is exhibited the medallion bust of the patron saint
of the little State, old Roger Williams, wearing his typical
sugar-loaf hat. A magnificent stair-hall lighted from above
is a feature of this impressive building; and from the surmounting tower there is a fine view over the city and surrounding regions and far down the bay toward the ocean.
A soldiers' monument stands in the public square in front
bearing the names of hundreds who fell in the war, and
having well-executed bronze statues representing the different arms of the service. General Burnside, who was the
leading Rhode Island general, faces it—a statue in heroic
bronze. All these are artistic works, but the city of Providence has a priceless gem of another kind in the exquisite
little picture of "The Hours," painted on ivory in London
by Malbone of Newport—the three Grecian nymphs representing the Past, Present, and Future. This is one of the
famous and most admired paintings in America, and is
carefully kept in the Atheneum, a solid granite house built
on the hillside not far from the Baptist church. Brown
University has its campus and row of buildings farther up
this hill—the great Rhode Island Baptist college which
bears the name of one of the leading families of the
wealthy manufacturing house of Brown & Ives. Around
this college and all through the extensive suburbs are the
splendid homes of the capitalists and mill-owners of the
State, who have made this hill, which rises between the
Providence and Seeconk Rivers, the most attractive residential section. These textile millionaires have lined
Benefit Street on this hill with their palaces.

In fact, Providence is a town of many hills and hollows,

11

and the vast aggregation of frame houses it displays would seem to offer a great temptation for fire. Extensive sections can be traversed without seeing a single brick or stone building. There is little trade by sea, excepting bringing coal and cotton, but it has a large railway-traffic. Like all the Rhode Island towns, it has many mills and it is a centre of much capital. There seem to be about forty banks in the place, and it evidently is a wealthy community; its mills make steam-engines and locomotives, cigars, textiles, and silver ware, rifles, stoves, and jewelry, and a "pain-killer" for the ills of humanity that is consumed by the hundred thousand gallons in all parts of the world. The "pain-killer" factory is one of the lions of the town. In Providence was built the great Corliss engine for our Centennial Exhibition, now at Pullman, near Chicago. Here are also made on an extensive scale the cotton-seed and peanut oils that pass current as the genuine "olive oil," they are of such rare flavor. This is the headquarters for gimlet-pointed wood screws, for tortoise-shell work, and cocoanut dippers. But Providence, beyond all other fame, is devoted to the memory of Roger Williams. A little old house on Abbott Street, having a quaint peaked roof and built in the seventeenth century, is carefully preserved as a precious relic, being reverenced as the place where he held some of his prayer-meetings. His bronze statue ornaments the Roger Williams Park, long the home of one of his remote descendants, Betsy Williams, who gave it to the city as her tribute to her great-great-grandfather in 1871—a beautiful tract of about one hundred acres surrounding her old gambrel-roofed house of the last century. Here you sail on Crystal Lake and get refreshments at "What Cheer Cottage." But the landing-place of "What Cheer Rock," alongside the Seeconk River, is the most treasured memorial of the founder—a pile of slaty rocks enclosed by a railing, near the foot of Williams Street, down by the water-side.

Providence is at the head of one of the finest harbors on the New England coast. Narragansett Bay stretches far up into the land to receive the waters of the many rivers that turn the Rhode Island mill-wheels, and it is the great attraction of the State. The bay opens broadly south of Providence, the shores being most beautiful, lined with water-worn cliffs and low crags, in front of which are lovely little rocky islets, several of them bearing lighthouses to guide the mariner into the harbor-entrance. Along the coasts and upon the larger islands are the pleasure-resorts that every season draw thousands of visitors to enjoy these charming cliffs and the clear and sparkling waters rolling in upon the pebbly beaches. Within its embrace are several islands of great fame, while out in the Atlantic off shore is Block Island. The largest island of Narragansett Bay is Aquidneck, or Rhode Island, thus named from a fancied resemblance to the Isle of Rhodes, and furnishing the first half of the long name of the little State—"Rhode Island and Providence Plantations." It is about fifteen miles long, and of much fertility, having the best farm-land in New England, and at the southern end the noted watering-place of Newport. The memory of the old Narragansett chieftain, Conanicut, is preserved in Conanicut Island, west of Rhode Island, and seven miles long, having between the two islands the famous anchorage-ground of Newport harbor. Old Roger Williams has also been down here distributing his stock of names, for Prudence, Patience, Hope, and Despair are other islands in the bay, and most of them popular resorts. The sail upon Narragansett Bay from Providence to Newport is very attractive, and exhibits the universality with which the natives gather the prolific crop of these waters—the clam. Men and boys in boats are dredging all the coves and shallows for clams, seizing enormous numbers by the skilful use of their double rakes. The people are proud of their home institution, the "clam-bake," which is given at all the shore-resorts, and is considered a connecting link binding them with the ancient Narragansetts, who originated it. To conduct the "clam-bake" properly a wood-fire is built in the open air upon a layer of large stones, and when these are sufficiently heated the embers and ashes are swept off, the stones covered with a layer of seaweed, and clams in the shells, with other delicacies, are put upon it, being covered by sail-cloths and also by masses of seaweed to keep in the steam. The clams are thus baked by the heated stones and steamed by the moisture from the salt seaweed. The coverings are then removed, the clams opened, and the feasting begins, and with appetite whetted by the delicious breezes from over the bay the meal is relished beyond description. There are millions of clams thus consumed all about these waters and those of New York and Long Island Sound, and where all of them are produced is a mystery, for the shores are so assiduously dredged one would think the clams would not have time to grow. Of the Narraganset-Bay resorts the chief are Rocky Point—a forest-covered promontory having a huge "clam-bake" dining-hall—and Narragansett Pier on the western shore, down by the open sea. This was anciently a fishing-village, and has a sea-battered and ruined pier originally built for a break-water. It has become very fashionable as a seaside resort, and has many large hotels spreading in imposing array along the shore. The smooth sands of its bathing-beach look out upon Newport far over the bay in front, and they have on their southern border precipitous cliffs against which the Atlantic Ocean breakers dash, the last rocks on the American coast until the Florida reefs are reached.

XXIII.

CHARMING NEWPORT OF AQUIDNECK.

WE have sailed down the pleasant waters of Narragansett Bay and landed at the queen of our seaside resorts, Newport. The south-western extremity of Aquidneck, or Rhode Island, broadens into a wide peninsula of almost level and quite fertile land, which makes a plateau elevated about fifty feet above the sea. This plateau rests upon rock, and the rocky layers make cliffs all about the plateau, with coves worked into them, presenting smooth beaches and intervening bold promontories. The south-eastern border of this plateau has toward the Atlantic an irregular front of little bays and projections, with the waves dashing against the bases of their bordering cliffs and among the rocks that are profusely strewn beyond them. Brenton's Point is behind the western extremity of the island, and projects in such a way as to protect the inner harbor of Newport. And here are the wharves and the ancient part of the town, its narrow streets and older houses covering considerable surface. This was "charming Newport of Aquidneck," as the colonial chronicler recorded it, then a leading seaport of New England. Thames Street fronts the town, and in the last century was one of the busiest highways in America. Upon Brenton's Point, protecting the harbor-entrance, is built Fort Adams, which was a formidable work before modern improvements in gunnery superseded the old systems, and, next to Fortress Monroe, it is now the largest defensive work in the United States. It was built during the Presidency of John Adams, as the other was during the Administration of James Monroe, each being named for the President who directed its construction. Curiously enough, Fort Adams was hurried to completion as a defence against France, then believed to meditate war against the republic she had so recently assisted in creating. Under the guns of Fort Adams the graceful yachts now ride at anchor that represent Newport's chief ocean commerce, while two or three men-of-war moored beyond give notification that the United States has a navy. All around this ancient town, and spreading broadly over the plateau to which the land slopes up in gentle ascent from the harbor, is the modern Newport of fashionable life and its most exclusive resort. From the older town, southward across this plateau, stretches Bellevue Avenue through the fashionable section.

Unlike most of our watering-places, Newport is not a city of hotels, but is pre-eminently a gathering of the costliest suburban homes this country can show. Built upon a space about three miles long and one or two miles broad, modern Newport consists of a galaxy of most elaborate country-houses, each in an enclosure of lawns, flower-gardens, and foliage, all highly ornamental and exceedingly well kept. Many of these houses are palaces that have cost enormous sums, and in front of them for several miles along the winding brow of the cliffs that fall off precipitously to the ocean's edge is laid the noted "Cliff Walk." This is a narrow footpath just at the edge of the lovely greensward that has the waves dashing against the bases of the rocks supporting it, while on the land side of the smooth and well-kept lawns are the costliest palaces of Newport, a broad surface intervening between them and the edges of the cliffs, while they have a grand and unobstructed outlook over the ocean. Each building is a type of different architecture, and, no matter how elaborate, each is called a "cottage." The methods of construction of these Newport villas are of every conceivable kind—French, Gothic, Swiss, Flemish, Elizabethan, every sort of ancient house known to Great Britain or continental Europe, being imitated and improved upon, while in some remarkable cases widely varying styles are condensed into one. In this way some of these "cottages" have become elaborate aggregations of buildings, with all kinds of porticos, doorways, pavilions, dormers, oriels, bow-windows, bays and turrets, chimneys, towers, and gambrel roofs, all piled together. In one noticeable case the villa has been elongated into the stable, both making a remarkably appearing but single extended house, and just where the one ends and the other may begin it is hard to determine, as the family, horses, and hounds, with the domestics and grooms, are all practically living under the same roof. Much attention is paid to the flower-beds and grass-plots, but out on the lawns of the ocean front it is difficult to make the trees grow, as the high winds coming without a protecting barrier from over the sea uproot them, so that the "Cliff Walk," with its bordering greensward, is bare of shade. These level lawns of most delicious green spread to the very brink of the cliffs, so that they break off abruptly at the tops of the rocky buttresses against whose bases the sea is constantly washing.

NEWPORT GRANDEUR AND NEWNESS.

Upon the palatial mansions of Newport have been lavished, in construction and decoration, large portions of the greatest incomes of the millionaires of Boston and New York, and hither they hie to enjoy the summer and autumn in a sort of fashionable semi-seclusion, for these are the seaside cottage-homes of the Vanderbilts, Astors, Goelets, Lorillards, Bennetts, Osgoods, Belmonts, Hamiltons, Stewarts, Havemeyers, Stevens, Brewers, Wetmores, Schermerhorns, and others whose desire and ability to spend money upon the elaborate decoration and maintenance of their summer palaces seem almost limitless. The superb dwellings facing the "Cliff Walk" in its miles of beautiful course along the winding outer edge of the Newport buttress of rocks protecting the place against the waves, present a display of residential magnificence that in its way is unexcelled.

These princes of inherited wealth have made Newport
peculiarly their own. Its genial climate first drew them
to the place, and it has the added attraction of soil of unexcelled fertility right at the edge of the sea, growing luxuriant flowers and grasses, while within the island are the
finest trees, although the substratum is rock. This fertility
wedded them to Newport, which has since been made the
fashionable seaside home for the millionaire class. Nowhere
else are gathered for protracted residence, as a recreation,
so many of the nabobs created by the American facility of
quickly amassing enormous wealth, and, their expenditures
being on a scale commensurate with their millions, the improvement and growth of the newer part of Newport have
been extraordinary. In the choicest locations the price of
land is advanced to fifty thousand dollars an acre (William
K. Vanderbilt has just bought eleven acres for five hundred
and fifty thousand dollars for his son George), whilst the
poorest and most remote surfaces of forbidding rocks away
from the sea are held at four thousand and five thousand
dollars. The taxes are said to be low, but some of these
mansions with a few acres of lawn will pay twenty-five
hundred to thirty-five hundred dollars annually. The
costliest villas—there being none, however, with more than
five or six acres—are valued at fabulous sums, although
nothing probably would induce their owners to sell. The
most elaborate of these Newport "cottages" cost six hundred thousand dollars to build.

There is, however, throughout this extremely exclusive
quarter everywhere the impressive air of newness. Trees
have hardly yet grown, as this requires more generations
than have been evolved since the fortune was founded. The
great houses are all recent constructions. It is true, the
architecture reproduces quaint and ancient forms, being
elaborated wherever possible to please the eye, but the
paint seems yet fresh and the ancestral ivy has hardly
begun to cling to the walls. When, in a generation or

two, maturer years shall have caused the trees to grow, all
this magnificence will have assumed more grandeur. Yet
there are, even now, older bits in Newport, and, if not so
costly, still many exquisite places far more attractive, even
if they do not so glaringly display the millions that created
them. Back from the sea-front some of the estates existing
many years already show the charms of maturity. The
houses are in style subdued and small and plain, compared
with the palaces of Aladdin out on the Cliffs, but their ivy
spreads and their trees are grown. They are comfortable
and home-like, and seem to hold happy people, whose hearts
beat in unison with those around, although their owners'
wealth may be limited. Some of the tree-embowered lanes
leading through the older suburbs of Newport are charming in leafy richness, their bordering walls and footpaths
and the canopies of foliage overhead combining to make
exquisite rural beauty.

NEWPORT CHARACTERISTICS.

William Coddington, whose name is preserved in various
ways, but whose descendants were degenerate, founded Newport. It is said that in early times the place was chiefly settled by people of various religious sects who were driven
out of the strictly Puritan New-England settlements. The
Puritans having abandoned England because they objected
to a State Church, they forthwith set up in Massachusetts
what was very like a State Church of their own, and proceeded immediately to make it hot for the alleged unbe-
lievers. They drove out both William Blackstone, who
founded Boston, and Roger Williams. Blackstone, when
he found that he had to get across the border into the wilderness and live a hermit on the bank of Blackstone River,
said, "I came from England because I did not like the
Lords Bishops, but I can't join with you, because I would
not be under the Lords Brethren." After Blackstone and
Williams, many others came to Rhode Island and settled at

Newport, for there they enjoyed the completest liberty of
conscience. The Quakers were unmolested, and came in
large numbers; the Baptists built a meeting-house; the
Hebrews established a synagogue; the sternest doctrines
of the Calvinists were preached; the Moravians held their
love-feasts; and orthodox Churchmen prayed for the king.
All shades of belief and dissenters of all ilks, with many
having no belief at all, abounded; so that the fair town of
Aquidneck became pervaded with such an atmosphere of
religious irregularity that even so late as the opening of the
present century a prominent Connecticut divine declared
that an alleged laxity of morals in Stonington was due to
"its nearness to Rhode Island." Still, despite these religious differences, the colony got on well, and in time Aquidneck came to be designated as the "Isle of Peace" and
the "Eden of America." Dean Berkeley from England
visited Newport in its early days, and gave the young colony an elevated literary tone. An Utopian plan for con-
verting the Indians brought him over, but, discovering it to
be impracticable, he returned home and was made a bishop.
His favorite resort is yet shown at the part of the Cliffs
called the "Hanging Rocks," and it is said he there composed various works, including the noble lyric closing with
the patriotic prophecy immortalized in Leutze's grand painting in the Capitol at Washington:

> "Westward the course of empire takes its way:
> The four first acts already past,
> A fifth shall end the drama with the day;
> Time's noblest offspring is the last."

There were about forty-five hundred people in the town
when the dean was at Newport, and by the opening of the
Revolution they had grown to twelve thousand, when the
port enjoyed a commerce far exceeding that of New York.
That war almost ruined the place, it being first held by
the English, and afterward by the French, both battering

and maltreating it, so that it emerged from the conflict in a condition of dilapidation and poverty, with the population reduced to barely five thousand. The French loved the island, and sought after the war to have it annexed to France, but this was not to be. Business growth since has been fitful, as the trade is gone, but Newport is an important naval station and the seat of the torpedo-school, so that there are always men-of-war in the harbor.

THE OLD STONE MILL.

The fashionable world, however, give Newport its chief fame and have made it such a noted resort. The popularity is due to the balmy climate and moderate changes in temperature, conducing alike to health and fertility. The Casino is the centre of fashionable Newport, a building in the Old English style, fronting some two hundred feet on Bellevue Avenue. There are reading-rooms and a theatre in it, with a garden and tennis-court at the back. During the season Bellevue Avenue is the daily scene of a stately procession of handsome equipages of all styles, as it is decreed that fashionable Newport always rides. Richly-dressed ladies sit back in the state befitting the multi-millionaires who thus seek dignified recreation, and they pass and repass during the afternoons in splendid review. To lengthen the outing, a circuit is taken of the "Ocean Drive" around by the bay-side, where there are pleasant views over the rocks and the sea. Thus surrounded, the island is soon recognized as possessing the similarity to the Isle of Rhodes that named it Rhode Island. The Indian name of Aquidneck, meaning "floating on the water," was also appropriately given, for the distant approach makes it almost seem to stand out between sea and sky, as if the delusion of a mirage had raised it above the clear waters.

In the early times the town's chief benefactor was Judah Touro, who gave it Touro Park. His father was the rabbi of Newport synagogue, and Judah spent fifty years in New

Orleans amassing a fortune, which was bequeathed to various charities. He aided the building of Bunker Hill Monument. The old synagogue was the first built in this country, dating from 1762, and is now not often used. It, with the beautiful garden adjacent which is the Jewish cemetery, is maintained in perfect order. Touro Park is a pretty enclosure in the older town, and has the noted memorial around which Newport's antiquarian treasures cluster—the "Old Stone Mill," a small round tower supported on pillars, between which are arched openings. Some of the wise men endeavor to prove that it was built by the Norsemen when they first found Vinland, centuries before Columbus, but the more practical townsfolk generally incline to the belief that some of the original Dutchmen from New Amsterdam, who abounded with the others on the island in the early days, may have put it up for a windmill to grind corn. Nevertheless, it is the shrine—whether ancient or modern—at which Newport worships, and, like the "Charter Oak" and "What Cheer Rock," embodies the local patriotic pride of the place. Like most of our seacoast rocks, the Newport Cliffs show wonderful formations of "spouting rocks" and chasms, while an endless panorama of white-winged vessels and swift and graceful steamers sail past them. And as we look out from them across Narragansett Bay, far off to the westward stretches into the sea the long, low sand-spit of Point Judith. This dangerous cape was named from Judith Quincy, who was the wife of John Hull, the coiner of the ancient "pine-tree shillings." Judith was long ago laid to rest, but her great landmark, the extremest southern land of the State of Rhode Island, ever exists at the entrance of Long Island Sound, and is a headland that is always the sailor's dread.

XXIV.

FROM NARRAGANSETT TO THE SEA.

WE leave the pleasant Isle of Aquidneck, and, passing northward over its fertile farms, the Old Colony Railroad carries us from Newport, along Narragansett Bay and the Taunton River, toward the New England metropolis, Boston. The energetic manufacturing city of Fall River stands upon one of the pleasant arms that make the head of the bay, possessing the unusual advantage of a great water-power at the edge of a good harbor. Consequently, there have gathered upon the hillsides sloping down to the border of the bay a population of sixty thousand, and a galaxy of big mills having more spindles swiftly turning in the manufacture of cottons and prints than any other place in the country. Fall River, which gives this industrious city its name, while but a small stream, yet has a large volume of water, drained from a series of ponds upon the extensive plateau above. It is scarcely two miles long, and within half a mile distance falls one hundred and thirty-six feet. Resting upon terraces rising one above the other back along this incline, the enormous mills are built upon the rocky banks of the stream, and stand up in platoons almost like the ranks of a regiment. There are extensive granite-quarries in the adjacent hills that have furnished the materials for these huge buildings, owned by over a score of manufacturing companies, having thirty million dollars invested and employing twenty thousand operatives, who make one hundred and seventy-five thousand pieces of print cloths in a week. Steam aids in driving the machinery, as the water-power was long since outgrown; and here flourish the French Canadians as on the Blackstone River, and also the Irish. Fall River is in Massachusetts, and across the Taunton River it looks out upon Mount Hope in Rhode Island, King Philip's ancient home. Above, at

Dighton, is the famous " Dighton Rock," an elongated mass of granite, half submerged by the tide, having rude inscriptions upon it in an unknown language which antiquarians have attributed to the Norsemen. These sculptured records, which have attracted great attention, a copy having been taken by the Scandinavian investigators to Copenhagen, are gradually fading with the lapse of time. Farther northward the railway gradually curves around through the long town of Taunton, with its pleasant cottages and gardens—another hive of industry. The rapids of the Taunton River make a water-power that originally attracted factories, and they now make both locomotives and tacks there, and also stove-linings, copper-ware, and screws, besides much iron-work. These people are particularly noted for their tacks, turning out no less than seven hundred kinds, varying from a heavy boat-nail down to the most minute particle used in microscopic work, of which fully four thousand are requisite to weigh an ounce.

QUINCY AND ADAMS.

We are again in Massachusetts, and the railway runs among the hills and rocks and wooden houses over the farm-lands of Raynham and Easton. More than half the shovels used throughout the whole world come from the great Ames factories at North Easton. This Ames family is one of the most powerful and noted in the " Old Bay State." In the early days of the republic the eloquence of Fisher Ames made him the most distinguished orator of his time. It was the energy of Oakes Ames that chiefly pushed the building of the first Pacific railway. Oliver Ames is the governor of Massachusetts. Their family villas abound at Easton, but we soon leave them behind, and, gliding past sundry shoemaking villages set among the hills, with some stone-quarries and patches of farm-land, we reach the classic grounds of Quincy. Here is a

picturesque agricultural town of some twelve thousand
population stretching down to the sea, with a broad fringe
of salt-marshes in front. It is famous as the home of the
greatest families of the original colony of Massachusetts
Bay—Quincy and Adams. Its antique church, known as
the Adams Temple, has in the yard the graves of the two
Presidents, father and son, the elder and younger Adams,
while their family, in yet younger generations, is still distinguished in Massachusetts. That wonderful old fellow
whose fame was made immortal by the " big round hand "
with which he leads the signatures to the Declaration of
Independence—John Hancock—was a native of Quincy.
This was among the earliest Massachusetts settlements,
having been colonized by companies of Episcopalians at
a place called " Merry Mount." They were such jovial
people that the strict Puritans at Plymouth were aghast,
and sent Miles Standish, with the entire army of the
colony, against them, and, capturing the leaders, shipped
them captives home to England. This severe treatment
had to be administered a second time before they were subdued. Thomas Morton of this colony, who was among
those twice banished to England, was the author of the
New England Canaan, giving a curious account of the Indians, saying: " The Indians may be rather accompted as
living richly, wanting nothing that is needful, and to be
commended for leading a contented life, the younger being
ruled by the elder and the elder ruled by the Powahs, and
the Powahs are ruled by the Devill ; and then you may
imagine what good rule is like to be amongst them." This
theory seems to have been generally prevalent among the
early colonists, for Cotton Mather wrote that " the Indians
are under the special protection of the Devill."

To the westward of Quincy rise the " Blue Hills of Milton," their highest dome-like summit being elevated six
hundred feet and giving a splendid view over sea and land
for many miles around. These are granite hills, the Quincy

granites being sent far and near and used in some of the finest buildings of our chief cities. It was to get out this granite that the earliest rude railway in this country was built, a line three miles long, constructed in 1826 from the Quincy quarries out to Neponset River, the cars being drawn by horses. It is now the "Granite Branch" of the Old Colony road. The geologists say these hills of Milton are an older formation than the Alps, and their earliest English name, designated, it is said, by King Charles, was the "Cheviot Hills."

MASSACHUSETTS BAY.

To the eastward of these noted hills the shore runs out in bold bluffs, overlooking Boston harbor. The sea-coast of Massachusetts is of very irregular formation, and the deep indentations have given it the well-known name of the "Old Bay State." The chief of these indentations is Massachusetts Bay, thrust up deeply into the land, with the granite buttress of Cape Ann stretching far out into the Atlantic for its northern boundary and the broad ocean spreading in front. Far off to the southward the land makes the wide sweep around to the east and then to the north that forms the curious hook of Cape Cod, enclosing Cape Cod Bay. Across the neck of this cape, and deeply indented on its southern side, is Buzzard's Bay. Upon one of its numerous arms is the town of New Bedford, the head-quarters of what is left of the American whale-fishery, which is still doing, in the decay of that noted industry, more whale-catching than all the rest of the world combined. This was the ancient Acushnet of the Indians, settled by Quakers on lands owned by the English family of Russell, whose chiefs are the dukes of Bedford, and hence the name of the town. Next to Boston, New Bedford has the best harbor on the Massachusetts coast. Massachusetts Bay, however, through its deep indentation into the land makes the finest of all these harbors. One of the boldest bluffs

thrust into it is the peninsula of Squantum, thus named in
memory of the old sachem who ruled all the country round
about when Boston was first colonized, and who had his
home on a hill near by.   From this circumstance was derived the name of Massachusetts.   The land was shaped
like an Indian arrow-head, which in their language was
called Mos, while the Indian for hill is Wachusett.   Hence
the sachem's home was called " Moswachusett," whence was
derived " Massachusetts " as a name for the bay and State.
Sturdy old Squantum was the firm friend of the colonists,
and when he was dying he besought Governor Bradford to
pray for him, " that he might go to the Englishman's God
in heaven."

MARSHFIELD AND DUXBURY.

We skirt along the southern coast of Massachusetts Bay,
beyond Squantum, bound to the " Old Colony " of Plymouth,
the earliest New England settlement, located upon the border of the first harbor south of the bay, about forty miles
from Boston.   On the coast below Nantasket Beach are the
rocky shores of Cohasset and Scituate, the former a favorite
summer resort for American actors, who have established
there several pleasant villas by the sea, and where the rocks
yield abundant mosses.   Minot's Ledge, a dangerous reef
in the offing, is guarded by the leading beacon of the New
England coasts.   To the southward there are broad salt-
marshes, and among them we come to Marshfield, the home
of Daniel Webster, whose remains lie in an ancient graveyard on an ocean-viewing hill not far away.   His two sons
—Edward, killed in the Mexican War, and Fletcher, killed
at Bull Run—lie beside him; but the old homestead has
gone to strangers, the house has been burnt, and a modern
ornamental villa replaces it.   The grave of the Pilgrim
governor Winslow is close by Webster's, and the quaint old
Winslow House, where he lived, is near by.   We are within
the domain of the " Old Colony," and everything is redo-

lent of Puritan memories. A short distance beyond is one of those long peninsulas of sand and rocks that abound on the Massachusetts coast, projecting about six miles south-eastward into the sea, and terminating in a knob called the "Gurnet," with hook turned inward. This elongated sand-strip is Duxbury Beach, having within it the northern portion of Plymouth Bay, with the town of Duxbury upon the mainland inside, a fishing village having about three thousand population. This place is probably best known as the American terminus of the French Atlantic cable.

It was at Duxbury that Ralph Partridge was the first regular pastor, whom Cotton Mather described as having "the innocence of a dove and the loftiness of an eagle." The region was allotted by the Pilgrims in the first settlement to their youngest member, John Alden, and to their military chieftain, Captain Miles Standish. Its name came from Duxbury Hall, Lancashire, in England, the old seat of the Standish family. The redoubtable Miles, whom Longfellow has made the hero of his poem, and whose alleged love-affairs have had much to do with Italian operas and New England romances, commanded the Pilgrim standing army of twelve men. He did not belong to their Church, but he had seen much service in the wars in Flanders, and was described as "a short man, very brave, but impetuous and choleric, and his name soon became a terror to all hostile Indians." Standish lived upon the "Captain's Hill" out on the peninsula, the highest land thereabout, and rising one hundred and eighty feet upon a broad point projecting into Plymouth Bay. As we are carried by the railway-train along the western shore of Kingston Bay within this point, the bare-topped, broad, oval-shaped hill is seen rising across the water, with an unfinished monument to Miles upon the highest point. This may have been a splendid lookout to watch for hostile savages, but it seems a rather bleak place to select for a home. Not a tree appears on the top, but there is some scrub timber on the sides, with grass growing above. Beyond this hill the long Duxbury Beach projects out, ending in the high Gurnet with twin lighthouses, and then hooking inward to another bold terminating bulb, the headland of Saquish. To the northward is Clark's Island, a similarly round-topped mass rising from the water. As we skirt around Kingston Bay these three knobs keep constantly in view, but change their relative positions, while inland the coast runs up into more hills, and to the southward the long ridge of Manomet projects out to the sea. We swiftly enter Plymouth, with its great cordage-factory down by the railway, while on an eminence a short distance behind it is the huge granite monument surmounted by the colossal stone statue of Faith, which has been erected to the memory of the Pilgrim forefathers, and thus guards their earliest settlement.

XXV.

THE OLD COLONY.

WE have come to Plymouth, the earliest settlement of New England, which saw the beginning of the greatest race that has made its impress upon the American character. Here the Pilgrims landed upon Plymouth Rock in December, 1620, to found, amid the winter hardships of a bleak and inhospitable coast, the hardy and energetic Yankee race. This "Old Colony" has a little landlocked harbor behind a long and narrow sand beach projected northward from the ridge of Manomet below, and, like a breakwater, protecting the wharves from the waves. This harbor has only shallow water, however, and does not seem to get much attention in "river-and-harbor bills," so that there is little trade by sea. The town of Plymouth spreads upon the bluff shores of the harbor and back across a plateau to the hills in the rear. About seven thousand five hundred people live here, the descendants of the Pilgrims being active manufacturers. Besides their great cordage business, they make nails and tacks and also weave cotton and wool, with other things, and quite a fishing fleet belongs to the place. The first impression made on the visitor by this famous Pilgrim settlement, it must be confessed, seems disappointing, for this oldest town in New England looks almost as if newly built. Yet the devotion to the memory giving the town its deathless fame is marked, for every one appears imbued with its spirit, and the Forefathers are probably better thought of in Plymouth to-day than ever before, as everything remaining as relics of them is being restored and perpetuated. There is not much, however, that can be seen of the olden time. The ocean is here, and the little harbor and the hills and original streets, but nothing else excepting a few carefully-cherished relics of the Mayflower's passengers that have been gathered together. It seems that the choice of Plymouth as their landing-place was due mainly to necessity, when protracted explorations had failed to find a better place and the coming of winter had compelled a landing somewhere. The actual location appears to have been illy considered, the Pilgrims themselves being far from satisfied with it; and this explains why Plymouth has declined in importance and been so greatly overshadowed by its neighbors.

After the little ship Mayflower entered Cape Cod Bay several weeks were passed in making explorations, and finally, upon a Sunday in December, 1620, there was a landing made upon Clark's Island, where religious services were conducted, being the first held in New England. Upon the most elevated part of this island there is a huge boulder about twelve feet high, which is called, from some local event, the "Election Rock." Upon its face are carved the words, taken from *Mourt's Relation*, the ancient chronicle describing the voyage of the Mayflower:

"Upon the Sabbath-Day wee rested, 20 December, 1620."

There were eighteen of them who thus "rested" after their shallop in making the landing had been almost shipwrecked. Upon the next day they sailed across the bay to the mainland, and their first landing was then made at Plymouth, while upon the second day, December 22d, the entire company came ashore and the settlement began.

THE PILGRIM HALL.

Within "Pilgrim Hall," a neat fireproof building upon the chief street, are kept the precious relics of the Mayflower, with authentic portraits of the leading Pilgrims and several fine paintings illlustrating this great event. Among the most interesting relics are autograph writings establishing a chain of acquaintanceship connecting the Pilgrims with the present day. The first-born of the infant colony was Peregrine White, born on the Mayflower after she came into Cape Cod Bay, in November, 1620, and he was only a month old when the Pilgrims landed. This baby, surviving all their hardships, lived to a ripe old age, and "Grandfather Cobb," who was born in 1694, knew him well. Cobb in his day lived to be the oldest man in New England, his life covering space in three centuries, for he exceeded one hundred and seven years, dying in 1801. William R. Sever, born in 1790, knew Cobb and recollected him well, and, living until he was ninety-seven years old, died in 1887. Thus three lives connected the Pilgrim landing with the present day through a longevity that is remarkable, and united they cover a period of two hundred and eighty-seven years. The old cradle that rocked Peregrine White on the Mayflower and after he was landed is still preserved—an upright, stiffbacked, wicker-work basket upon rude wooden rockers.

The chief paintings upon the walls of the Pilgrim Hall represent the departure from the Delft in Holland, the signing of the memorable compact on the Mayflower, and the landing. The latter is a reproduction of the painting in the Capitol Rotunda at Washington. Some of the old straight-backed chairs of the original Puritans, with their pots and platters, also Miles Standish's sword, and much else of antiquarian value, are kept in the hall. The court-house, this being the county-seat, has the original records of the Plymouth Colony, the first allotment of lands among the settlers, their deeds, agreements, and wills; so that there is a perfect foundation in these records for the land-titles. Here also is displayed the patent given the colony by Earl Warwick in 1629. The curious handwriting of these quaint old records, with the ink partly fading out, also tells how they divided their cattle when it was determined to change from the original plan of holding them in common. The signatures of the Pilgrims are attached to many of these valuable documents, and one of them in old Governor Bradford's penmanship is the famous order establishing trial by jury in the colony.

THE PILGRIM ROCK.

Every one knows Mrs. Heman's beautiful hymn of the landing of the Pilgrims, beginning,

> "The breaking waves dashed high
> On a stern and rock-bound coast."

Yet, unfortunately for the poetry about this "stern and rock-bound coast," there is sand everywhere, and scarcely a rock or boulder can be seen for miles, excepting the little one on which they landed. Down by the water-side is this most noted stone—the "Forefathers' Rock," the sacred stone worshipped by all the Pilgrim descendants. It is a gray sienite boulder, oval-shaped and about six feet long. Some time ago it was unfortunately split, and the parts have been cemented together. This boulder lay on the sandy beach of the bay at the time of the landing, and was almost solitary among these sands. Unlike the coast north of Boston and the verge of Manomet to the southward, this sandy shore was then as now almost without rocks of any kind. This boulder had been dropped here in one of the early geological periods, and lay partly in the water, thus making a boat-landing that was naturally attractive to the water-weary Pilgrims who came coasting along in their shallop from Clark's Island, so that they stepped out upon it to get ashore dryshod. It has since been elevated several feet to a higher level than that originally occupied, but otherwise has been continued in the same local position. This sacred rock has been surmounted by an imposing granite canopy, and is railed in for protection from the vandalism of the relic-hunter. There is a sort of fissure in its face that seems like the impress of a foot, and the numerals "1620" are rudely carved upon its side. Behind the rock and its canopy rises the bluff shore into Cole's Hill, having its steep slopes neatly sodded, this having been the place up which the Pilgrims climbed after their landing. A wharf is built out in front of the rock, and this takes care of most of the commerce of the port. Across the bay in front spreads the narrow sandspit protecting the harbor, while on the right hand is the long ridge of Manomet, and distant sand-dunes appear along Duxbury Beach over the water to the left. Bordering the harbor are a number of frame houses of little pretension, and in them is conducted much of the business of the town. In the distance, off to the northward, rises the "Captain's Hill" of Duxbury, surmounted with its unfinished monument. Upon Cole's Hill, behind the rock, was the Pilgrims' first burial-place, and here were interred about half the intrepid band, who died from the privations of the first winter. Their bones have been occasionally washed out by heavy rains or found in digging for the foundations of buildings; but all these have been carefully collected, and several of the dead thus exposed have again been entombed in the granite canopy over the noted rock on which their feet had pressed. There is a street a little way to the southward—Leyden Street, running from the water's edge back up the slope for some distance to the side of the "Burial Hill" which was the earliest cemetery in this country. This street was the first highway laid out in New England, although it did not get its present name until long afterward. Upon this street the Pilgrims built their first rude houses, the lots stretching from it farther southward to the "Town Brook," just beyond, which supplied them with good water, and was the main cause of selecting this place for the settlement.

THE PILGRIM STORY.

Mourt's Relation, written by one of the actors in this rare historical drama, tells the story of the landing. He describes their protracted explorations and final hasty selection of this place, and thus continues: "So, in the morning, after we had called on God for direction, we came to this resolution, to go presently ashore again and to take a better view of two places which we thought most fitting for us; for we could not now take time for further search or consideration, our victuals being much spent, especially our beer, and it being now the 19th of December. After our landing and viewing the places so well as we could, we came to a conclusion, by most voices, to set on a high ground, where there is a great deal of land cleared and hath been planted with corn three or four years ago; and there is a very sweet brook runs under the hillside, and many delicate springs of as good water as can be drunk, and where we may harbor our shallops and boats exceeding well; and in this brook fish in their season; on the farther side of the river also much corn-ground cleared. In one field is a great hill on which we point to make a platform and plant our ordnance, which will command all around about. From thence we may see into the bay and far into the sea, and we may see thence Cape Cod. Our greatest labor will be the fetching of our wood, which is half a quarter of an English mile; but there is enough so far off. What people inhabit here we yet know not, for as yet we have seen none. So there we made our rendezvous and a place for some of our people, about twenty, resolving in the morning to come all ashore and to build houses."

They began about a week afterward to construct their fort on the hill, and allotted their plots of land on the highway afterward named Leyden Street. Thus began the town, behind which rose two hills, the one now known as the "Burial Hill" being at the head of this street, and elevated about one hundred and fifty feet above the sea. This was an admirable place for a fort, and Miles Standish with his military eye soon selected its site, overlooking Leyden Street and the "sweet brook" beyond, as the location for their permanent defensive work. Here, in 1622, was built the square timber block-house that made them both a fort and a church, the entire settlement as it then existed being enclosed by a stockade for further protection. This caused the hill to be then named Fort Hill, and it was not until years afterward that it was used as a cemetery and called "Burial Hill," the first interments being some of the original Pilgrims after the graveyard on the slope of Cole's Hill down by the water-side was abandoned. On this hill also was built the "Watch-House," where an outlook was kept for the Indians. Stones now mark the places both of the fort and watch-house, and surrounding them are the graves of several of the Mayflower's passengers, with many of their descendants, the dark slate gravestones having been brought out from England. These old stones are now carefully encased in zinc, to prevent relic-hunters from chipping off and running away with what is left of them. From this lofty Burial Hill there is a splendid outlook over the harbor and the open sea beyond to the distant yellow sand-streak of Cape Cod, and also landward over the adjacent valleys.

Northward about half a mile is the other hill, rising somewhat higher, and upon it has been placed the great monument to the Pilgrims which was dedicated on August 1, 1889, and is seen from afar on entering the town. This is a massive granite shaft surmounted by the largest stone statue in existence—a colossal figure of Faith. This splendid memorial is adorned by other statues around the base emblematical of the principles of the settlement, and upon it are representations of the landing of the Pilgrims, their names, and the great compact they made on the May-flower. It was into the infant colony of Plymouth, after some weeks of careful parley and investigation, that the stalwart Indian Samoset strode, and paved the way for the subsequent treaty and alliance with Massasoit, which was for many years scrupulously observed by both parties, and was not broken until after he died. Soon afterward Canonicus sent a sheaf of arrows bound with a rattlesnake's skin to Governor Bradford as a token of hostility. The sturdy old governor quickly filled the skin with powder and shot and sent it back to Canonicus, who understood the grim challenge and restrained his tribe. But differences followed, culminating in "King Philip's War," in which both sides fiercely fought for extermination. To-day, two hundred and sixty-nine years after their feet pressed the sacred rock, this landing-place of the Pilgrims is a peaceful, industrious town, the home of busy millworkers, like so many other New England towns, and in summer a favorite resort for hundreds then seeking the seaside. Here began the New England settlement which was the dawning of the nation ruling America, with the founding of the greatest race on this continent.

XXVI.

THE MODERN ATHENS.

THE railway approaching the great New England metropolis from the south, skirts the harbor and crosses the narrow Fort Point channel separating South Boston from the city proper, and enters the terminal station just beyond. To the northward the city rises gradually, ridge above ridge, until the centre culminates in the famous Beacon Hill, surmounted by the brightly-gilded dome and lantern top of the Massachusetts State-House. From all sides the land, with its varied surfaces of hill and valley, slopes toward the water-courses running into the deep indentation of Massachusetts Bay, and thus adding to the facilities of Boston harbor. The rounded peninsula forming the original Boston was the Indian "Shawmut," or the "sweet waters," a name preserved in many ways in the modern city. It is said that hunting for good water by the first colony led to this settlement at Shawmut, the colonists who had come from Salem crossing over from Charlestown in 1630, and finding William Blackstone, of whom I have already written, as the sole white inhabitant of the place, he having lived there in solitude for about five years. The old gentleman was not partial to having near neighbors, so they finally bought him out and got the whole town-site for about one hundred and fifty dollars, which was the value of all Boston in 1634, when Blackstone, disgusted with the Puritan "Lords Brethren," avoided them by going farther into the wilderness. The two leading men of the colony came from Boston in England, and hence the adoption of the name, but the younger city has far outstripped the elder, as more than half a million people are now living around Boston harbor in the various towns and suburbs that make up the "Hub of the Universe." When this first colony was established in 1630 one of the depressed

settlers described Shawmut as "a hideous wilderness, possessed by barbarous Indians, very cold, sickly, rocky, barren, unfit for culture, and like to keep the people miserable." Yet the settlement, though so inauspiciously begun,
persisted in growing, and, as an early historian says, "Philadelphia was a forest and New York was an insignificant
village long after its rival, Boston, had become a great
commercial town." In 1663 a visitor from England described the place, and wrote that "the buildings are handsome, joining one to the other as in London, with many
large streets, most of them paved with pebble-stones. In
the high street toward the Common there are faire houses,
some of stone." The young colony encouraged commerce
and became possessed of many ships, the earliest built at
Boston being the bark Blessing of the Bay, of thirty tons,
which soon got into lucrative trade. This noted vessel,
which was considered a wonder in her time, belonged to
Governor John Winthrop, for many years the ruler of
Boston. He is described as an amiable gentleman, who
believed in moderate aristocratic principles. In one of his
messages, which always contained solid chunks of wisdom,
was the announcement that "the best part of a community
is always the least, and of that part the wiser are still less."
His descendant in the sixth generation, Hon. Robert C.
Winthrop, still lives in Boston at a venerable age, one of
the leading citizens. He was formerly Speaker of the
House at Washington.

BOSTON HARBOR.

The harbor of Boston covers a surface of about seventy-
five square miles, having various arms, such as South Boston Bay, Dorchester Bay, and the estuaries of the Charles,
Mystic, and Neponset Rivers. There is much natural beauty
in the harbor, heightened by the adornments of buildings
and other improvements, its surface gradually narrowing
toward the city and dotted with craggy, undulating islands

having long stretches of bordering beaches, interspersed with jutting cliffs, broad promontories, and both low and lofty shores. The coasts are lined with villages that gradually merge into the suburbs of the great city. In this extensive harbor there are at least fifty large and small islands, and most of these, which were bare in Winthrop's day, are now crowned by lighthouses, forts, almshouses, hospitals, and other institutions, several of them being most striking buildings that give a pleasing variety to the scene. The splendid guiding beacon for the harbor-entrance, Boston Light, stands upon Lighthouse Island at about one hundred feet elevation, with a revolving light visible sixteen miles. George's Island, near the entrance and commanding the approach from the open sea, has upon it the chief defensive work of Boston, Fort Warren, about two miles west of Boston Light. Farther in is Castle Island, with Fort Independence, the successor of the earliest Boston fort, the "Castle," built in 1634. Opposite and about one mile northward is Governor's Island, containing the incomplete works of Fort Winthrop. This island was originally the "Governor's Garden" of old John Winthrop, and he paid a yearly rent of two bushels of apples for it. The part of the island not held by the Government is said to still continue in possession of his family. These forts are nearly all constructed of Quincy granite, but none of them have yet seen practical warfare beyond the imprisonment of Confederates in Fort Warren. Upon Long Island, which covers considerable area and is a high, craggy place, there is another lighthouse. To the eastward is a low, rocky islet bearing as a warning to the mariner a curious stone monument which is known as "Nix's Mate." Here, it is said, the colonists used to hang the pirates caught off the New England coasts. There are also Deer and Rainsford Islands, occupied by the city hospitals and reformatory institutions. Upon Thompson's Island, which is fantastically shaped like an unfledged chicken, is an asylum and farm-school for indigent boys. Spectacle, Half Moon, and Apple Islands have got their names from their shapes. The narrow ship-channel leading up through the harbor passes between, and can, if necessary, be readily defended by the forts upon, Castle and Governor's Islands.

THE BOSTON SUBURBS.

At the inward or western extremity of the harbor is the Shawmut peninsula of Boston, having waterways all around it. Upon the one side is South Boston and upon the other Charlestown, the comparatively narrow intervening watercourses of Fort Point channel and Charles River being in parts almost roofed over with bridges that grudgingly open their draws to let through the schooners laden with lumber and coal. To the north-east, upon another peninsula which formerly was an island, is East Boston, having Chelsea beyond. Toward the north-east, across the broadened estuary of Charles River, is Cambridge, and the branch of this estuary that comes in at the west end of Boston, and is known as the Back Bay, has been largely encroached upon to create more land for the crowded and spreading city. The outlying suburbs of Roxbury and Dorchester are to the southward, and to the westward are Brookline, Brighton, and Somerville. Upon the Shawmut peninsula the original limits of Boston covered only seven hundred and eighty-three acres, but by filling in various flats and reclamations from the Back Bay this has been much more than doubled. To help make South Boston, the city absorbed Dorchester Neck, and it took in Noddle's Island to make East Boston, so that by filling up their flats and marshes it thus got eighteen hundred and thirty-eight acres more surface. Then it subsequently absorbed Roxbury, Dorchester, Charlestown, and Brighton, so that to-day it covers nearly forty square miles and is about thirty times the area of the original Boston. What with cutting down hills, the improvements made everywhere, and the great changes wrought by fires that have obliterated the older narrow and crooked streets, it is now said that Boston has become entirely changed, so that the alignments of the ancient maps can scarcely be recognized.

Scarcely a vestige thus remains of the Boston of early colonial times. Its Shawmut peninsula was then the " Tri-mountain," which has been shortened into "Tremont," now a common Boston designation. As the first settlers saw the place from Charlestown, whence they came athirst to seek the "sweet waters" of the Indians, Shawmut seemed to chiefly consist of three high hills, which were respectively named Copp's, Beacon, and Fort Hills. The highest of these, the Beacon Hill, was in itself a sort of "tri-mountain," having three well-developed surmounting little peaks. These, however, were afterward cut down, although the massive elevation of Beacon Hill, whereon the colonists burnt their signal-fires, still remains to bear upon its tops and slopes the weight of the most exclusive aristocracy of Boston. The younger generation, of later wealth and more modern aggrandizement, however, is being generally gathered into the more imposing and newer residences recently built upon the filled-in lands reclaimed from the Back Bay. The city's sturdy growth requires constant expansion.

BOSTON COMMON.

Boston, as now developed, is clustered around the well-known park that has come down from the colonial days as " Boston Common," and upon its northern verge this park rises toward Beacon Hill. The city, no matter by what route approached, has the appearance of a broad cone with a wide base, ascending by a gradual plane to the bulb-like apex of the gilded State-House dome. The surface is occasionally broken by a tall building looming above the mass, or is pierced by church-spires or fanciful towers of modern architecture or by a high chimney pouring out black smoke over the aggregation of houses. Thus it becomes a symmetrical scene in the general view, though made up of irregular details, and the observer, when looking at this severely regular cone-shaped city rising by easy and steady advances to the central summit, can scarcely believe that in its various parts it is so remarkably uneven. Toward this same central summit of the State-House dome the Common rises from the south and west by a graceful plane, interspersed with hillocks, whose sides peep through the openings in the trees. The Common also has broad, open spaces, used for outdoor sports and military displays, which sometimes gather the sight-seers by thousands. The Common is rich in noble trees, and it covers a surface of about fifty acres, while to the westward there is an additional park of half its size known as the Public Garden, and separated by a wide street opened to accommodate the cross-town traffic. We are told that this noted Boston Common was the ancient Puritan pasture-ground, and it comes down to the present generation rich in traditions of bygone times. Here in the colonial wars the hostile Indians, when captured, were put to death, and their grinning heads impaled on stakes for a public warning. Murderers were gibbeted here, witches burnt, and duels fought. The impassioned George Whitefield in the middle of the last century preached here in the open air to a congregation of twenty thousand. An English traveller of about two centuries ago described the place as "a small but pleasant common, where the gallants, a little before sunset, walk with their marmalet-madams till the bell at nine o'clock rings them home." Sometimes it has been a fortified camp, and always a pleasure-ground, while during the great Boston fire a few years ago enormous piles of saved goods filled the eastern portions. The eastern boundary of the Common is Tremont Street, with Boylston Street on the southern side and Beacon Street on the northern. Rows of stately elms are planted upon its walks along these streets and upon the pathways leading across the Common and making convenient "short cuts" for pedestrians in various directions. There are also some noble works of art. Flagstaff Hill, the most prominent eminence, is surmounted by the Soldiers' Monument, rising ninety feet high to a colossal statue of America, which overlooks the city. This is one of the most imposing memorials of the Civil War among the many in this country. The Brewer Fountain, a munificent gift from a prominent citizen and famous for its magnificent bronzes, pours out its limpid waters near the eastern boundary. There is a colossal equestrian statue of Washington of great merit adorning the Public Garden. These attractive grounds are additionally embellished by pleasant little lakes, one of them being the noted "Frog Pond," so dear to the hearts of the older Boston boys, whose whitening locks are telling in these later years of the rapid flight of time.*

* A valued correspondent calls the author's attention to the derivation of the name of Boston from "St. Botolph's Town." The original Boston in Lincolnshire, England, grew around the monastery of the Saxon saint Botolph, and hence, according to the historian Lombard, "the name of Botolph's Town, commonly and corruptly called Boston." The English Bostonians presented a Gothic window (from the ruins of old St. Botolph's) to Trinity Church (Rev. Phillips Brooks). This correspondent refers to the general politeness of the crowds in Washington Street, Boston, shown by the drivers as well as pedestrians. "There seems," he writes, "to be a quiet and polite assertion of right of way, and at the same time a courteous acknowledgment of the rights of others. Even the very horses seem to be imbued with this spirit. I actually saw a horse, whose driver was inattentive, suddenly come to a stop before collision, because another horse passing from Milk to Water Street, across Washington, got half a head in first."

13

XXVII.

A RAMBLE THROUGH BOSTON.

As we have been strolling about Boston Common we have climbed its northern edge upon Beacon Hill to cross Beacon Street to the State-House. This famous building stands upon ground that in the last century was John Hancock's cow-pasture, his residence that was for many years alongside being now replaced by the ornamental "swell fronts" of the aristocratic Somerset Club. This rounded swell front is a distinctive feature of Boston residential architecture. The State-House is the home of the Massachusetts Legislature, and is coeval with the present century. The portraits and busts of the great men of the Commonwealth adorn the rotunda, and are surrounded by the battle-flags carried by the Massachusetts regiments during the Civil War. From the lantern surmounting the gilded dome is the finest view in Boston, the elevation giving a magnificent outlook over the city and its suburbs, with the mass of estuaries penetrating the land on all sides, the harbor and the distant islands, and over the neighboring country for many miles. The legislative halls are light and airy, but the Representatives' Chamber, which accommodates a numerous body, is rather crowded. Upon its upper wall, just under the roof and in full view of the Speaker and the members, hangs a significant emblem of the "Old Bay State"—the noted carved codfish, typifying a great Massachusetts industry. It was upon St. Patrick's Day, March 17, 1785, in the original State-House preceding this one, down on Washington Street, that Representative Rowe, who is also said to have been the suggester of throwing overboard the tea in Boston harbor, according to the records, moved "That leave might be given to hang up the representation of a codfish in the room where the House sit, as a memorial of the importance of the cod-fishery to the welfare of the Commonwealth, as had been usual formerly." Then, said motion being seconded, the question was put, and leave given for the purpose aforesaid. This emblem was brought to the new State-House and hung on the wall, and just at this time of fishery discussion it has peculiar interest. It further suggests, according to a local newspaper, that while our statesmen are trying to settle the fishery-problems, they might also undertake to solve one of long standing that has perplexed New England : "Does the codfish salt the ocean, or the ocean salt the codfish?"

BRIMSTONE CORNER.

A short distance from the State-House, on the eastern edge of the Common, at the corner of Park and Tremont Streets, is the famous old "Brimstone Corner," where stands the citadel of orthodoxy, the Puritan meeting-house, "Park Street Church." Adjoining this, upon land evidently once part of the Common, is an ancient graveyard, the "Old Granary Burying-Ground," where lie the remains of some of the most famous men of the colony of Massachusetts Bay—John Hancock, Samuel Adams, Paul Revere, Peter Faneuil, many of the governors, and also the parents of Benjamin Franklin, a prominent monument marking the graves of the latter. This quiet burial-place adjoins one of the busiest spots in Boston, and the rows of ancient, dark-looking, and half-effaced gravestones are an antiquarian novelty. There are around it many noted buildings, and along Tremont Street are found some of the most attractive resorts, including the Masonic Temple, various publishing-houses, and the "Piano Row," wherein is concentrated music of all kinds. In front moves a steady procession of street-cars leading to all parts of the city and suburbs. Here are the Tremont Temple and the Horticultural and Music Halls, all of them popular public assembly-rooms. The first Episcopal church established in Boston, the "King's Chapel," is also on Tremont Street, although this is not the original building. Adjacent to it is the oldest burial-place of the colony, where lie the remains of John Winthrop and his sons and other first settlers. Some of the people who formerly ruled over this graveyard have, strangely enough, taken all the ancient gravestones away from the graves, and without reference to their proper positions reset them as edge-stones along the paths. One of these odd old stones of a greenish hue marked the grave of William Paddy, who died in 1658, and it bears these quaint words recorded in an unique poetical effusion :

> " Hear sleaps that blessed one
> Whoes lief God help us all
> To live that so when tiem shall be
> That we this world must liue,
> We ever may be happy
> With blessed William Paddy."

This old-time region, thus recalling the early days of the colony, is bordered by the splendid Boston City Hall, which grandly rises beyond the graveyard. This fine building in the Italian Renaissance, with a surmounting louvre dome of imposing proportions, has in front statues of Benjamin Franklin and Josiah Quincy.

THE OLD SOUTH CHURCH.

Strolling down into the heart of the city, the intricacies of its remarkable method of highway construction are more and more realized. Such an engineering comedy of errors as originally planned and laid out the Boston streets probably nowhere else exists. The highways and intersections seem to be ever at cross-purposes, most of the thoroughfares in the older portion gyrating so strangely over the ground that, while the Bostonian may know all the convenient short-cuts that ease his peregrinations, the visitor usually gets bewildered, and travels through them around to the place where he started. Many of them are culs-de-sac or

blind passages, and no experience in other cities can teach
the stranger a rule whereby to find a destination in Boston.
Imagine the perplexity of the square-cornered and rectangular Philadelphian when set down in this labyrinth. Nevertheless, Boston is not so large but that a moderate amount
of this uncertainty is pleasurable, although one realizes in
wandering about the enormous population that concentrates
from the suburbs into this business section during the day
from the crowded condition of the streets and the steady
rush of people in all directions. Locomotion is at times
uncomfortable amid the busy, jostling throngs. Going
through any of the many routes leading eastward, one
passes from Tremont Street into Washington Street, these
two chief highways in a certain sense being parallel. Washington Street is the main thoroughfare of Boston, having
the leading theatres, the newspaper offices, and many of the
largest stores, and it finally leads over into the "South End,"
being a wider and straighter street in this newer portion.

Just a little way off of Washington Street, where now
stands the office of the Boston *Post*, formerly stood the
little old dwelling where Benjamin Franklin was born.
Alongside is the "Old South Church," fronting on Washington Street, the most famous church of Boston, now, however, chiefly an historical relic and museum of Revolutionary antiquities, the congregation having recently built themselves a magnificent new temple upon Boylston Street, in the
fashionable "West End." This ancient church is a curious
old building, with a tall spire and a clock, to which it is said
that more eyes are upturned than to any other time-piece in
New England. The interior of the building is square, with
double galleries on the ends, and its original condition has
been entirely restored. This church was the colonial shrine
of Boston, wherein were held the spirited meetings of the
exciting days that hatched the Revolution, and within it
were arranged the preliminaries leading to the march of
the party of disguised men who went down to the wharf

and threw the tea overboard. Behind the pulpit is the famous window through which climbed Joseph Warren in 1775 to make the oration on the anniversary of the "Boston Massacre" that had so much to do with creating the state of feeling which produced the final defiance of the British soldiery, culminating in the battle of Lexington. Here Whitefield preached and Franklin was baptized, and within this noted church were delivered, for nearly two centuries, the annual "election sermon" before the governor and legislature. It was only by almost superhuman exertions that the venerable building was saved from the ravages of the great fire of 1872, which was halted at its edge. This grand historical relic has deep interest for every visitor, standing as a landmark of the original colony amid the surging throngs all about which form the busy life of modern Boston.

FANEUIL HALL.

The "Old State-House" is also on Washington Street, an oblong building at the head of State Street which was the quarters of the provincial government. The "Boston Massacre," where the troops fired upon the populace, occurred in the street on its eastern side; after which Samuel Adams, voicing the indignation of the town, made within this building, in an address to the Executive Council, his memorable and successful demand that the British soldiery should be removed outside the city. In the upper portion is a collection made by the Bostonian Society, containing much of interest in connection with early Boston history. The British "Lion and Unicorn" of the colonial time on the front of the building has been replaced by our "bird of freedom," a brightly-gilded eagle.* Dock Square is a short distance away, and near here, viewed through the openings made

---

* The author is reminded by a correspondent that the British Lion and Unicorn have recently been restored to the wings of the roof over the south front of the "Old State-House."

by an intricate system of crooked, radiating passageways, is the Boston "Cradle of Liberty," Faneuil Hall. Old Peter Faneuil built it for a market and presented it to the town, and afterward it was unfortunately burnt. Within it were held the early town-meetings, many being of sterling interest, and it was enlarged in 1805 to the present size. This famous hall is a plain rectangular building about eighty feet square inside, the lower portion being a market and the upper part an assembly-room. It stands, with surmounting cupola, in an open square, and here are still held the public meetings of Boston when anything excites the people, and it is crowded by standing audiences, there being no seats. Across the end of the hall is a raised platform for the orators, behind which, on the wall, is Healy's large painting representing the Senate listening to a speech by Daniel Webster, the occasion being his oration in the earliest secession days of 1832, when South Carolina adopted the policy of attempted "nullification" of unwelcome acts of Congress and Webster was the champion of the Union. Upon the walls hang many historical portraits. Faneuil Hall is never rented for money, but is open for all whenever certain regulations are complied with by a sufficient number of persons. In front of it, extending toward the harbor, is the Quincy Market, one of the busiest parts of Boston.

At the corner of Washington and School Streets is another ancient building, the "Old Corner Bookstore," which has come down for generations as the noted bookshop of this literary community. Here was the house of Allen & Ticknor, a firm that passed through various changes until it became the noted house of Ticknor & Fields, the ancestors of the present firm of Houghton, Mifflin & Co., who now have more spacious quarters elsewhere. The gambrels and gables of the old house recall an architecture that is almost out of vogue. Prolonged northward, Washington Street runs to Haymarket Square, and Charlestown Street is beyond this, passing by Copp's Hill. Upon this hill, which has been considerably reduced in size, is the oldest church in Boston—Christ Church in Salem Street—from whose steeple on the eve of the battle of Lexington were displayed the lights giving warning of the movement of the British troops starting for Concord. These lights notified Paul Revere over the Charles River, who made his famous midnight ride that roused the country. The silver plate, service-books, and Bible belonging to this church were gifts from George II., and in its churchyard are the graves of the three reverend doctors Mather who had so much to do with the early colony—Increase, Cotton, and Samuel.

THE BOSTON FIRE.

Reference has been made to the destructive Boston fire of 1872 that was stopped with so much effort at the Old South Church. Closely following the great Chicago fire, this conflagration continued two days, ravaging the wealthiest district of Boston, and burning seven hundred and seventy-six buildings and property valued at nearly eighty million dollars, the flames extending over fifty acres of the business quarter. There were many lives lost and there was much suffering, but the people set to work quickly reconstructing their city in far better style, straightening and widening the narrow, crooked streets, and putting up much finer buildings. This once-desolated region east of Washington Street is now the centre of enormous business operations that fully occupy many noble structures, so that every trace of the great fire was long ago effaced. Among the finest of the new buildings is the magnificent post-office, of Cape Ann granite, that cost the Government over seven million five hundred thousand dollars. As the visitor traverses the section devoted to trade the evidences of Boston's extensive business operations are more and more impressive. Enormous office-buildings, elevated many stories toward the skies; huge insurance-offices; extensive blocks of stores; scores of banks; innumerable mercantile houses; and the endless processions of trucks moving upon excellently paved streets,—show the wealth and trade of the vigorous town. Stretching down from the old State-House to the harbor is State Street, the home of the brokers and bankers. The greatest boot- and shoe-marts in the world are in Pearl and Bedford Streets, selling the vast product of the Massachusetts shoe-factories. In a half dozen neighboring streets is the dry-goods district, controlling and selling the output of hundreds of New England cotton- and woollen-mills. The merchants, the lawyers, and all the railway-offices are congregated in the region between Tremont and Washington Streets and the harbor.

I have described Beacon Hill and referred to Copp's Hill. To give better business and commercial facilities the third eminence of the "tri-mountain," Fort Hill, was cut down, and its earth and rocks were used to fill in and grade the magnificent marginal street fronting the harbor—Atlantic Avenue. This broad street, carrying the rails of the steam-railways, thus crossing the heads of the long docks and giving facilities for shipment, is of the greatest advantage to Boston commerce. In front of it the piers project, in some cases as much as eight hundred feet, into the harbor, having rows of capacious storehouses in their centres, while on either side are docks of large size filled with shipping. Here is conducted an extensive traffic with all parts of the world, and to these wharves come the hardy fishermen with their yacht-like fishing-smacks and flocks of dories to unload their cargoes of cod and mackerel and take in supplies for another voyage. Fleets of these trim little vessels are in the docks with piles of fish in the stores, and the crews preparing for new voyages to the fishing-banks. This fishing industry is of great importance to New England, and invaluable to the country as an educator of the sailor; and any one strolling about these wharves can fully realize the local significance of the carved codfish hanging in the Massachusetts State-House.

XXVIII.

BOSTON CHARACTERISTICS.

THE development in many ways of the great public spirit of the people is a prominent characteristic of Boston and its suburbs. They take pride in their city and its high rank in the country, its culture, energy, history, and achievements. The wealthy townsfolk, both while living and after death, have devoted their fortunes to the benefit of the community by gifts of fountains and statues, public halls, libraries, and educational endowments, many being of most princely character. There are more libraries, schools, colleges, art and scientific collections, museums, conservatories of music, technological institutes, and all the wide range of educational foundations, in and near Boston than in any other American city. Next to the Library of Congress, the Boston Public Library is the largest in America, the spacious edifice being constantly crowded with book-borrowers and readers. The love of the fine arts was long ago developed among the Bostonians, and the frequent open spaces at the street-intersections, as well as the public grounds, are adorned by admirable statues of prominent men and groups representing historical events of national renown. When not overweighted with the pressure of business cares the people of Boston seem to be always studying and investigating, the women as well as the men alike pursuing the difficult paths of abstruse knowledge with indomitable Yankee perseverance, so that armies of them, thoroughly equipped, scatter over the country every year to impart their learning to less-favored communities and guide the newer settlements in the Far West in their start upon the road to wealth and knowledge. Of this is the "Modern Athens" largely composed, and Boston is proud indeed of such a prominent characteristic.

When the great fire of 1872 had been quenched and an estimate was being formed of the enormous losses, the significant statement was made that "the best treasure of Boston cannot be burnt up. Her grand capital of culture and character, of science and skill, humanity and religion, is beyond the reach of flame. Sweep away every store and house, every school and church, and let the people with their history and habits remain, and they still have one of the richest and strongest cities on earth."

The Boston people also demonstrate their public spirit by liberal gifts for the erection of magnificent buildings, and these grand structures are scattered with prodigality all around the town. These are the homes of art, science, and education, as well as of business. There are many fine churches, especially in the newer districts of the West End, whither have removed into grand temples of modern artistic construction quite a number of the wealthy congregations that were noted in the olden time. Boston has its clubs also, of which there are endless varieties, formed for every conceivable purpose, and not the least attribute to which many of them pay particular if not exclusive devotion being periodic feasting. In fact, one robust Bostonian told me that the "Hub" seemed in danger of being "clubbed to death." Its sturdy devotion to social enjoyments in some respects is quite as pronounced as the development of education and philanthropy.

THE BACK BAY AND THE SUBURBS.

One is not many days in Boston without discovering that the city long since became too cramped for the rapidly-expanding population. The municipality has consequently grown over an extensive network of outlying suburbs across the flats and ponds and waterways environing the original town, from which a vast mass of humanity pours in every morning to transact business. There are eight railways leading out from the city over causeways and bridges, and carrying enormous traffic to the suburban districts. In beautifying and extending the city itself, however, Boston could not have done a better thing than filling in what is known as the "Back Bay," an extensive tract, originally marsh and lowlands, adjacent to Charles River and west of the Common. During more than thirty years this improvement has been going on, making a spacious new district in the West End, now containing the best streets, with the finest churches and hotels and elaborate rows of elegant "swell-front" dwellings of the favorite Boston style of rounded construction, which are the homes of the modern aristocracy. Through this splendid district for over a mile stretches the grand Commonwealth Avenue, two hundred and forty feet wide, its centre being a tree-embowered park adorned by statues and having on either side a magnificent boulevard. The residences are fronted by delicious gardens, and fashionable equipages roll over the smooth pavements. Fine streets at intervals cross this grand avenue at right angles, their names being arranged alphabetically as one proceeds westward by the adoption of these well-known English titles: Arlington, Berkeley, Clarendon, Dartmouth, Exeter, Fairfield, Gloucester, Hereford, etc. Parallel to the avenue are also laid out Boylston, Marlborough, Newbury, and Beacon Streets through this favorite residential district of more modern Boston.

Beyond this, and for five miles through the growing suburb of Brookline, there is being constructed a noble driveway, combining all the attractions of park, garden, boulevard, and footwalk, with also a special bicycle-track upon the latest approved method, Boston being the first city to thus properly recognize the rights of this useful and popular vehicle. Leading out to the southern and south-western suburbs, it finds in Roxbury and the hills beyond, and in Brookline and Brighton, a region of wondrous development and beauty. The surface is undulating and superbly wooded, dotted with crystal lakes, and displaying a succession for miles of costly country-houses and villas that are constructed upon every artistic style and varying fashion. Their hedges and groves and gardens and greensward are at this season in full-leafed midsummer glory. This favorite region spreads beyond the limit of close settlement, with as much verdure as the rocky condition of the land will permit, up to the great water reservoir of Chestnut Hill, which holds eight hundred million of gallons and is the storehouse for the city's needs. Here the villa-covered surface is constantly enlarging as the people are able to devote more money to its adornment. The attractive driveway in this district is around the great reservoir, a broad road being laid on its surrounding embankment, which is at times raised to a higher level where the hillside permits, so that the scenery of woods and water and over the distant landscape is very fine. Jamaica Pond and Jamaica Plain are near by, and beyond the latter are two of Boston's attractive cemeteries, Mount Hope and Forest Hills.

BUNKER HILL.

A prominent feature of Boston is the location of one of the world's great historical battles within the city—Bunker Hill, marked by a noble monument rising on the centre of the hilltop north of Charles River, where the British stormed the Yankee redoubt in June, 1775. This battle-field was then in the Charlestown district, out in the open country, beyond Charles River, but it has long since been covered with houses as the city spread, excepting upon the small open space reserved for a little park around the monument on the summit of the hill. The granite shaft rises two hundred and twenty-one feet upon the highest part of the eminence, which is elevated sixty-two feet

above the level of Charles River.   Facing Boston, in front
of the monument, the direction from which the attack came,
is the bronze statue of Colonel William Prescott, who commanded the Continental troops, the broad-brimmed hat
shading his earnest face as with deprecatory yet determined gesture he uttered the memorable words of warning
that resulted in such terrible punishment of the British
storming-column : " Don't fire until I tell you ; don't fire
until you see the whites of their eyes." The traces of the
hastily-constructed breastworks, thrown up during the pre-
vious night, can be seen on the brow of the hill, and a stone
marks where Warren fell ; for the noted Dr. Joseph Warren,
who made the impassioned speech in the Old South Church
that did so much to kindle the Revolutionary feeling in
Boston, was among the slain at Bunker Hill.   The top of
the tall monument gives a splendid view in all directions
over the harbor and suburbs of Boston—mapping out the
maze of water-courses and railroads, with the many towns
and villages, the fields and forests, and the shipping clustering at the wharves or moving over the waters.   This
grand outlook embraces a wide expanse of country, showing the vast growth and busy industries of the complex
mass of humanity clustering upon the coasts of Massachusetts Bay.   There is only one apparently idle locality.
Adjoining the harbor and surrounded by a high stone wall
is an enclosure with its storehouses and docks fronting the
water and covering an extensive surface behind, yet almost
utterly lifeless, so far as can be seen.   There is an old hulk
moored off the shore, but the shops and docks show little
sign.   This is the Charlestown Navy-yard, covering about
a hundred acres and having an extensive frontage on the
river, with a grand dry-dock and fine ropewalk.   It needs
a reinvigorated United States navy to give it occupation.

HARVARD UNIVERSITY.

A street-car journey upon the long causeways crossing the wide expanse of Charles River where it spreads out to form the "Back Bay," and passing in front of the new improvements on the filled-in lands of the West End and beyond the adjacent flats, takes the visitor to the academic suburb of Cambridge and the great Boston university. This populous town, so far as it is known to fame, is mainly the college, but at its outskirts upon the banks of Charles River is Boston's most noted burial-place, the romantic Mount Auburn Cemetery. This fine enclosure covers about one hundred and twenty-five acres of hill and vale, with a grand development of tombs and landscape. The tower upon the summit of the mount gives a beautiful outlook over Charles River Valley, the Brighton and Brookline villa districts being opposite, with the distant view closed by the Blue Hills of Milton. Harvard University is in the centre of Cambridge, its grounds covering about twenty-two acres, with adjacent fields for athletic sports. Many buildings of ancient and modern construction fill the college yard, as the dormitories and lecture- and recitation-halls, some of them being large and attractive structures. Two hundred and fifty-three years ago the Massachusetts General Court, as the colonial legislature was styled, voted four hundred pounds for the establishment of a school at Cambridge. Two years afterward, in 1638, John Harvard, who had been a pastor in Charlestown, died and bequeathed this school his library and about eight hundred pounds more. Then the Cambridge school was made a college, and named Harvard by the General Court. Cast in heroic bronze, the youthful patron now sits upon a capacious chair in front of the Memorial Hall in the college yard. This university far antedates its rival, Yale, at New Haven, for its first class was graduated in 1642. In fact, Harvard was founded only ninety years later than the greatest college of the old English Cambridge—Emmanuel. John Harvard and Dunster, who was the first president of Harvard, with several other prominent Boston colonists, had been scholars of Emmanuel, and thus from the older Puritan foundation came the younger, and they brought with it the name of the "University City." The first New England printing-press was set up here, and in the University and Riverside presses of to-day it has been succeeded by two extensive bookmaking establishments. Holmes, Lowell, and Long-fellow have been members of the faculty, and it has sent out thousands of famous graduates. It is liberally endowed, and has thus been enabled to erect its many magnificent buildings, which are usually named in memory of the benefactors. The Harvard government formerly was a strictly religious organization, most of the graduates becoming clergymen; but recently it has been secularized, so that no denominational religion is insisted upon, and but a few comparatively now enter the Church. There are schools of law, medicine, divinity, and the arts, all the learned professions being provided for, but everything is elective.

In the various departments at Harvard during the session there are over fourteen hundred students and about fifty-five professors, with many instructors. Much attention is given outdoor sports and athletic training, the college having the finest gymnasium in this country. The most elaborate building of the university, and the best in Cambridge, is the Memorial Hall, which cost four hundred thousand dollars. It is a splendid structure of brick and Nova Scotia stone, three hundred and ten feet long, having a cloister at one end and a massive tower rising at the other. It was recently built in memory of the Harvard graduates who fell during the war, and in the vestibule which crosses the building like a transept, having a marble floor and a rich vaulted ceiling of ash, and grand windows at either end through which pours a mellowed light, there are tablets set in the arcaded sides bearing the names of one hundred and thirty-six dead of Harvard.   Upon one side of this impressive vestibule is the Sanders Theatre, a half amphitheatre, used for commencements and other public services, and seating thirteen hundred persons.   The statue of the venerable Josiah Quincy, once president of Harvard and mayor of Boston, adorns this theatre.   Upon the other side of the vestibule is the great hall of the college, one hundred and sixty-four feet long and eighty feet high, with a splendid roof of open timber-work and magnificent windows.   This is the refectory of the students, and here centre the most hallowed memories of the university, portraits and busts of the distinguished graduates and benefactors adorning it, and the great western window in the late afternoon, as we viewed it, throwing a flood of rich sunlight over the charming scene.   Tables cover the floor when the dinner-hour approaches, and here the students are fed at a cost of about four dollars per week. Such is the noted Boston university, patterned after the original Cambridge, and thus adding much to the English style of most things seen about the great Massachusetts capital.   It was here, when Sir Charles Dilke visited them a few years ago, that the people told him that they spoke "the English of Elizabeth," and at the same time congratulated him upon using what they said was "good English for an Englishman."

XXIX.

THE MASSACHUSETTS NORTH SHORE.

THE northern coast of Massachusetts Bay is a rock-ribbed region of interspersed crags and sand-beaches, stretching far away from Boston toward the north-east to terminate in the massive granite buttress of Cape Ann.

It is largely a region of modern sea-coast villas and of old-time fishermen, of shoemakers and sailors, and in many portions is passing through the interesting stage of transition development caused by the recent inroads of fashionable life. The attractive formation of Boston harbor I have heretofore mentioned, with its numerous islands and the curiously-shaped peninsulas jutting from the mainland. These seem to be scattered about with an apparent irregularity that is very picturesque, yet more closely examined they manage to arrange themselves in three concentric rings. Of these, the inner circle appears to be made by Castle and Governor's Islands in alignment with the peninsulas of East Boston and South Boston. Another and larger circle is a short distance farther eastward. The Squantum peninsula, of which I have already written, juts out from the southern shore between Dorchester and Quincy Bays, and without much difficulty it might be prolonged through Moon and Long and Deer Islands to another of these curiously-formed peninsulas thrust out from the north shore and making the bluffs of Winthrop and a narrow projecting strip that terminates in the rounded headland known as Point Shirley. This is an attractive seaside resort, and was named in memory of Governor Shirley of the Massachusetts colonial province, who once commanded all the British forces in North America. Deer Island is almost connected with this point, and we are told was so called "because of the deare, who often swim thither from the maine when they are chased by the wolves." It has been many years, however, since deer or wolves (of this kind) have been seen around Boston.

There is yet another and outer circle, which may be regarded as the eastern boundary of Boston harbor. On the north shore, in front of Lynn, there stretches out for several miles the curious formation of Nahant, and in line with it southward are the reefs known as the "Graves" and the group of islands whereon is Boston Light. To complete

the segment of this outer bounding circle, comes out northward from the south shore Nantasket Beach, acutely bend-
ing from the north around to the south-west to make the
hook whereon is Hull, and leaving at the extremity of the
peninsula Paddock's Island. All these odd formations help
in making the Boston surroundings very picturesque. The
modest village of Hull nestles under a hill near the extremity of this outer Nantasket peninsula—a construction
that seems as if put just where it is by human hands to
make a breakwater protecting Boston harbor from the
Atlantic storms. The northern projection of this curious
formation is Point Allerton, and the narrow Nantasket
Beach connecting it with the mainland of the south shore
is a ribbon of hard white sand four miles long, upon which
the surf perpetually beats. This region is a popular summer resort, Hingham village being on the main land, while
stretching farther east along the coast is the noted Jerusalem
Road, lined by the splendid seaside villas of wealthy Bostonians that have their lawns spreading out to the edge of
the sea. Hingham is a somewhat antiquated locality that is
being modernized into a summer resort. Its pride is in the
possession of the "oldest church in Yankeedom," a square
house with a steep roof sloping up on all the four sides to a
platform at the top, surrounded by a balustrade and surmounted by a little pointed belfry.

THE SHOEMAKERS OF LYNN.

But we must start from Boston for the north shore.
Crossing over a ferry to East Boston in the early morning, we are met by the crowds pouring into the city to
their daily labor. As the boat moves along, the harbor
passes in review, with its grain-elevators and the extensive wharves of the European steamship lines, its tugs,
steamers, and ferry-boats. The Bunker Hill Monument
is elevated high behind the huge ship-houses of the Charlestown Navy-yard, seen off to the north-west up Charles

River. To the eastward is Governor's Island, with Fort Winthrop upon it, and beyond are the network of peninsulas and the craggy islands enclosing the harbor, while farther off are the long, undulating rocky coasts and sand-strips making the southern shore, with the projecting hook of Nantasket that does so much to protect the place from ocean storms. We land in East Boston, and a swift railway-train is soon spinning along through the town and out upon the edge of the water, across flats and marshes and among the frame houses built upon the hill-slopes sharply rising inland, while on the seaside are successive sand-beaches. The vegetation is sparse, but shore-houses are numerous, and "chowder" and bathing establishments plenty, having cottages clustering around them. The remarkable formation of the Winthrop peninsula is thrust out broadly seaward, having its long, thin, and bulbous southern projection of Point Shirley and the outlying Deer Island with summer hotels upon it. We cross its neck and skirt along Revere Beach, and then there appears in front Lynn Bay, and across it, to the eastward, the narrow sand-strip that leads out to Nahant, one of the strangest formations on this curious coast.

Upon the mainland ahead of us is the city of Lynn, stretching far along the shore with its mass of white and yellow wooden houses and broadly spreading up the background of hills. There are forty thousand people in Lynn, who chiefly devote their time to the manufacture of women's and children's shoes, a Welshman named Dagyr having started this important industry here in the middle of the last century. The whole place is redolent of the pungent odors of morocco and leather; the main streets are lined with the offices of shoe-merchants; there are two hundred or more shoe-factories, great and small, scattered through the place; the myriads of frame houses covering the plain near the sea and the adjacent hills are mainly the homes of thousands of shoemakers, men and women, who

work in the "teams" in the factories; and here are made
more women's shoes than in any other place in the world,
there sometimes being turned out in a single year fifteen
million of pairs that are sent everywhere. As may naturally be expected, here flourishes in all its glory the powerful society of the "Knights of St. Crispin" which rules
the shoe trade and largely controls the politics of the town,
and its members have made Lynn a special citadel of American labor by successfully discriminating against most of the
foreigners who are so numerous in other New England manufacturing centres. Much of the work on the shoes is done
by machinery. It was from Lynn-Regis in England that
the first flock of colonists were brought by their pastor in
1629 to Lynn, and hence its name. It is the chief town
of Essex county, for we have crossed over the border from
Suffolk, the county containing Boston. The attractive city
hall of Lynn is seen from afar, being prominently built of
brick and brownstone and fronting on the narrow common.
The fish-sellers, who represent another Massachusetts industry as important as shoemaking, go about its streets announcing their vocation by lusty blasts on resonant horns,
and there are many fishing-boats drawn up on the shores
of the bay. A magnificent display of costly villas is made
out in front of the eastern portion of Lynn, having the
ocean in full view and Nahant seen across the bay. Here
live the shoe-and-leather princes of the town and also many
business-men from Boston. Having excellent roads embowered with trees, and the surf beating in upon the sloping shore in front, this is a lovely spot for a home; and
when the busy people tire of their shoe-factories they need
not go far to get the recreation given by a pleasant view
across the deep blue sea.

VILLA-CROWNED NAHANT.

The long and narrow sand-strip that goes out to Nahant
stretches seaward in front of Lynn. On either side the surf

briskly beats, and would soon wash the strip away were not
the beach of hard sand and gravel sustained by a stiff backbone of rocks beneath. This ribbon of sand is barely a hundred yards wide, having Nahant Bay on its ocean side to the
eastward and Lynn Bay to the westward. On the outer edge
of the bay to the eastward stands up the isolated, oval-
shaped Egg Rock, rising nearly one hundred feet high,
with the guiding beacon-light that surmounts the summit
seen far away over the water. In front, as we go out along
the sand-strip, are the rocks and hills forming Nahant,
seeming almost bare and having a few trees and many
villas upon them. Nahant, which means the "Lovers'
Walk," is a curious formation. The narrow sand-beach
tying it to the shore, and thus thrust out directly into the
ocean, is nearly four miles in length. At the outer extremity a mass of rocks and soil rises to a considerable height
above the sea, being of very irregular shape, nearly two
miles long and half a mile broad, and covering about four
hundred and fifty acres. Its shores are mostly lined with
rocks, many being of unique character, making caves and
spouting fissures as the waves dash in. A short distance
within the outer peninsula a smaller mass of about forty
acres crosses the connecting sand-strip and is called Little
Nahant. The Bostonians have made Nahant, which is
within easy access, one of their favorite summer resorts,
occupying the whole of the place with villas, whose red
roofs rise upon all the hilltops, having the neat tower of a
pretty little white church (like all New England hamlets)
on the highest ground, near the centre of the strangely-
shaped locality, apparently for the chief landmark. The
cottages are comfortable, and many are roomy and some
quite ornamental, though the elaborate and even effusive
use of wealth in decoration and building that is so extensively displayed by the millionaires of Newport is not seen
at this popular Boston resort, where the people may have
similar tastes, but are evidently more happy in possessing

less overgrown fortunes. The highways that are laid out upon this curious peninsula are excellent, the arching elms in most charming manner rising gracefully over them. Many pretty landscapes are displayed from the higher grounds, and there are views across the sea in almost every direction. Several old-time houses are still found among the lawn-environed villas, relics of the earlier days, before modern fashion had seized upon Nahant. All around the ocean side are huge buttresses of rock, where the waves long since washed out all the sand and soil, although there have been left many pretty coves among the rugged projections of the cliffs. The dark-blue water sparkles under the brisk wind, which raises profuse spray and "white-caps." Seen across the sea, far away to the southwest and hazy at the horizon, is the distant city of Boston, having the prominent gilded State-House dome rising at the top of the broad, flat cone the city makes. As we go about Nahant, watching the waves beating upon the rocks and dashing into the little intervening coves, and winding with the pleasant road among the villas, there constantly stands up the little white-towered church as the central landmark. Returning to the mainland over the long, narrow isthmus, the broadly-extended Massachusetts shore in front is seen to be fringed with villages, their white wooden houses dotted along the edge of the water and spreading almost the whole way from Boston, past Winthrop, being all in full view, and finally developing into the larger town of Lynn immediately before us, with its towers and spires and the conspicuous city hall, having a long background of hills. Then the fringe of villages spreads off to the eastward, into Swampscott and Marblehead, while far beyond there loom up the granite hills among which the famous fishing-port of Gloucester nestles, the view finally ending in the distant rocky headland of Cape Ann.

XXX.

THE GRANITE BUTTRESS OF CAPE ANN.

From Lynn our eastward journey is renewed along the picturesque northern coast through the frequent fishing-settlements that are undergoing a modern evolution into seaside summer resorts. Cottages border the little bays, where the fishing-boats are drawn up on the sand-beaches, and villas are hung upon the hillsides rising high at the back. Around the many swamps and marshes here abounding crags protrude, for we have entered another Boston summer suburb—Swampscott—as fashionable as Nahant and as populous. In all directions the rocks raise their jagged and battered, furrowed sides, and cottages are set on top or nestle among them. Some of these summer-houses are of large size and built in very strange styles, for their designers like nothing better than to get up odd kinds of architecture. Some of the more startling houses are perched high on the rocks, with stairways leading up to them. There are huge hotels out near the water-side, and Swampscott merges into Clifton, with the ocean washing in front; and as we move farther along more and more rocks appear, and the whole surface seems to have been formerly covered by the boulders that have been gathered to construct the stone fences, and it is still covered with myriads of smaller rounded and water-worn stones. As we go among these rocks, with a field or two disclosing a doleful attempt at farming, the distant Marblehead steeples appear in front rising from that ancient and most curious town.

QUAINT OLD MARBLEHEAD.

An uneven backbone of granite, covering about six square miles, is thrust out into the Atlantic Ocean in the direction of Cape Ann, and is hedged about with rocky islets. On the one side this granite peninsula forms the harbor of Salem, while on the other side a miniature haven is made by a craggy appendage to the south-eastward that is attached to the main peninsula by a ligature of sand and shingle. The quaint old town of Marblehead occupies the greater part of the surface, while the appendage, now the yachtsmen's headquarters, is known as Marblehead Neck. Formerly this place was a great resort of sailors and fishermen. The crooked, narrow streets in the older portion run in all directions over the rocks, lined by frame houses, their uneven sides generally being without footwalks, and the buildings are crowded together in an inconvenient manner. This once pre-eminently nautical town was formerly the second port in Massachusetts, but its marine interests have almost passed away, and it has since, like so many other Massachusetts communities, gone largely into shoemaking, the big shoe-factories being scattered through it. Among the many wooden buildings rocks appear in all directions, and have certainly gained the mastery. When the preacher, George Whitefield, visited Marblehead, he gazed in astonishment upon the superabundant rocks, and asked in surprise, "Pray, where do they bury their dead?" The English Channel Islands furnished many of the original settlers, and their peculiarities of dialect still prevail among their descendants. The old-time houses, coming down from the colonial days, and the nautical flavor of almost everything, even though shoemaking is now permanent among this seafaring people, recall the time in the last century when the seaport of Marblehead was almost a rival of Boston. The superannuated little Fort Sewall, that once protected the port, is out on the headland, and its position commands the harbors upon either side. Built upon the projecting crag, with the water washing it upon both sides, the surface has been sodded over, and, although the walls are decaying, the precious old fort is preserved as a memento of the past. From it there is a charming outlook at the rocks and promontories, the little bays between, and far out over the sea. There is Lowell Island, with its summer hotel; and the more distant view is along the extended north shore, with its modern summer resorts expanding and overshadowing the older fishing-towns at Beverly, Manchester-by-the-Sea, and, finally, the New England fishermen's great port of Gloucester and the ponderous rocks of Cape Ann. Though it may have ceased to be a defensive work, this ancient fort is now a picturesque ruin, and a contribution-box hangs on its gate for aid in its restoration. There are red-roofed villas, some of unique and attractive construction, perched on the rocks all about this quaint yet charming town that has had so much to do in educating the American sailor.

THE ANCIENT PORT OF SALEM.

There stretches westward of the Marblehead peninsula into the mainland another noted haven of the olden time—Salem harbor, which divides into two arms, known as North and South Rivers, having between them the town, mainly built upon a peninsula about two miles long. Passing around the rocky edge of an intervening bay, we enter the ancient city of the witches by going through one of those typical New England streets of which so many have been seen upon this tour, with its long rows of stately overarching elms making a grand aisle of interlaced branches far above. Bordering this attractive street are pleasant homes standing in spacious grounds, while on the waterside their smooth green lawns stretch down to the harbor's edge. This was the Indian domain of "Naumkeag," a name that has been preserved in many titles here, and is said to mean the "Eel Land." This was the mother-colony on Massachusetts Bay, the first house having been built in 1626. Old John Endicott got a grant from the Plymouth settlers for the colony, and came out and founded the town two years afterward, naming it "Salem, from the peace which they had and hoped in it." Despite this original peacefulness, however, the pious Salem colonists soon developed warlike tendencies. The settlement had not long existed when they scourged and cut off the ears and banished Philip Ratcliffe for "blasphemy against the First Church." In the infancy of the colony a trade report showed annual imports of one hundred and ten thousand dollars in arms and cannon and ninety thousand dollars in furniture, building materials, and everything else. The "First Church," formed in 1629, is said to have been the earliest church organization in the United States, and it still exists and flourishes. In that year the early history records that there were ten houses in the town besides the governor's house, "which was garnished with great ordnance;" adding, "thus we doubt not that God will be with us, and if God be with us, who can be against us?" It was from Salem in 1630 that John Winthrop migrated to found Boston.

In former times this remarkable old town was the leading New England port for foreign trade, but its glory has departed, this trade now being attracted by the superior inducements of the more energetic Boston merchants. Salem in 1785 sent out the first American vessel that doubled the Cape of Good Hope, and during a half century afterward it held almost a monopoly of the China and East Indies trade with the United States, having at one time fifty-four large ships thus engaged. Salem ships also went to the southern seas, to Japan and Africa, so that seventy or eighty years ago it was in the first rank of American ports, its harbor being commodious, with deep water, and convenient. The town is yet wealthy, but it stands almost still while other towns around it grow. Passing a green old age in quiet restfulness, its venerable merchants and sea-captains live in the comfortable mansions surrounding its attractive common enclosed by rows of the stately elms that also line the chief streets. These make the aristocracy of Salem, having lost their occupations, while the younger and more active generation, like so many of their neighbors along these coasts, have taken to shoemaking and other industries. The population is standing almost still at twenty-eight thousand. The most noted man of Salem was George Peabody, born in the suburb of Danvers, and his remains rest here. This suburb changed its name to Peabody, and in the Peabody Institute, which he founded there, Queen Victoria's portrait, her gift to him, is kept as a sacred relic. Among other prominent natives of Salem have been General Putnam, Nathaniel Bowditch, William H. Prescott, and Nathaniel Hawthorne.

The East India Marine Hall is the most noted institution of Salem—a fine building on Essex Street, filled with a valuable Oriental collection gathered during the many voyages made by the mariners of the town, and also having a Natural History Museum, showing the development of animal life. In the Essex Institute is contained the original charter given by King Charles I. to the colony of Massachusetts Bay. There is also carefully kept near by the original "First Church," built in 1634 (for the organization formed in 1629), and of which Roger Williams was the pastor before the Puritans banished him. When the expanding congregation afterward built a larger church, this curious little house, with its high-pointed roof, diamond-paned windows, and gallery, which is revered as the shrine of Salem, was removed to its present place, and is carefully preserved. In Essex Street is also the old "Roger Williams House," a quaint, low-roofed structure, with a little shop in front, which has acquired additional fame as a relic of the witchcraft days, for in it was held the court that tried the witches who were afterward taken to the bare-topped Gallows Hill, on the outskirts of the town, to be put to death. This witchcraft delusion began in the Danvers suburb in 1692, and it soon overran most of New England. During more than a year the persecutions continued, and nineteen proven witches were put to death, while one, under the ancient English law, was pressed to death for standing mute when told to plead. Old Cotton Mather, the zealous historian and divine, was among the leaders in the movement against the witches, and when the frenzy was at its height a large part of the Salem people fled in panic from the town.

THE EXTREMITY OF THE CAPE.

Beyond Salem harbor the north shore stretches far away toward the north-east down the cape, with its old-fashioned fishing-towns in a transition state under the modern stimulus of Boston villa-life, that brings in all kinds of strange architecture to enhance the picturesqueness of Beverly and Manchester-by-the-Sea. The old-time trawlers and harpoon-men and skippers of Cape Ann are agog at the change made in most things here by this recent invasion of fashion and artistic building, though they don't object to the way in which it has put up the price of town-lots beyond anything ever imagined even in the best days of the fisheries. At Beverly lived Nathan Dane, the eminent New England jurist,whose memory is preserved in Dane Hall, the Harvard Law School. Beverly also, in these degenerate days for the fishermen, keeps in the swim by giving much attention to shoemaking. The magnificent headlands and splendid beaches of this coast have been making it more and more attractive to the summer visitor, so that it is spotted with clusters of villas. Crags overhang and rocks encompass them about, while behind, the land rises into the dreary hills making the backbone of the peninsula, which is well called "the ridge of rocks and roses," terminating in the gaunt headland of Cape Ann. This cape is a mass of sienite, forming low hills, over the surface of which the rock is generally exposed to view, the fields being strewn with boulders, many of large size, while beds of pure white sand inter-

vene. There are quarries worked, and the sand and granite are extensively exported, much of the latter coming to
Philadelphia for paving.

It is among these granite rocks of the cape, deeply indented, about four miles south-west of its extremity, that
we find the harbor of the chief New England fishing-port
—Gloucester. This well-protected and capacious harbor is
safe in all weathers and easy of access, having a sufficient
depth to float the largest vessels. Its inmost recesses are
guarded by Ten-Pound Island, and it is usually filled with
fishing-smacks. There are twenty-five thousand people
living here, but the prevalent odor of salt fish has not
prevented the fashionable invasion of villas and summer-
houses that is such a conspicuous feature throughout the
north shore. Yet, unlike so many of the other places,
Gloucester has not been led away from the fisheries by
the tempting allurements of Massachusetts shoemaking. It
sturdily clings to its cod and mackerel trades, and is by far
the leading port in the number of its fishermen and vessels
and the value of the catch, while its manufactures are almost entirely confined to articles pertaining to the fisheries.
It has seventy wharves and six marine railways. In the
compactly built and handsome town surrounding the harbor and among the adjacent granite hills are concocted
shrewd methods of securing fish despite the international
entanglements of the vexing fishery question. But this
fascinating trade is full of dangers, and Gloucester loses
many lives and vessels every year, so that it has the fatal
celebrity of containing the largest population of widows
and orphans of any city in the United States. It was here
in 1713 was built the first vessel of the favorite American
rig known as the schooner, a class of easy navigation now
making up the largest portion of our merchant marine.
It has always been a great school for the sailor, and the
tone and temper of its people show that it hopes to keep
on with the fisheries, come what may. Beyond this model

fishery-town is the extremity of the cape, where the ponderous rocky buttresses have been broken down by the
Atlantic to form another small but well-sheltered harbor.
Upon its shores, at an elevation of about ninety feet above
the sea and standing about six hundred yards apart, are
the two fixed lights of Cape Ann, the well-known beacons
marking the great headland thrust out into the ocean
which makes the northern limit of Massachusetts Bay.

XXXI.

GOING DOWN EAST.

For a good while we have been steadily journeying
toward the rising sun, and ever on the search for that
mythical and elusive region known as " Down East." We
of Philadelphia are accustomed to regard the land beyond
New York as the veritable " Down East." But when we
got among the Connecticut Yankee notions, and inquired
if we were in the true locality, the people looked doubtful
and pointed farther onward. Likewise in Massachusetts
we are still chasing the golden treasures underlying the
end of the brilliant rainbow arch, for the natives look wise
and tell us the true " Down East" is still farther toward
the rising sun. Now we pass beyond the great headland
of Cape Ann, yet bent upon the search: it is beyond us.
Samuel Adams Drake tells of putting the momentous
question to a Maine fisherman who was getting up his sail
on the Penobscot: " Whither bound?" Promptly came
back the answer: " Sir, to you—Down East." This mythical land we thus ever pursue, and it ever eludes us; but
enough has already been learnt on this tour to conclude
that the true " Down East" must be far beyond the New

England border, and among the "Kanucks" and "Blue Noses" of the Canadian maritime provinces.

Resuming the Eastern journey beyond Cape Ann, we cross the broadening North River out of Salem, and pass among the wooden houses and shoe-factories of its ancient suburb of Beverly, with their environment of truck-gardens, and the high reservoir on the hill to the south-east, where Salem stores her water-supply drawn from Wenham Lake. This noted ice-producer, with its capacious ice-houses, is near the railway, while upon the ocean front spread the splendid beaches of Beverly, Manchester, and Magnolia. Then we cross the valley of Ipswich River, with the pretty town covering both sloping banks, with scattered cottages among the foliage, and having the grave-yard perched on the opposite hill—a region of green fields and prolific orchards, seeming almost like an oasis amid the desert of sands and rocks left behind us. Not far in the interior is the town of Andover, where the thrifty fathers of the Church, having bought the domain from the Indians "for twenty-six dollars and sixty-four cents and a coat," established the noted theological seminary of the Congregational Church, where its ablest divines have been taught in what has been called "the school of the prophets." Here on "Andover Hill" abstruse theology has been the ruling influence since the opening of this century, and intense religious controversies have been waged, some three thousand clergymen having been graduated. The seminary buildings, the local guide tells us, cause visitors to wonder "if orthodox angels have not lifted up old Harvard and Massachusetts Halls and carried them by night from Cambridge to Andover Hill." Ipswich, too, has its seminary, but it is for the opposite sex, although fully as noted. One reason we are told for the popularity of Ipswich Female Seminary is that it tends to soften the rigors of study, for this is the place "where Andover theological students are wont to take unto themselves wives of the daughters of the

Puritans." The shore of noble Ipswich Bay, indented north of Cape Ann, was the ancient Agawam, where the redoubtable Captain John Smith coasted along in 1614, and made a record in his narrative of "the many corn-fields and delightful groves of Agawam," then a flourishing Indian village.

CROSSING NEW HAMPSHIRE.

But the brief Ipswich oasis is soon passed, and, crossing moors and salt-marshes and among patches of scrub timber with protruding rocks, we reach the Massachusetts eastern boundary at the noted Merrimac River and Newburyport. Rounded hills surround the town, and, tunnelling under these, the train runs into the collection of wooden houses so largely composing it. The Merrimac flows from the westward past the famous factory-towns of Lowell and Lawrence, Nashua and Manchester—a river of frequent waterfalls, furnishing immense power to the mills. It is a narrow stream carrying a powerful current, and broadens into a spacious harbor at its mouth, where Newburyport is built on the southern shore, having its splendid High Street, one of the noted tree-embowered highways of New England, stretching for several miles parallel to the river down toward the sea, bordered with the stately mansions of the olden time. This is a quiet town, standing almost still in the modern march of progress, its decayed foreign commerce and shipbuilding being largely replaced by manufactures, as in most of these New England coast-cities. Here lived in the last century the eccentric merchant Timothy Dexter, who is said to have shipped a cargo of warming-pans to the West Indies, and made a fortune out of that and similar odd business ventures. Here also lived Caleb Cushing and John B. Gough, and the noted preacher George Whitefield is buried in its old South Presbyterian Church, while behind this church is the little wooden house where William Lloyd Garrison was born.

15

We cross the Merrimac on an elevated bridge affording
fine views both up and down the river, which sweeps out in
a broad curve to the ocean three miles below, seen through
the gauzy trusses of a wagon-bridge in front of us. Thus
is the State of New Hampshire entered, rocks being thrust
up everywhere through the thin covering of soil in its
border-town of Seabrook, whose inhabitants are hereabout
known as the "Algerines." Salt-marshes, winding streams
leading down to the sea (appropriate to the name of Seabrook), forests and rocks, vary the view with long sandy
beaches bordering them out on the ocean front, and the
foaming line of breakers rolling in as we gaze off at the
distant clusters of seaside hotels and cottages, with the
exhilarating salt air blowing upon us. The first passed is
Salisbury Beach, one of the noted New Hampshire coast
resorts, where the people by many thousands congregate on
a day late in August to have a good time, thus annually
renewing a custom they have observed for more than two
centuries. Here Whittier pitched his *Tent on the Beach* he
has so graphically described. Next comes Hampton Beach,
and then the famous Rye Beach, the latter being the most
fashionable, and their sojourners crowd in and out of the
railway-train. It was at the little village of Hampton
that occurred in 1737 the parley which resulted in giving
the infant colony of New Hampshire its narrow border on
the sea-coast. This region had been settled by Massachusetts, and that province was bound to possess it, although
the king had made an adverse grant. Into Hampton rode
in grand state the governor of Massachusetts at the head
of his legislature and escorted by five troops of horse, for-
mally demanding possession of the maritime townships.
He met the governor of New Hampshire in the George
Tavern, and the demand was refused. The latter governor
sent a plaintive appeal to the king, declaring that "the
vast, opulent, and overgrown province of Massachusetts
was devouring the poor little, loyal, distressed province

of New Hampshire." The royal heart, we are told, was touched, and the king commanded Massachusetts to surrender her claim to two tiers of townships, twenty-eight in number, thus giving New Hampshire her present sea-coast, a narrow strip of only eighteen miles width. The seaside hotel and cottage, developing farther inland into farms with stately old mansions, are the universal development of this region. The plains near the coast do not, however, stretch far into the interior, for the surface soon becomes broken and rugged, rising into higher and higher hills until they culminate in the magnificent scenery of the White Mountains. In fact, between its popular sea-beaches, splendid lakes, and grand mountain-district New Hampshire is an almost universal resort for the tourist and summer saunterer, and is filled with hotels and boarding-houses, some bearing most aristocratic names. It is not singular, therefore, that the shaft of satire should have been levelled during the recent moist season at one of the many hotels of this scenic State:

"In a certain part of New Hampshire,
  Where the true name should be 'Dampshire,'
Where the chills and fever run the summer through,
  A tavern unpretentious
  Has a host so conscientious
That he calls his boarding-house the 'Montague.'"

PORTSMOUTH AND KITTERY.

It does not take long for the railway-train to cross the narrow strip of New Hampshire—only about thirty-five minutes—between Newburyport and Portsmouth, from the Merrimac to the Piscataqua River, between which it is enclosed. In a brief space we are upon the border of Portsmouth, and pass "Frank Jones & Son's Brewery," emitting a strong odor of not very fresh beer, and a reminder of the man who is a robust opponent of prohibitory laws and is said to chiefly own this part of New Hampshire. He has been shrewd enough to recently sell his great brewery to an English syndicate for a round sum. Portsmouth is a small town, quiet and quaint, the river flowing past with rapid tidal stream, and having upon an island of the opposite shore the well-known Kittery Navy-yard of Maine. This river is really a strait, broadening into a bay some distance above Portsmouth, and thus carrying such an enormous tidal current that the harbor is always free from ice. In this venerable and tranquil place, which has stood still for a good while, commerce has about surrendered sway to the superior attractions of the modern summer resort, and one almost envies the home-like charms of the comfortable old dwellings that slumber in their extensive gardens. To this spot came "the founder of New Hampshire," Captain Mason, who had been the governor of the South Sea Castle in Portsmouth harbor, England, and at his suggestion the settlement, originally called Strawberry Bank from the abundance of its growth of wild strawberries, was called Portsmouth. He wrote that it was "a name most suitable for the place, it being the river's mouth, and as good as any in the land." The old town to-day has barely nine thousand people. Its quietness and ancient ways have been too tame for the younger generation, who have gone elsewhere to seek their fortunes. Portsmouth harbor is bordered by islands, and in fact the whole region adjacent to the Piscataqua seems interlaced with waterways, dividing it into many islands with picturesque shores, some of them yet bearing the remains of the old forts that defended the port in the troublous colonial times. Upon Continental Island is the Kittery Navy-yard, near which is the village of Kittery Point, where was born and is buried the greatest man of colonial fame in these parts, Sir William Pepperell, the famous leader of the expedition that captured Louisburg from the French in 1745, for which he was knighted.

"LADY WENTWORTH OF THE HALL."

Among the islands adjoining Portsmouth harbor, and having a broad beach facing the sea, is Newcastle Island, which for the annual fee of three peppercorns was incorporated by King William III. and Queen Mary. Here lived in semi-regal state the Wentworths, who were the colonial governors, and their memory is preserved in the colossal Wentworth Hotel, whose vast proportions are visible far over land and sea. Newcastle Village to-day is a straggling fishing-settlement, but the Wentworth mansion at Little Harbor, wherein was held the provincial court, still remains—an irregular, quaint, but picturesque building of considerable size, having within it the council-chamber and some interesting old portraits. Far away to the northward rises the isolated peak of the adjacent Maine coast, the broad-topped Mount Agamenticus, which was the throne of the Indian sagamore Passaconoway, whom the local legends describe as St. Aspenquid. To the southward is the wide sweep of Ipswich Bay, enclosed by the long, slender arm of Cape Ann, and having in its graceful curve the Rye and Hampton Beaches. The most noted occupant of Wentworth House was the courtly but gouty old governor Benning Wentworth, who named Bennington, Vermont, and whose wedding on his sixtieth birthday has given Longfellow one of his most striking themes. As we read his graceful poem one can almost see Martha Hilton as she goes along the street swinging her pail and splashing with the water her naked feet. Mistress Stavers in her furbelows, the buxom landlady at the inn, feels called upon to give her sharp reproof:

> "'Oh, Martha Hilton! fie! how dare you go
> About the town half-dressed and looking so?'"

To this the gypsy laughed and saucily replied:

> "'No matter how I look, I yet shall ride
> In my own chariot, ma'am.'"

In course of time Martha came to be employed at Wentworth House as maid-of-all-work, not wholly unobserved by the old governor, as the sequel proved. He arranged a feast for his sixtieth birthday, and all the great people of the colony were at his table. Of it the poet sings:

" When they had drunk the king with many a cheer,
   The governor whispered in a servant's ear,
   Who disappeared, and presently there stood
   Within the room, in perfect womanhood,
   A maiden, modest, and yet self-possessed,
   Youthful and beautiful, and simply dressed.
   Can this be Martha Hilton? It must be!
   Yes, Martha Hilton, and no other she!
   Dowered with the beauty of her twenty years,
   How ladylike, how queenlike, she appears!
   The pale, thin crescent of the days gone by
   Is Dian now in all her majesty.
   Yet scarce a guest perceived that she was there,
   Until the governor, rising from his chair,
   Played slightly with his ruffles, then looked down,
   And said unto the Reverend Arthur Brown:
'This is my birthday; it shall likewise be
   My wedding-day, and you shall marry me.'

" The listening guests were greatly mystified:
   None more so than the rector, who replied,
'Marry you? Yes, that were a pleasant task,
   Your Excellency; but to whom? I ask.'
   The governor answered, 'To this lady here,'
   And beckoned Martha Hilton to draw near.
   She came and stood, all blushes, at his side.
   The rector paused. The impatient governor cried,
'This is the lady. Do you hesitate?
   Then I command you as chief magistrate.'
   The rector read the service loud and clear:
'Dearly beloved, we are gathered here,'
   And so on to the end. At his command
   On the fourth finger of her fair left hand
   The governor placed the ring; and that was all:
   Martha was Lady Wentworth of the Hall!"

XXXII.

THE ISLES OF SHOALS.

ONE of the strangest places on the Atlantic coast is the collection of crags and reefs out in the ocean off Portsmouth harbor known as the Isles of Shoals. We start from the wharf on a little steamer to go out there. The tidal current of the Piscataqua River moves swiftly past the almost idle wharves of the town, where two or three schooners are unloading Pennsylvania coal. The front of the port gives evidence that a large commerce once existed, but has passed away, for many of the quays are now abandoned and overgrown with weeds. Yachts and row-boats dot the water, as pleasure-seekers are numerous, and over opposite is the State of Maine, its shores being a succession of islands, the white buildings of the navy-yard, its shiphouses, and dock spreading broadly across the view. The flag floats from a tall staff, and a little steam-launch briskly crosses the river toward us, making a sort of ferry, but the navy-yard itself seems almost idle, a vessel or two being outfitted, and the vast establishment, much like League Island, is waiting for the new American navy to be created, so that it may get business. The green and sloping shores of the surrounding islands frame it in and make a pleasant picture, while a corvette moored in front has her flag flying apeak, ready to go to sea. We steam down the crooked river, threading our way among the islands of the harbor, passing the abandoned forts below the town, and skirting the attractive shore of Newcastle Island and its fishing village, with the huge Wentworth Hotel rising against the southern sky. Soon we pass the lighthouses, and, leaving Whale's Back Light on our left, are out at sea. Ahead, and about six miles off shore, looms up the dim and shadowy outline of the islands, lying like a cloud along the edge of the horizon. The prow is turned toward them as we go bounding over the long rolling billows that come up before the fresh southerly wind. As the steamboat approaches, the islands gradually rise and expand to view as they separate into their respective forms, the chief being Appledore, which rises from the sea much like a hog's back, and hence the original name of Hog Island.

There are nine islands in the group. The largest is Appledore, covering about four hundred acres, and the whole of them do not aggregate much over six hundred acres. Star Island has one hundred and fifty acres. Haley's, or Smutty Nose, with Malaga and Cedar, which are connected by a sort of bar or breakwater, together have about one hundred acres. There are four smaller islets—Duck, White, Seavey's, and Londoner's—and upon White Island is the lighthouse for the group, with a great revolving light having alternating red and white flashes, elevated eighty-seven feet and visible fifteen miles out at sea. A covered way leads back over the crags from the tower to the keeper's cottage. The Isles of Shoals are a remarkable formation—rugged ledges of rock out in the ocean, bearing scarcely any vegetation. On some of them not a blade of grass is seen. Four of them, stretching in a line, make the outside of the strange group—bare reefs, with water-worn flinty surfaces, against which the sea beats with all the force of thousands of miles of gathering waves. Not a tree grew on any of the group until a little one was planted on Appledore in front of the hotel, and another dwarf was coaxed to grow in the little graveyard on Star Island. Their best vegetation was low whortleberry-bushes until somebody thought of gathering soil enough to make some grass patches for a cow or two. No one can describe the utter desolation of these rocks, thus cast off, apparently, from the rest of the world.

THE STRANGE FORMATION OF THE ISLES.

Yet the Isles of Shoals have their admirers. Celia Thaxter the poetess was the daughter of the lightkeeper, and to her glowing pen much of their fame is due, which has culminated in establishing on these wind-swept rocks an abiding-place for summer fashion. "Swept by every wind that blows," she writes, "and beaten by the bitter brine for unknown ages, well may the Isles of Shoals be barren, bleak, and bare. At first sight nothing can be more rough and inhospitable than they appear. But to the human creature who has eyes that will see and ears that will hear Nature appeals with such a novel charm that the luxurious beauty of the land is half forgotten before one is aware. The very wildness and desolation reveal a strange beauty to him. In the early morning the sea is rosy and the sky; the line of land is radiant; the scattered sails glow with the delicious color that touches so tenderly the bare, bleak rocks."

The curious name of these islands first appears in the log of their early discoverer, Champlain, the geographer for the noted Frenchman, Sieur des Monts, who had a grant for all this region. Champlain found them as he coasted along in 1605. From the earliest times they were prolific fishing-grounds, and the name of the Isles of Shoals is generally believed to have been given from "the shoaling, or schooling, of the fish" around them. In a deed from the Indian sagamores to John Wheelwright and some others in 1629 they are called the "Isles of Shoals." The redoubtable Captain John Smith, who had so much to do with early American exploration, visited and described them in 1614, and tried to attach to them the name of "Smith's Islands," but he was not successful. The State boundary-line between New Hampshire and Maine passes through the group between Star and Appledore. Owing to their peculiar grouping, quite a good harbor, and the only secure one, is formed between these two, opening to the westward, and being enclosed by Smutty Nose, Star, and Cedar Islands, so that it is amply protected from the sea. Into this our steamer glides, halting first at Apple-dore and then at Star Island to land its passengers. The curious development of rocks and desolation, relieved by a little artificiality in the form of flower-beds, strikes the beholder with amazement. These rugged crags resemble the bald and rounded peaks of a sunken volcano thrust upward from the sea, with this little harbor forming its crater. When Nathaniel Hawthorne was induced to come out here he gazed upon their curious and impressive forma-tion, and then wrote, "As much as anything else, it seems as if some of the massive materials of the world remained superfluous after the Creator had finished, and were care-lessly thrown down here, where the millionth part of them· emerge from the sea, and in the course of thousands of years have become partially bestrewn with a little soil." The savagery of these isolated rocks during violent storms, when surrounded by almost perpetual surf and exposed to the ocean's greatest fury, becomes almost overwhelming, and they actually seem to reel beneath one's feet. The peculiar novelty of the position impresses the visitor. The eternal plash and boom of ocean's waters on every side are the constant sounds, and it is easy to believe you are far out at sea.

THEIR ODD HISTORY.

Star Island has some history, and until they were sent away and their cottages removed to make way for the sum-mer hotel it had a village of fishermen. It was the town of Gosport, and has its little church, visible with its tiny bell-tower many miles over the water. The original Gos-port church was built of the timbers from the wreck of a Spanish vessel in 1685, and was rebuilt shortly afterward, and burnt by the islanders in 1790. The present little stone church is as old as this century. This charge had several faithful clergymen, who are buried on the island. It was here that Rev. John Brook ministered, of whom the quaint historian Cotton Mather relates this anecdote illustrating the efficacy of prayer: A child lay sick and so nearly dead those present believed it had actually expired, "but Mr. Brook, perceiving some life in it, goes to prayer, and in his prayer used this expression: 'Lord, wilt thou not grant some sign before we leave prayer that thou wilt spare and heal this child? We cannot leave thee till we have it.' The child sneezed immediately." On the highest part of Star Island is the broken monument erected to Captain John Smith, which was put up by his admirers not many years ago. It was a triangular shaft of marble rising from a triangular base of hewn stones placed upon the crag. It bore three heads—representing three Moslems slain by Smith and seen on his escutcheon—but vandals have thrown the structure down and the broken fragments lie there, making the monument as desolate as its bleak surroundings. Likewise the old graveyard. The little fort that defended Star Island in colonial times has been abandoned for a century, and nestling beneath it is the little graveyard, part of the walls remaining. It is overgrown with grass and weeds, and has a few gravestones which are gradually reeling over, as gravestones will when no loving hands care for them. A sorry-looking, dilapidated picket-fence tries to fill some of the gaps in the walls. All the original inhabitants of the island are dead, their descendants scattered, and fashionable pleasuring now replaces their fishing-huts and nets and boats on this rocky desert and its environment of restless waters.

As might be expected, a place like this was a favorite haunt for pirates in the colonial days. When they were caught and condemned, the old-time Puritan parsons, as a sort of preparative before they were hanged, would have them brought into church, and then preach long and powerful sermons to them on the enormity of their crimes and

the deserved torments awaiting them in the other world.
Around these islands cruised Hawkins, Phillips, and Pound,
notorious pirates two centuries ago. It is related of Phillips that he seized a fishing-vessel named the Dolphin, and
made her sailors all turn pirates. Among them was John
Fillmore, who rebelled, and, starting a mutiny, killed the
pirate chief, afterward successfully taking the Dolphin back
to Boston. This brave man's great-grandson was President
Millard Fillmore. Another pirate, Low, captured a fish-
ing-smack off the islands, but, disappointed of booty, first
had his captives flogged, and then gave each one the alter-
native of being hanged or of three times vigorously curs-
ing old Parson Cotton Mather. With alacrity, it is said,
they did the latter. Captain Kidd sailed these shores and
buried his treasures here, as he did in many other places,
and the ghost of one of Kidd's men is reported to still
haunt Appledore. The renowned Blackbeard also haunted
the Isles of Shoals. When the pirates disappeared these
reefs degenerated into the haunt of the smuggler, for whose
stealthy calling they seem appropriately adapted.

THEIR GRAND OUTLOOK.

Gazing shoreward from these islands at the close of day
there is a sight worth seeing. Far away are the White
Mountains with sunset hues behind them. The foreground
gives the broad-spreading New England shore-line, with
Agamenticus and its attendant summits off to the northward, and in front the steeples of Portsmouth and Newburyport and their intervening beaches. The smoke of
many inland villages rises in the distance, and the colossal
Wentworth Hotel has its galaxy of electric lights in front
of Portsmouth, while the eye sweeps with the south coast
around Ipswich Bay to Cape Ann thrust far out into the
ocean. At our feet is the little harbor bearing its galaxy
of yachts and skiffs, that vary their sailing and fishing

with the flirtations of the place to make a round of amusements. The sun sinks and twilight comes. Then

> " From the dim headlands many a lighthouse gleams,
>   The street-lamps of the ocean."

Whale's Back Light, at the Portsmouth entrance, flashes
six miles away, and the monster twin-lights of Thatcher's
Island send their steady radiance out to us twenty miles
across the waters from Cape Ann. Almost at our elbow
White Island alternates its red and white revolving blaze.
Far away to the north-east a single white star appears. It
is eleven miles off, on the solitary rock of Boon Island out
in mid-ocean, where not a pound of soil exists excepting
what has been carried there. One of the worst wrecks
ever known occurred here before this lighthouse was built.
The Nottingham, from London, was driven ashore, the
crew with difficulty gaining the rock when the ship broke
up. They had no food, and day by day their sufferings
from cold and hunger increased. The mainland was in
full view, and they built a boat of pieces of the wreck to
try and get there, but the waves dashed it to pieces. They
saw vessels and signalled, but could not attract attention.
They sank gradually into an almost hopeless band of
miserable wretches, but thought to make another effort.
A rude raft was constructed, and two of them tried to
reach the shore. It, too, was wrecked, being found two
days later on the beach, with a dead man lying near by.
Then hope entirely failed them, and to sustain life they
had to become cannibals, living on the body of the ship's
carpenter sparingly doled out to them by the captain.
But eventually they were rescued, the wrecked raft being
their preserver. When it was found, the people on shore
started a search for the builders, and they were taken off
after passing twenty-four days in starvation on the island.

As we muse upon this horror the fog, the bane of our
northern coasts, closes in about us, the lights disappear,

and in their place from far over the sea come the distant deep-voiced blasts of the fog-sirens, another warning to the mariner. Then the fog breaks to the northward—for it often goes as quickly as it comes—and again gleams out the steady white star from Boon Island:

> " Steadfast, serene, immovable, the same
>   Year after year, through all the silent night
> Burns on for evermore that quenchless flame,
>   Shines on that inextinguishable light!
>
> " A new Prometheus chained upon the rock,
>   Still grasping in his hand the fire of Jove,
> It does not hear the cry nor heed the shock,
>   But hails the mariner with words of love.
>
> " ' Sail on !' it says—' sail on, ye stately ships !
>   And with your floating bridge the ocean span ;
> Be mine to guard this light from all eclipse ;
>   Be yours to bring man nearer unto man !' "

XXXIII.

ENTERING THE PINE-TREE STATE.

Much of the State of Maine is covered with forests, and cutting and floating the logs down her great rivers and preparing their product for market make the livelihood of many of her people. Crossing the Piscataqua River from Portsmouth, New Hampshire, we enter the border-town of Kittery, sacred to the memory of her colonial chieftain, Sir William Pepperell. Here are the remains of the old Fort Pepperell guarding the river-entrance, which had its quaint six-sided block-house loopholed for musketry. Here is his old mansion, with its gambrel roof and broad lawn, whence he had an unrivalled view over the sea and the islands of the river. He was the great man of his day, his vast landed estates stretching from the Piscataqua eastward to the Saco

River, and his name is reproduced in these parts in banks, mills, and hotels, even Kittery Town having once been called Pepperellville. But the train soon plunges into the forests, plenty of pine trees adorning the land, with piles of cord-wood cut for fuel. It glides among the attendant foot-hills of Mount Agamenticus, the isolated mountain standing by the sea as a sentinel on the outpost of Maine. The country is sparsely settled, and much of its surface rough, with saw-mills in the woods working up the timber from the clear-ings. Occasionally farms are passed, with grand hay-fields, and spacious mansions seeming to have come down in good preservation from the fine estates of the colonial times. The railroad winds among the hills and forests, which are bor-dered on the ocean front by the famous beaches of the Maine coast. Here is its place of earliest settlement in 1624, the quiet old town of York, "the ancient city of Ag-amenticus," almost shadowed by that mountain, and once a thriving, busy port. At the eastern end of York Beach, Cape Neddick is thrust out into the sea, with the curious rocky islet of the Nubble off its extremity, and a deep channel between. There projects beyond the frowning promontory of the Bald Head Cliff and its lofty Pulpit Rock an almost perpendicular wall rising ninety feet, with the breakers beating at its base. Then comes the town of Wells, with more magnificent beaches, having hard and firm sands that are fine, white, and sharp, being greatly prized by builders. The farmers haul these sands away as bed-ding for cattle and also to mix with too heavy soils. Plenty of seaweed comes ashore, being used for fertilizers, furnish-ing soda, lime, and salt. Above the verge of the sands the pebbles heap up in long rows by the action of the waves. The broad road furnished by these successive beaches is the chief highway along the coast, always kept in elegant repair by old Neptune. There are occasional piles of shingle, and rocky ledges protrude, while the boom of the breaker and the roar of the sea are the eternal accompaniment.

As the train rolls along there comes a break in the forest, and suddenly through the hills and woods flows down the charming little Kennebunk River, rushing away past falls and saw-mills to its town and the sea. Then we approach the broader Saco River, with the steeples of Biddeford rising among the trees—one of them, the French Catholic church, having two little trees, a willow and a poplar, growing high up out of its spire. The Saco comes down from the White Mountains, where it flows through the famous Notch, and its cataracts give valuable power to the twin factory-towns of Biddeford and Saco. As the train crosses the bridge there is a good view of both, with the river between them. Logs are rafted in the boom spreading under the railroad-bridge, and the locality is redolent with the pungent odors of pine timber and sawdust. All these rivers make good harbors at their mouths. Beyond the Saco are more forests, with stretches of salt-meadows spreading down to the ocean-beaches, where the ancient fishing-settlements are all being converted into fashionable summer resorts. The beach fronting Saco dissolves into Old Orchard Beach, stretching nearly ten miles from Saco to Scarborough River, the finest beach in New England, over three hundred feet wide, and named from an apple orchard that stood there, of which the last ancient tree died before the Revolution. Through more forests and over more salt-meadows we go, crossing Cape Elizabeth, and finally coming out of the woods on the edge of one of Maine's many splendid harbors, the magnificent Casco Bay. The train crosses an arm of the bay and halts in the new union railway-station on the western edge of Portland, which has been only recently opened—an artistic building reflecting credit on its constructors.

THE CITY OF PORTLAND.

Portland is Maine's metropolis and the winter port of Canada, which has to use its harbor when the St. Lawrence is closed by ice. It is built upon a peninsula about three miles long, projecting eastwardly into Casco Bay. The surface of the peninsula is quite elevated, and at each extremity the land rises into commanding eminences, the western being Bramhall's Hill and the eastern Munjoy's Hill. Around both have been made spacious promenades for outlooks. The city being almost surrounded by water, and the bay having bold shores enclosing many beautiful islands, the magnificence of the views in every direction may be imagined. This chief city of the Pine-tree State, with its streets elegantly shaded, mainly with elms, has not inappropriately been called the "Forest City." It was the Indian land of Machigonne, settled by the English in 1632. There still remain noble trees of that day, and they are one of the charms of its pleasant park of the Deering Oaks at the West End, from which State Street leads into the best residential section, its double rows of bordering elms making a grand overarching bower for the highway. Here in a circle at the confluence of several leading streets is the noble bronze statue of Longfellow, who was a native of Portland, the poet sitting meditatively in his chair. The city has an air of comfort, and its broad-fronted, vine-clad homes look enticing, while the general quietness and restful aspect betoken both wealth and content. Congress Street, passing lengthwise along the peninsula, is the chief business highway, having upon it the city hall, while opposite is the sign of the "City Liquor Agency," a reminder of the Maine liquor law, there not having recently been a chance to vote "wet" in Maine. But though Portland is legally "dry," its spiritic humidity is not unlike that of some other American cities. On the day we were there the Portland *Press* announced "there were thirty-six arrests made last week, twenty-four of which were for drunkenness." It further reported the verdict of a coroner's jury upon a man killed on a railway, declaring decedent's injuries "were sustained while in a state of intoxication, and were due to his own

16

carelessness." Though legally "dry," Portland seemed just then to be practically quite "wet."

As we move about, the charm of Portland's ample water-environment is displayed, for almost every street discloses at its end a beautiful vista view over the bay to some distant island or pleasant landscape. The eastern promenade, encircling Munjoy's Hill, where they are constructing a new water-reservoir, gives splendid views over the city and harbor. The town nestles in the depression between this and Bramhall's Hill, two miles westward, rising grandly in the distance and surmounted by the Maine Hospital. All around there is an outlook over Casco Bay and its arms, with the many islands rising pretty and bold, with trees fringing their rocky summits. On the eastern verge of the bay Falmouth Foreside stretches down to the distant ocean, while on the western shore is the broad peninsula terminating in Cape Elizabeth, south of the harbor-entrance. In a beautiful spot on this noble outlook is the monument erected to the founder of Portland, bearing the inscription, "George Cheeves, Founder of Portland, 1699." There are wonderful capabilities in developing this charming spot into a splendid park at small expense, for it has a commanding prospect over one of the most bewitching scenes in America —this island-studded Casco Bay with the ocean beyond. There lies, surmounted by the wide Ottawa House, the famous Cushing's Island, the outermost of the archipelago, guarding the entrance from the sea. Upon other islands down the bay are the three forts, two practically abandoned, while the flag flying from the more modern works of Fort Preble shows that we still have an army even in this remote region. The tall white lighthouse beyond guides the mariner into the channel, while nearer to us the breakwater stretches in front of the inner harbor, with the diminutive beacon-light on the end. The arms of the bay spread behind it into the land, making the harbor with its branching creeks, and here, having ample room and railway facilities, the wharves and shipping are located in front of the lower parts of the town.

THE SEA-FIGHT.

On Munjoy's Hill is the old cemetery, and here rest alongside each other two noted naval officers of the last war with England—Burrows and Blythe. They commanded the rival war-ships, the American Enterprise and the British Boxer, that fought on Sunday, September 5, 1814, off Pemaquid Point, near the mouth of the Kennebec, the adjacent shores being covered with spectators. The Enterprise captured the Boxer and brought her a prize into Portland harbor. Both commanders were killed in the engagement, and their bodies were brought ashore, each wrapped in the flag he had so bravely defended, and the same honors were paid to both in the double funeral. Longfellow recalls this as a memory of his youth:

> " I remember the sea-fight far away,
> How it thundered o'er the tide,
> And the dead captains as they lay,
> In their graves o'erlooking the tranquil bay
> Where they in battle died."

Bramhall's Hill has the splendid estate of Portland's leading townsman, some time ago deceased—Brown of sugar-making fame. Around it is the western promenade, overlooking the noble western view. As we stand up here the arm of the bay known as Fore River is at our feet, with the railways coming out of the forests beyond and crossing it to get into the union station, which is almost beneath us, while far away are the ranges of distant hills and the hazy background of New Hampshire, closed in by the cloudlike outlines of the White Mountains, making another view of wondrous beauty. The clangor of the locomotive bells and the roar and rumble of the trains come up from below as we gaze upon this unrivalled land-

scape. Thus both upon its eastern and western borders
Portland has gorgeous views well worth coming all the
way from the Keystone State to see.

FROM PORTLAND TO THE PENOBSCOT.

From Casco Bay we journey across the peninsula to the
Androscoggin River at Brunswick through a rolling wooded
region, much of it a rough country liberally supplied with
steep and vexatious-looking hills. These must be the despair of the farmers, yet they manage to scratch some subsistence out of their fields that seem almost set on end. As
Brunswick is approached the surface becomes more level,
and the twin spires of Bowdoin College rise above the
trees with a dense growth of pines behind them. The
Androscoggin comes down from Umbagog Lake and the
White Mountains to tumble over the falls that turn the
mill-wheels of Brunswick, and then it flows on to unite its
waters with the Kennebec in Merry Meeting Bay. Bowdoin is the chief college of Maine, chartered in the last
century, and having had Hawthorne and Longfellow
among its graduates, the latter being its professor of
modern languages before he was called to Harvard. We
leave its spires behind, and are soon approaching at Bath
the Kennebec, the great river that sends its prolific crops
of ice and timber throughout the world. The Kennebec
flows out of the largest lake in Maine (Moosehead), and,
descending a thousand feet in its course of one hundred
and fifty miles, making valuable water-power, it enters the
Atlantic through Sheepscott Bay, an irregular indentation
of the coast studded with many islands.

The town of Bath has long been famed as the great shipbuilding port of Maine. Here, more than anywhere in
New England, has been the practical realization of Longfellow's invocation:

"Build me straight, O worthy master,
  Staunch and strong a goodly vessel

That shall laugh at all disaster,
And with wave and whirlwind wrestle."

The town has its front border of shipyards, unfortunately until recently without much employment, their occupation being curtailed because most of the world seems to prefer building its ocean tonnage of iron and steel, rather than of wood, which is the great Maine staple.   The railway-train is ferried across the noble Kennebec to Woolwich on the opposite shore, giving a fine view of Bath fringed for two or three miles along the western bank, while on either hand the rocky shores slope steeply down as the river flows between.   Again we plunge into the forests to traverse the peninsula between the Kennebec and the Penobscot, the two great rivers of Maine, crossing various streams and arms of the sea, and passing the towns of Wiscasset, Dama-riscotta, Waldoboro', and Thomaston to Rockland.   Dama-riscotta was named for Damarine, the old sachem of Saga-dahoc, who was called "Robin Hood" by the whites who bought his domain to make the site of Bath.   The route crosses the Sheepscott and St. George's Rivers and skirts the head of Muscongus Bay, passing through the counties of Lincoln and Knox, bearing famous Revolutionary names, while Waldo county is to the northward.   After leaving the Kennebec the crop of rocks is even more stu-pendous, huge crags thrusting out from every hill, with trees clinging to them, excepting where the surface refuses to give either soil or roots a foothold.   Yet these rocks have their virtue.   They make the purest water.   These hills are full of springs, feeding many pretty lakes and streams, and adding to the beauties of the forest landscape as we wind among the hills and skirt the bays and harbors on the route eastward toward Penobscot Bay.   Then, glid-ing down to the edge of that great bay, we halt at its flour-ishing port of Rockland, on Owl's Head Bay, looking out upon the Penobscot, with its guiding light upon the point called the Owl's Head. These are more of Maine's famous bays and havens, of which Whittier sings:

"From gray sea-fog, from icy drift,
　From peril and from pain,
　The homebound fisher greets thy lights,
　O hundred-harbored Maine!"

XXXIV.

THE RIVER OF NORUMBEGA.

WE have come to the chief river of Maine, the Penobscot, draining the larger portion of its enormous forests and emptying into the ocean through the greatest of the many bays that are thrust into its rugged coast. Three centuries ago this was the semi-fabulous river of Norumbega, thus named by the Spaniards and Portuguese, who sent the earliest explorers to these prolific fishing-grounds of America. At that time Europe knew of no stream that was its equal, and no bay with such broad surface or such enormous tidal flow. Hence many were the tales and great the wonder about weird Norumbega, whence many adventurers went to examine and colonize. The Penobscot is the most extensive bay on the sea-coast of Maine, which in many respects is the most remarkable coast in the country. It is jagged and uneven, seamed with deep inlets and serrated with craggy headlands projecting far out into the ocean, while between are hundreds of rocky and, in many cases, romantic islands. This coast is composed almost entirely of granites and sienites and other metamorphic rocks that have been deeply scraped and grooved ages ago by the huge glaciers, which, descending from the north and stretching many miles into the sea, were of such vast thickness and ponderous weight as to plough out the immense valleys and ravines in the granite floor. The chief of these ridges and furrows extend almost north and south, so that the shore-line of Maine is a series of long, rocky peninsulas separated by deep and elongated bays, within and beyond them being myriads of islands and sunken ledges having the same general trend as the mainland. Thus the Maine coast, while stretching in a straight line two hundred and seventy-eight miles from Kittery Point to Quoddy Head, has no less than two thousand four hundred and eighty-six miles length in the sinuosities of its shore-line. There are also large rocks and boulders strewn over the land and upon the bottom of the sea, where they have been left by the receding glaciers. These fragments are piled in enormous quantities in various places, many of the well-known fishing banks, such as George's Shoals, being these glacial deposits. These rocks and sunken ledges are covered with marine animals, making the favorite food of many of our most important food-fishes, so that the coasts are the resort of many species known as "bottom-feeders," such as the cod and haddock. While the map makes the Maine coast a jagged seaboard of stern headlands and green archipelagoes, yet it teems with fish and has many good harbors, while the capacious bays conduct rivers of great volume to the ocean, bearing the product of her forests.

THE PENOBSCOT.

The greatest of these rivers is the noble Penobscot, which from its sources to the sea is about one hundred and seventy-five miles along, the two branches that form it uniting about one hundred and thirty-five miles from the mouth. Its embouchure broadens out into an enormous bay filled with islands, and the wedge shape of the lower river, by gathering such a vast flow of waters which are suddenly compressed at the Narrows, just below Bucksport, sixteen miles from Bangor, makes a rapidly-rushing tide and an ebb and flow rising seventeen feet at Bangor. Champlain early entered this broad, deep bay, and Captain George Weymouth came in 1605, setting up a cross near where is now the city of Belfast, and taking possession in the name of England. Weymouth marvelled greatly at what he saw, writing home that "many who had been travellers in sundry countries and in most famous rivers affirmed them not comparable to this—the most beautiful, rich, large, secure harboring river that the world affordeth." But while its fame went abroad, the English were fated to make no permanent settlements on the coast of Norumbega, though several colonies were attempted there and elsewhere. Subsequently the French got possession, and the land adjacent to the Penobscot and beyond became the French Acadia, where have been left many French names still existing to tell of their occupation and to recall the mortal enmity and many conflicts between them and the English. Norumbega in the seventeenth century was famous both as a river and a city, there being on its shores a populous Indian settlement of the Tarratines, one of the tribes of the Abenaqui nation. These Indians inhabited all of Maine, and were firm friends of the French, who early sent Jesuit missionaries among them from Canada. They called the great river "Pentagoet," or "the stream where there are rapids," while its shores were the "Penobscot," appropriately meaning "where the land is covered with rocks." Both these names clung to the river, but subsequently the French built Fort Pentagoet on a long narrow peninsula on the eastern shore of the bay, so that this name was finally diverted to that region. Both of these are pure words of the Abenaqui tongue, which is said to be one of the completest Indian languages and the "aboriginal Greek of America." As one progresses up the Penobscot he finds plenty of this Indian Greek, for it receives many tributaries with ponderous names—albeit they are of the purest dialect—such as the Penduskeag, Piscataquis, Mattawamkeag, and Passadumkeag.

THE RED MEN OF THE EASTERN LAND.

The Abenaquis, or "men of the Eastern Land," were a famous and warlike Indian nation, their tribes extending from the Merrimac to the St. John River, and at one time as far west as the Connecticut. Upon the Merrimac they were known as the Pennacooks, and upon the Kennebec as the Canabis, whence the name of that river is derived. Both the English and the French colonists sought alliance with them, but the French priests, who had converted most of them to Christianity, were the more influential, and, becoming close allies, they sided with the French in all the colonial wars. In those days of bigotry and border ferocity, as might be supposed, the French lost no opportunity of inflaming these savages against their English enemies. Old Cotton Mather, the quaint Puritan preacher and early historian I have occasionally quoted, relates that one of the fiercest Canabis chiefs told him that some of the friars said to his people that "the Blessed Virgin was a French lady, and the English had killed her son Jesus." The Jesuit Father, Sebastian Rale, was the most powerful missionary among these Indians—a priest and instructor who came from Nismes in France, where he had been a teacher of Greek in the university. He came in 1695, and lived among them thirty years, making a complete dictionary of their language which is now preserved in Harvard University. He held them always firmly to the French alliance, and the English on the border ascribed all their quarrels with the Abenaquis to his influence, accused him of instigating their raids upon the settlements, and finally set a price upon his head. His church and village were at Old Point on the Kennebec, above Norridgewock, and for twenty years expeditions were sent against him repeatedly, burning his church and destroying the village; but he always escaped, and the tribe was sure to wreak fearful vengeance upon the English settlements afterward. In one of these raids the English stole his dictionary and carried it off to Boston. Rale was said to have a superb consecrated banner, emblazoned with the cross and a bow and sheaf of arrows, floating from a staff in front of his church. In the border warfare this crusading standard was often borne by his tribe in their forays against the Puritans. In the final attack against Father Rale, so stealthily did the Puritan rangers and their Mohawk allies surround the Abenaquis town in August, 1724, that the first knowledge its people had was a shower of bullets sweeping through it. Some escaped, but all who were caught, men, women, and children, were massacred. When Rale heard the tumult he fearlessly exposed himself, hoping to draw the fire and save his flock with his own life. The English saw him, gave a shout and a volley, and he fell dead, pierced by a hundred bullets. Seven chiefs who had endeavored to shield his body fell beside him. When the captors had plundered the village and left, the fragment of the tribe which escaped returned and found Rale's body horribly mutilated at the foot of the mission cross. They buried him where the church altar had stood, and within the present century a granite obelisk has been erected to mark the spot.

THE NOTED SETTLEMENT AT CASTINE.

Penobscot Bay has an even more stirring history. On the narrow Pentagoet peninsula is the famous town of Castine, abounding with relics and scarred by the wars caused by no less than five national occupations. The Plymouth Company first established here an English trading-post. Then the French captured it, built Fort Pentagoet, and their Catholic and Huguenot chieftains quarrelled and alternately held possession. Afterward the Dutch took it; the French recaptured it; the English plundered and finally held it during the Revolution and the War of 1812; and now it peacefully vegetates in wealthy decadence as a summer resort in a remote part of the United States. This old Pentagoet town has its pleasant romance, for it was named for Vincent, baron de St. Castine, lord of Oléron in the French Pyrenees, who came over with his regiment to Canada and Acadia in 1667, and, inspired by a chivalrous desire to spread the Catholic religion among the Indians, went into the wilderness to live among the fierce Abenaquis. As Longfellow tells it:

> "Baron Castine of St. Castine
> Has left his château in the Pyrenees,
> And sailed across the Western seas."

Pentagoet was then a populous Indian town, ruled by Madockawando, grand sachem of the Tarratines, this being the famed city of Norumbega of which Europeans had heard so much. The baron tarried there and soon found friends among the savages. As in Virginia, the sachem had a susceptible daughter, and the dusky Pocahontas of Pentagoet, captivated by the courtly graces of the young and handsome baron, fell in love with him:

> "For man is fire, and woman is tow,
> And the Somebody comes and begins to blow."

The feeling was mutual, so that it was not long before—

> "Lo! the young baron of St. Castine,
> Swift as the wind is, and as wild,
> Has married the dusky Tarratine—
> Has married Madockawando's child!"

The sequel might be expected. This marriage made him one of the tribe, and he soon became their leader. The warlike and restless Indians almost worshipped the chivalrous young Frenchman; he was their apostle, and then became their chieftain and led them in repeated raids against their English and Indian foes. But he ultimately tired of this roving life in almost fabulous Norumbega, and returned to "his château in the Pyrenees," taking his Indian bride along. Then came the wonder of his French tenantry :

"Down in the village day by day
 The people gossip in their way,
And stare to see the baroness pass
On Sunday morning to early mass;
And when she kneeleth down to pray,
They wonder, and whisper together, and say,
'Surely this is no heathen lass!'
And in course of time they learn to bless
The baron and the baroness.

"And in the course of time the curate learns
A secret so dreadful that by turns
He is ice and fire, he freezes and burns.
The baron at confession hath said
    That, though this woman be his wife,
He hath wed her as the Indians wed—
    He hath bought her for a gun and a knife!"

Then there was trouble, but it was soon cured, for the curate made all things right by a Christian wedding:

"The choir is singing the matin song;
    The doors of the church are opened wide;
The people crowd, and press, and throng
    To see the bridegroom and the bride.
They enter and pass along the nave;
They stand upon the father's grave;
The bells are ringing soft and slow;
The living above and the dead below
Give their blessings on one and twain;
The warm wind blows from the hills of Spain,
    The birds are building, the leaves are green,
    And Baron Castine of St. Castine
Hath come at last to his own again."

But this was not all. The son of the baron by his Tarratine princess became the chief of the tribe, and ruled it until, in 1721, he was captured by the English and taken prisoner to Boston. He is described as brave and magnanimous, and, when taken before the Boston council for trial he wore his French uniform and was accused of attending an Abenaqui council-fire. He sturdily replied: "I am an Abenaquis by my mother; all my life has been passed among the nation that has made me chief and commander over it. I could not be absent from a council where the interests of my brethren were to be discussed. The dress I now wear is one becoming my rank and birth as an officer of the Most Christian king of France, my master." After being held several months a prisoner he was released, and finally he too returned to the ancestral estates in the Pyrenees. Lineal descendants of the St. Castines still rule the Abenaquis, but the nation afterward dwindled almost to nothingness. Fort Pentagoet, honoring these memories, became Castine. In and around its harbor in the many wars it has seen have been fought no less than five important naval battles. Remains of its fort and batteries are yet preserved, and a miniature earthwork commands the harbor. All the Abenaqui tribes were firm allies of the Americans during the Revolution. There are some remnants of them in Canada, but the best preserved is the settlement of Penobscot Indians on Indian Island in the river at Oldtown, above Bangor. For their fealty during the Revolution they were given an extensive reservation, where about four hundred of them, receiving a small revenue from the State, now live in a village around their Catholic church. They have a town-hall and schools, with books printed in their own Abenaqui tongue. The settlement maintains tribal relations, being ruled by a governor, lieutenant-governor, two captains, and four councillors. This remnant of a once great and warlike nation now gets a modest subsistence by catching fish and lobsters and rafting logs on their native river of Norumbega.

XXXV.

THE GREAT PENOBSCOT BAY.

WE have come through the forests to the edge of Penobscot Bay—one of the crowning glories of "hundred-harbored Maine." Its shores and islands bear many noble trees, and its head-waters traverse an immense territory covered with forests of pine, spruce, and hemlock. Two hundred millions of feet of lumber will be surveyed at its chief port of Bangor in a single season. The visitor wanders in these great woods and thinks of Longfellow's lines:

"This is the forest primeval. The murmuring pines and the hemlocks,
  Bearded with moss, and with garments green, indistinct in the twilight,
  Stand like Druids of old, with voices sad and prophetic,
  Stand like harpers hoar, with beards that rest on their bosoms.
  Loud from its rocky caverns the deep-voiced neighboring ocean
  Speaks, and in accents disconsolate answers the wail of the forest."

This magnificent region of wood and mountain, bay and archipelago, to which we have come recalls many Revolutionary memories. The bold western shores of Penobscot Bay make the well-known Maine counties of Knox and Waldo. Its abutting lands were included in the noted "Muscongus Patent" which King George I. issued and which came to Governor Samuel Waldo. The colonists were sturdy fighters in those days, and at Thomaston, through which we have passed, on the picturesque St. George's River, the English built a fort early in the last century to hold this crown grant, and the French from Acadia must consequently attack it, the monks, it was said, leading their Indian allies, the warlike Tarratines, but being successfully repulsed. This extensive Muscongus Patent embraced a tract thirty miles wide on each side of the Penobscot, and General Waldo, who was colonial governor of Massachusetts, thus had a princely domain. But he died before the Revolution, and Waldo county and the town of Waldoboro' now preserve his memory. His patent afterward came to the noted Revolutionary general, Henry Knox, through his wife, and thus Knox became the patroon of Penobscot Bay, building a palace at Thomaston, where he lived in baronial state, maintaining all the dignity and ceremonial of the most aristocratic court, and spending so much money in maintaining his princely scale of living and generous hospitality that he bankrupted himself and almost ruined his Revolutionary compatriot, General Benjamin Lincoln, who became involved with him. General Knox was a splendid man, but he was literally "land poor," although he owned much of the best part of the then province of Maine, which at that time was part of the State of Massachusetts. His descendants and successors have since divided up his extensive principality.

AN EXPLORATION.

Upon part of General Knox's domain, the beautiful waters of the magnificent Penobscot Bay and its many dotted islands, whose rocky contours make the most attractive and capacious archipelago upon the Atlantic coast of the United States, we look out from the diminutive but most picturesque Owl's Head Bay at Rockland. This town of primitive development nestles behind the bold jutting point of the Owl's Head, whose strong and steady light and fog-signal guide the mariner entering the Penobscot. It is a town of sea-captains, fishermen, and lime-burners. Its rocks make the best lime on these coasts. They are quarried and burnt in kilns along the shore, where the product is put in barrels and shipped to market. A hundred kilns illuminate the hills at night, and a million barrels will be sent away in a year. Yet lime is not the only rocky product of this region. The adjacent islands are famous for their granites. Among them is Dix Island, a compact mass of granite, where the vessels load alongside the ledges whence the blocks are cut. This granite built our Philadelphia Post-office. Vinalhaven Island, down the bay, produces the Bodwell granite that built the grand new Army and Navy Department building in Washington. Fleets of schooners are now bringing this Maine granite in paving-blocks to Philadelphia to improve our streets. These granite islands and the pleasant shores and protruding points of land jutting into the bay at Rockland that have such a superb outlook are just beginning to feel the presence of the summer saunterer. Rustic cottages are going up, and a pretty club-house out on a promontory gives a feature to the view at Owl's Head; but these primitive people seem still too much wedded to the ways of their forefathers to very extensively patronize it. Salt fish and a noontide dinner still prevail in these parts over swallow-tail coats and a full-course banquet in the evening.

From Rockland we begin an exploration of this wonderful bay. An ancient stage-coach with four horses, which might have been patronized by General Knox himself, after sundry turnings skilfully managed is judiciously packed by a party of Quaker explorers from the city of Penn, and starts up the coast. We take a winding road among the cottages and bits of forest, giving splendid views out over the bay. We move north-eastward, and the towering and forest-crowned Camden Hills rise higher and higher as the stage-coach approaches that little town. More lime-kilns are along the shores, with their quarries inland, the old coach rocking and rolling as we jolt by them and swiftly slide down the winding way that leads into the steep ravine making the miniature harbor of Rockport, which supports another colony of lime-burners. The male population not thus employed are generally standing listlessly about with their hands in their pockets, mildly wondering who could have had the audacity to thus rudely invade their sleepy village. But we climb laboriously out

of the Rockport ravine, admiring the gorge through which
the stream comes down that has made it, and soon reach
Camden, with its bold shores around the pleasant cove that
forms its harbor, where enough of Maine's almost lost shipbuilding industry remains to allow of the construction of
two large vessels on the sloping bank. This town nestles
under the shadow of the towering Camden Hills, which
here make such a gorgeous background for the western
edge of Penobscot Bay, and round-topped Megunticook
Mountain rises fourteen hundred feet above the Camden
harbor. Visitors sometimes climb to its top to get the
grand view over the broad blue bay and its splendid archipelago, with the ocean at its entrance and the swelling
peaks of Mount Desert far to the eastward.

THE ARCHIPELAGO.

At Camden our Quaker party is carefully unpacked from
the ancient stage-coach to change from land to water navigation. The road brings us out high above the waters of
the cove, so that we carefully pick our way down the steep
steps and wooden sidewalks of the hilly streets of Camden
to get to the water-side, where a pleasant little steam-yacht
awaits us at the wharf. Soon the party, not forgetting the
commissariat, are upon the Barbara, ready for a sea-voyage.
She swiftly moves out of the diminutive harbor, rocking
gently as the quick pulse-beats of her busy little engine
keep time with the waves. In a few minutes she has passed
out upon the broad bay. In front are the bold forest-clad
shores of the islands two or three miles off, spread in grand
array broadly across the view. Behind us, as the Barbara
briskly paddles along, rise the noble Camden Hills higher
and higher, the sloping shores in front of them a mass of
delicious green, having little villas peeping out among the
trees. We swiftly cross the rippling waters of the great
bay, getting a full view of its splendid sweep from the
ocean for miles northward and into the deeply-indented

harbor of Belfast, some distance above Camden. The Owl's Head lighthouse marks the limit of the southern view, while over opposite is another little white light-house tower nestling among the islands, making a land-mark toward which our nimble-paced Barbara is head-ing. Quickly crossing the bay and leaving its western mountain-backed shores, our active little craft enters the archipelago and passes among the pretty islands into Gilkey's Harbor, an almost completely landlocked sheet of water, where the largest ships can securely float, yet having such thorough protection from the islands enclos-ing it that the pleasures of the sailing yacht and row-boat can be enjoyed in perfect security. One might suppose this a miniature summer sea in the famed Grecian Archi-pelago. The sail is magnificent over the smooth waters bordered by the rocky, forest-covered island shores, where sheep browse in the clearings, with an occasional old-fash-ioned farm-house on the upland. Our little yacht has taken us in past the Ensign Island and Job's Island, and behind Seven-Hundred-Acre Island and Spruce Island, the latter containing a mass of firs of most gorgeous develop-ment, rivalling the noted groves of arbor vitæ that have been established at enormous expense on Lake Winder-mere in the English Lake District.

Soon we approach a little wharf which has just been built in a pleasant cove behind Grindle's Point on Long Island, and land. By recent purchases a large part of Long Island and some adjacent sections have become Philadelphia property for a summer resort. A primitive farm-house on the sloping shore about a thousand feet from the harbor, and elevated nearly a hundred feet above the water, becomes our temporary home. It is a low-spread-ing, comfortable building, filling the want so many tourists long for. All the rooms are front rooms, and the house is chiefly first floor. From the piazza is an unrivalled view in its combination of land-and-water loveliness. The green-

sward stretches down to the water, with a sunken border
of trees on either hand growing on the banks of ravines.
In front is the modest graveyard of the settlement, with a
score of white tombstones in a setting of evergreens. The
placid harbor lies beyond, with yachts at anchor to give
point to the scene, and the narrow and elongated projection of Grindle's Point enclosing it, with the white lighthouse at the entrance. This entrance is both deep and narrow, and the world's biggest vessels could come safely in
and ride at anchor. Spread in front, as the harbor stretches
for two or three miles to the southward, is the archipelago of protecting islands, with their intervening dividing
straits making other entrances, the whole enclosing as fair
a landlocked harbor as one can hope to see. Outside is
the broad Penobscot Bay with its splendid western background of the Camden Hills, their line of rounded peaks of
nearer green or more distant blue, over which the cloud-
shadows are chasing, stretching off toward Belfast. The
islands, the hills, the smooth and pleasant waters, are
reminders of the glories of the archipelago of Puget
Sound, with even more beauties, and having a bracing
summer air known only to these coasts of the Atlantic;
yet this elysium is much nearer to us than that noted
region of the Pacific coast, which people gladly go thousands of miles to see.

THE INSULAR TOWN OF ISLESBORO'.

The "insular town of Islesboro'," or Long Island as the
natives call it, was part of the princely domain of General
Henry Knox, and is the gem of Penobscot Bay. This
grand interior sea has dotted over its magnificent waters
probably five hundred islands, which, with its own enclosing shores, present a combination of more scenic beauties
than any other bay in the entire range of the Atlantic
coast. Islesboro' is an elongated strip of land in the centre of this charming bay stretching some thirteen miles,

and having on either hand the mainland distant from two to five miles, and with much of the intervening water surface varied by little islands. The long strip of Islesboro' rises into highlands and is of varying widths, being deeply indented, and in some cases almost bisected, by ravines and fissures, making pretty bays and coves that are almost circles, where the gentle waves flow in upon the pebbly beaches that fringe their sloping shores. Above rise bold banks crowned with evergreens, presenting the perfect pastoral landscape of water, field, and woodland giving such a charm to this portion of the New England coast-scenery. The long and narrow island covers some ten square miles of irregular contour, broadening or narrowing as the coves and harbors may indent it, and the surface rising in many places over a hundred feet into bold bluffs. Its hills and vales and wooded slopes give perfect views, while the bracing air, come from what quarter it may, blows freely over it, combining the healthful breezes of both mountain and sea and making a miniature paradise.

As we move about this attractive island with such charming surroundings, in all directions there are beautiful views over the water and over the land, with pretty islands, stretches of glinting sea, or distant green or blue mountains to make a superb background for the picture. To the westward the bold range of the Camden Hills looks down upon us beyond the range of islands enclosing our little harbor. To the eastward the eye has a grand sweep over the bay and around the horizon, with the massive Blue Hill standing up, an isolated guardian, behind the peninsula of Castine off to the northward, the church-spire of this noted town rising among the trees, and the sun shining on its pleasant white houses spreading over the broad and sloping point of land that encloses the deep harbor which has so much historical interest. All the land and all the water we are looking at, so peaceful now, has run red with blood from the fiercest fighting of the colonial times. Scattered about this East

Penobscot Bay are many islands, with the Fox Island group of about one hundred and fifty, North Haven and Vinalhaven to the southward, and beyond are the shores of Cape Rosier, making the eastern border of the bay, behind which rise the distant bisected, round-topped peaks of Mount Desert thirty miles away. Off through a vista among the many islands looms up the distant Isle au Haut, an outer guardian of the group upon the ocean's edge. Such is the splendid scene from Islesboro' over the East Penobscot Bay as scores of white-winged yachts, standing over with the strength of the fresh north-western breeze, are threading the many passages among these pleasant islands and dancing over the sparkling waves *en route* to Mount Desert. Everywhere growing upon this charming island of Islesboro' are groups of gorgeous Christmas trees—millions of them, big and little—the stately and symmetrical firs of this country, which people of our own region would give much to possess. They are beautiful beyond description in their native glory upon these rocky hills. Acres of ferns of many splendid forms and most delicate texture grow in shaded nooks. The primitive people of the island live in neat houses with broad fronts painted white, and the men are all sea-captains, their front doors opening upon steep stairways rising almost straight up, like a ship's companion-ladder, to the upper floors. Shells and sea-urchins are found upon the pebbly beaches, and fish-hawks circle about and scream above our heads. Scattered over the island are the little white-tombed graveyards where rest the forefathers of the place, whose descendants live to-day exactly as they did a century ago. The first sound of summer fashion knocking for entrance upon one of the fairest scenes in Nature has just awakened them to a realization that the world has moved.

XXXVI.

THE END.

STANDING upon the high land of Islesboro', just above the bewitching little fir-embowered cove of Dark Harbor, we watch the fleet-winged yachts, their white sails bulging before the stiff north-western breeze as they glide across the magnificent expanse of the East Penobscot Bay. They have come out from behind the Owl's Head, and scores of them are moving over the white-capped waves, whose foaming tops have been whisked off by the brisk wind, seeking a passage through the mazy thoroughfares among the many islands toward Mount Desert. As we survey this splendid view there is a noble background for our picture, seen thirty miles away across Little Deer Island and the mainland of Cape Rosier, the two distant blue mountains nestling on the edge of the horizon like a recumbent elephant, and marking that noted island which has recently captured so many Philadelphians. The yachts dance over the waves as they go through the complex labyrinth of passages in the attractive archipelago between Penobscot and Frenchman's Bays. They thread the reaches, and, rounding Blue Hill Bay, soon come in full view of the island beyond, which presents the only land along our Atlantic coasts where high mountains stand in the close neighborhood of the sea. It appears to-day just as it did to the early explorer, Champlain, when he first found it in September, 1604, and, being impressed with its desolate and craggy summits, appropriately named it the "Isle des Monts déserts"—the "Island of Desert Mountains." He then wrote of it: "The land is very high, intersected by passes, appearing from the sea like seven or eight mountains ranged near each other; the summits of the greater part of these are bare of trees, because they are nothing but rocks." As the yachts have skimmed over the water in their zigzag approach through the galaxy of attendant islands, the recumbent elephant of Mount Desert has resolved its two rounded summits into different peaks, and the fact is realized that this remarkable island, being so near the mainland that the narrow strait between them is bridged, is at the same time a ponderous mass of mountains, entirely overshadowing the lower surface of the adjacent shores.

THE APPEARANCE OF MOUNT DESERT.

In approaching overland from the northward by the railway-route to Mount Desert, which is most travelled, it is curious to watch how the gradually diminishing distance unfolds the separate mountain-peaks of the island. The whole range is finally displayed, there being apparently eight eminences, but upon coming nearer others seem to detach themselves that had at first blended with those higher and more distant. Green Mountain is the highest of them, rising over seventeen hundred feet, while Western Mountain terminates the range on the right-hand side, and at the eastern verge is Newport Mountain, having the fashionable settlement of Bar Harbor at its base. High up among these peaks there are several beautiful lakes, the chief being Eagle Lake. Beech and Dog Mountains have peculiarities of outline, while a wider opening between two pronounced peaks shows where the sea has driven in the strange and deeply-carved inlet of Somes Sound from the southern side to almost bisect the island. Forest fires have repeatedly overrun all these mountains, but a new growth of young trees is coming on. There are thirteen eminences altogether, and the eastern summits on the Frenchman's Bay side are the highest, terminating generally at or near the water's edge in precipitous cliffs with waves dashing against their bases. Upon the south-eastern coast, as a fitting termination to the grand scenery of these mountain-ranges, the border is a galaxy of stupendous cliffs, the two most remarkable being of world-wide fame—Schooner Head and Great Head—having the full force of Old Ocean coming thousands of miles across the broad Atlantic and driving the powerful breakers against their massive rocky buttresses. Schooner Head has a surface of white rock on its face that is fancied to resemble a small schooner when seen from the sea, apparently sailing in front of the giant cliffs. Great Head, two miles southward, is an abrupt projecting mass of rock, its bold and grim front having deep gashes across the base, evidently worn by the waves. This is the highest headland on the island. Castle Head is a perpendicular columned mass, appearing like a colossal castellated doorway flanked by square towers.

During more than a century after Champlain first looked at this Desert Island repeated but ineffectual attempts at settlement were made, but it was not until 1761 that any one succeeded in making a permanent home here. In that year old Abraham Somes, a hardy pioneer from Gloucester on Cape Ann, came along, and, entering the sound that bears his name, squatted on its inner shore and became the founder of a settlement. He came to stay, and his descendant still keeps the village inn at Somesville on the very spot of his earliest colonization. Thus the indomitable spirit of the Yankee colonist triumphed where both the French and English had previously repeatedly failed. Judicious cultivation of the cranberry and the gathering of prolific crops of blueberries kept the people alive on these rocks after Abraham had planted the colony. These are almost the only food-products of the moderate allowance of soil Nature has vouchsafed to Mount Desert. When population increased, about a century ago the island was divided into towns, the eastern portion being named, with sublime Yankee irony, Eden. The village of East Eden, on the edge of Bar Harbor, is to-day the fashionable resort. It has a charming outlook over the bay and its fleets of gayly-bannered yachts and light canoes and the enclosing Porcupine Islands, but the village itself is without a single feature of beauty. It is a wooden town of summer boarding-houses and hotels built upon what was a treeless plain, the outskirts being a galaxy of cottages, many of pretension, where the decree of fashion has pushed up the value of land to fabulous prices. But the combination of sea and mountain-air, the admirable harbor, and the general concentration of wealth and "social status" have made Bar Harbor and its Eden village one of the most famous resorts of the Atlantic coast.

THE FOGS AND THE AQUATICS.

The bane of Mount Desert Island is the fog. It comes quickly, envelops everything, and is frequent in summer, seriously interfering with tourists' pleasures. Sometimes, during days in succession, mountains and sea are wrapped in impenetrable mist. Here is the place where Neptune during last summer brewed most of those fog-banks that the east winds carried away to dissolve in daily deluge upon Philadelphia. But even fog, in its place of nativity, has charms. There are days when it lies in banks upon the sea, with only occasional incursions upon the shore, when under a shining sun the mist creeps over the water, swiftly ascends the mountain-side, then, one by one, envelops the adjacent islands, and finally blots out the whole landscape. But light breezes and warm sunshine soon disperse the mist, the mountains pierce the veil, the islands reappear, and once more bright sunshine gilds the splendid scene. The fog-rifts are wonderful picture-makers. Sometimes the mist obscures the sea and lower shores of the islands, leaving a long and narrow fringe of treetops resting against the horizon as if suspended in mid-air. Often a yacht sails through the fog looking like a colossal ghost, when suddenly its sails flash out in the sunlight like huge wings. Thus the mist paints dissolving views, so that the Mount Desert fogs are not the least attraction. Sometimes there comes through it the famed mirage, which Whittier describes:

"Sometimes in calms of closing day
  They watched the spectral mirage play;
  Saw low, far islands looming tall and high,
  And ships, with upturned keels, sail like a sea the sky."

When the fog lifts there can be seen the attendant islands. Off the entrance to Somes Sound are the Cranberry Islands with some others, making a picturesque outlook for the settlements at North-east Harbor and South-west Harbor at the entrance to the sound. The lighthouse stands on Baker's Island, the outermost of the cluster. Off the eastern shore, in Frenchman's Bay, are the five high rocky islands called the Porcupines, which form the chief attraction in the view from the Bar Harbor settlement. These islands enclose the waters of Bar Harbor, the nearest of them, Bar Island, being connected with Mount Desert at low ebb tide, and thus naming the harbor. They bristle with crested pines and cedars, and hence their name, Bald Porcupine also having some stupendous cliffs. It is within this pleasant bay that the yachts cluster, and its waters are covered with boats of all kinds, aquatic sports being the chief amusement. Here flourishes the modern craze for "canoeing," which has of late become so fashionable among the land-folk, who suddenly become full-fledged amateur sailors at the seaside. Many canoes ride on the water—the light, frail, dancing, dangerous canoes that are so likely to give their unskilled occupants an unexpected ducking, if not worse.

THE GREEN MOUNTAIN VIEW.

The picturesque at Mount Desert is divided in interest between the cliffs and the mountain-views. A journey of four miles takes the visitor from Bar Harbor to the summit of Green Mountain, there being an inclined-plane railway up the mountain-side. The sides of this, as of all the eminences, are precipitous and savagely rugged, a tangled forest growth covering the lower portions, while the tops are bare and riven rocks. The beautiful Eagle Lake adds a charm to the ascent, and when the mountain-top is reached and the fog permits there is a grand view over hill and vale and lake, with the deeply-cut Somes Sound penetrating almost through the island, whose contour is set out like a map. Behind us is the grand stretch of the Maine coast, seen with its bays, islands, and headlands extending from Penobscot to Passamaquoddy. Eagle Lake nestles among the mountain-peaks, and from almost alongside it comes up the railway that eases the traveller's ascent. There is also a carriage-road coming up, which was ruined by dynamite blasts to prevent competition a few weeks ago. In front of us spreads the open sea, limited only by the horizon, and like a speck, seen twenty miles away, is the lighthouse upon the bleak crags of Mount Desert rock, the most remote beacon in its distant isolation upon the coast of New England.

And here I close this pleasant story. During the summer we have been exploring some of the most interesting portions of our country. We crossed New Jersey from the Delaware River to the metropolis of New York, and viewed its active city-life, wonderful development, and attractive surroundings, its noble harbor, its parks and pleasure resorts, and some of its suburban attractions. Then we entered New England, admired its splendid scenery and its arching elms, visited its great hives of industry, its busy marts of manufacture and trade, traversed its coasts, scanned its fisheries, and, with a keen appreciation of its sterility and forbidding surface, saw the beginnings and studied the early history of the pushing, energetic, and indomitable Yankee race. Then, plunging into the forests of Maine, we have recognized another wonderful development, and enjoyed the beauties of

its unrivalled bays, islands, and archipelagoes, finally halting on its rock-bound shores. And yet at no time have we
been distant more than twenty-four hours' railway ride from
Philadelphia. Beyond us, farther eastward, there is yet a
little more of Maine, but not much that is novel—more
islands, more rocks and forests, more fishery-villages and
pleasant sea-expanses, until, finally, the serrated coast of
the grand old " Pine-tree State " ends with Quoddy Head
and its red-and-white striped lighthouse tower just at the
national boundary, which marks the limit of New England
and the entrance to the dividing St. Croix River and East-
port. These wanderings have been instructive, and it is
hoped their recital has been profitable to the reader. Somewhere I have heard a definition of the noun "tramp," which
has recently been incorporated into our American language,
that indicates a twofold form of that individual. One is the
vagabond who scares the womenfolk in the rural districts
into giving him undeserved food—a distressful, homeless,
aimless wanderer. The other is the more prosperous fellow,
who has a home, but don't want to stay there, and goes
rambling over the face of the earth in quest of novelty.
Possibly our tramp of this summer may have created in
the home-stayer who has read its history something of the
enjoyment given in making the record, and it may have
also produced new thoughts and aspirations to enhance
future pleasures.

Reluctantly bidding farewell to the rock-bound coasts
of Maine, our Eastern Tour is ended.

> "Still they must pass! the swift tide flows,
>   Though not for all the laurel grows.
>   Perchance in this beslandered age
>   The worker, mainly, wins his wage;
>   And time will sweep both friends and foes
>   When FINIS comes!"

INDEX.

THE END.

www.ingramcontent.com/pod-product-compliance
Lightning Source LLC
Chambersburg PA
CBHW030618030726
47497CB00006B/1553